the eleven

KYLE RUTKIN

DIED
FAMOUS

With Gratitude

Copyright © 2024 by Kyle Rutkin

All rights reserved.

No part of this book may be reproduced in any form or by any electronic or mechanical means, including information storage and retrieval systems, without written permission from the author, except for the use of brief quotations in a book review.

Published by Greater Path LLC

Died Famous Branding by Anamaria Stefan

ISBN: 978-0-9836833-8-4 (Paperback)

ISBN: 978-0-9836833-7-7 (E-book)

To those who have the courage to face their shadows

Authors Note

In an era where fiction can often be misconstrued as fact, I believe it's important to clarify the nature of this work. This novel is not an endorsement or reflection of any real conspiracy theories or harmful ideologies. My aim is to entertain and engage the reader's imagination, not to influence beliefs or actions. Please enjoy this journey into the speculative with this understanding.

LATIMES.COM

ACTRESS SAVANNAH BECK MISSING

Model and actress Savannah Beck has been reported missing after failing to show for a table reading of Showtime's hit show, *Kings*.

Sources close to the 44-year-old actress say that Beck was last seen three days ago at a cast party in Brentwood, where she seemed to be in good spirits and enthusiastic about the upcoming season.

Beck first got her big break in the 2000 film *The Offering*, playing the scheming seductress Erin Brooks in a career-defining role. Since then, Beck has had a prestigious modeling career, with a variety of guest appearances and TV roles before her casting in Showtime's dark and gritty adaptation of the Old Testament Book, *Kings*.

If you have any information as to her whereabouts, please contact the Los Angeles Police Department.

Kohl Reynolds

LOS ANGELES

For years, rumors have circulated amongst the Hollywood elite, whispers of a mysterious symbol veiled beneath the glitz and glamor of this town—XIIX. Many believe that the symbol leads the seeker to greatness, to golden statues and unparalleled riches.

The chance to become a Hollywood god.

Others claim that the symbol brings tragedy and destruction upon those it finds. That it is a mark from the devil himself. *Abandon all hope, ye who enter.*

Good or evil, I'll let you decide.

I stare at the InsideJuice.com masthead, pondering the dangerous assignment that awaits the reporter on the other end. If they are successful, this story will define their career. A mind-bending tale of love, murder, and mayhem.

I type in the generic email address from the website. I won't give them the reporter's name. Destiny will bring them to me. The symbol calls to them. Just like it called to me. I write:

I have the story of a lifetime, a wild conspiracy that will bring this town to its knees. I am offering your magazine an exclusive. In less than forty-eight hours this secret goes with me to the grave. Tick tock. Tick tock.

Sincerely,

Kohl Reynolds

May God have mercy on all our souls.

1

CONNER

"We are a celebrity gossip site, and we have nothing on the biggest fucking story in Hollywood right now!" Our editor-in-chief, Tom Arnold, slams his therapeutic stress ball onto the conference room table with a resounding thud. All seven members of the writing staff shift uncomfortably, doing their best to avoid Tom's heated glare.

Unlike my colleagues, I'm perched along the back wall, relishing the moment. This is my final meeting at the celebrity magazine where I've interned all summer, and I'm feeling nostalgic. I'm genuinely going to miss this place—from the wall of celebrity photos covered in Sharpie'd devil horns, to the pink box of stale doughnuts marinating since last week's meeting. Even the sound of Allie, my fellow intern and only friend at the magazine, slurping the last clump of Frappuccino from her Venti cup. For her and the rest of the interns, this gig marks the beginning of their Hollywood adventures. But for me, it's the end of the line.

By Monday, I'll be back to my quaint hometown of Breckinridge, Kansas, where the grand total of traffic lights is a mere seven. Where my future begins and ends with my uncle's small town construction company.

"Savannah Beck is missing, and our homepage is a reality star DUI!" Tom screams, raking his hands through his thinning brown hair. "So... Which one of you overpaid writers can deliver... Grace?"

Of all the things I'll miss about this place...

This morning, my workplace crush, Grace, is wearing a cozy gray cashmere sweatshirt with pinned-up hair and thick glasses that cover her freckled face. I'm not exactly sure what it is about Grace. Maybe the way she chews on the back of her pens when she's deep in thought, or her collection of ironic coffee mugs. I love that her desk is filled with real books, everything from the classics to romance, to hard fantasy and literary. She isn't like the rest of the writers here. She'd never report on Taylor Swift's nail care regimen, which is why she has the lowest clicks of any writer on staff.

"I'm working on the Jacob Perry story," Grace says, her eyes glued to her notebook.

Tom clenches his fists, seething. "You've been working on that conspiracy shit for months, hotshot. Moving on. I need Savanahhh Beck." He draws out her name. "If we can't get the real story, we'll start with the gossip. Red-carpet outfits. Gossip. Her damn Del Taco order!"

"Her co-star on *Kings* owes me," chimes senior reporter, Lane Davies. "I'll press him about her final days on set."

Tom nods in approval. "Getting warmer. What else we got?"

"I'll get dirt on that actor she went to the Golden Globes with," offers Angela, our romance columnist.

Tom looks thoughtful. "Can you make him into a suspect?"

Angela smirks. "I can do anything."

Tom gives her a thumbs up. "Anyone else? Peggy, any tips come through?"

Our senior office administrator clears her throat. "Not about Savannah. But I got a strange email from a screenwriter, Kohl Reynolds, at three this morning. Claims to have the biggest story ever to come out of Hollywood. He's offering us the exclusive." Peggy shrugs.

"Isn't that guy in rehab?" Tom shakes his head. "Doesn't matter. If it isn't about Savannah, I don't care. We can get fillers later. I want everyone chasing Beck right now."

An idea starts to form. My heartbeat hammers against my ribcage as I swallow back my better sense. Interns aren't permitted to pitch at meetings, and besides, the junior writer position has already been filled. What's the point of embarrassing myself? Out of the corner of my eye, I catch Grace glancing up from her notebook, staring in my direction. As though she realizes the dots I connected.

"We should take that story," I blurt out, and every head in the room swivels my way, then back to Tom, awaiting my execution. The window of silence extends. Tom regrips his stress ball, his eyes narrowing on me like a sniper.

"Kohl Reynolds wrote *The Offering*." I vomit the words. "That was Savannah's big hit movie." I turn to the room for validation. Everyone avoids my gaze. I add, "Shouldn't we chase every lead?"

Tom puts his glasses back on, assessing me intently. The silence is unbearable.

"What's your name?" Tom asks.

"Kansas intern. Nicknamed Jayhawk," Lane whispers in his ear.

"It's Conner," Allie retorts from the seat next to me.

"Fine, run with it, Jayhawk. But I'm pairing you with a senior writer. Lowest click count will supervise." He looks down at a metric report on the table, a grin sweeping across his face. "Oh, what a coincidence, Grace. You'll be overseeing this story."

"No, no, no." Grace shakes her head. "Absolutely not. I don't want anything to do with that washed-up screenwriter."

"If you want to keep your job here, you'll assist the intern. Make him do the grunt work. And in the meantime, get your clicks up and I won't make you babysit."

For the first time in eighty-seven days, Grace notices my existence. She looks like she wants to strangle me to death.

2

CONNER

"Look who got someone's attention!" Allie plops down at the desk across from me.

I open my laptop, ignoring the stares and whispers from the staff writers. The adrenaline from the meeting is still coursing through my veins. No matter how it happened, I'd snagged my first real story. A story about Kohl Reynolds with Grace as my supervisor. I glance over at her cubicle. She's engrossed in her work, punishing her springy keyboard with wild finger strokes. This morning's coffee mug reads, *World's Worst Coworker*.

Now might not be the best time for a pow-wow.

I google Kohl Reynolds, eager to dive in. On the screen's side, a cluster of images of the author and screenwriter. He's in his fifties with a rugged face and slicked black hair, a faded snake tattoo slithering up his neck.

I scroll down the page. There are a few articles in TMZ's archive from at least six years ago, one documenting his stint in rehab. Another documenting his divorce from actress Jane Lacy.

I scroll further.

His IMDb page is impressive, with writing credits for nearly twenty films. Blockbuster movies like *Love at First Flight*, *The Offering*, *Band of Thieves*, and *Impeachment*. He was nominated for an Oscar for that one. But that was seventeen years ago. He hadn't had a real hit in a decade. His most recent credited movie, *Vampires in Hollywood*, got a measly fifteen percent on Rotten Tomatoes. And that was the audience score.

"You're wasting your time."

I swivel my chair to find Grace standing behind me, arms crossed, foot tapping. This is the closest she's been near me all summer, and my body responds accordingly—dry mouth, clammy hands. Her deep green eyes are even more stunning up close.

"Listen, Jayhawk."

"Conner," I cough, clearing my throat of nerves.

"Whatever," she continues. "I can respect that you're trying to get a break here, but I'm telling you this is a dead end."

I involuntarily nod.

"Good." She unfolds her arms. "I tried using Kohl as a lead for the story I'm working on. Him and Jacob Perry came up in Hollywood together. But the guy's a total flake. Showed up to our meeting stoned, drunk, who knows. Complete asshole. You're better off leaving this alone."

Jacob Perry is the most iconic movie star in Hollywood... My mind drifts back to the Google search bar, anxious to get back to my research.

"Conner," Grace says firmly. "You're going to drop the story, right? I can tell Tom that I'm off babysitting duty?"

I manage a faint smile. "With all due respect, I'd like to give it a shot."

Grace's back stiffens, arms re-crossed. "Fine. Do what you've got to do. I expect twenty-five hundred words by Friday." She huffs off before calling over her shoulder, "Good luck, Jayhawk."

Allie sneers from her desk. "Did you just get a date?"

By seven p.m., I've exhausted all my leads. Not a single response from Kohl, his agent, manager, even his old publicist. My research was just as futile. Savannah and Kohl only worked together on one film, and the only evidence of an off-screen connection is an old photo posted from Savannah's social media account in 2002—the two backstage at a Blitz Cab concert. Kohl appears haggard in the photo, his eyes half-mast, arm slung around the stunning Savannah Beck, wearing tight jeans and a leather jacket, her teal eyes shining brightly. The caption: *Reunited with my favorite writer.* That was it. Maybe Grace is right. There's no story here.

I rub my bloodshot eyes, glancing around the office. There are very few signs of life. Grace is the only one at the writers' desk, still gnawing on a pen cap, her headphones in. She is by far the hardest working writer on staff. I shut down my computer and load up my messenger bag, offering a half wave in her direction. She leans closer to her computer screen—code for fuck off.

My studio apartment is five miles away from the office, a thirty-minute commute through Los Angeles. The apartment is tight quarters. The kitchen is next to the futon, which doubles as the bed. I collapse onto the worn-down cushions, pulling out my phone—three voicemails from my Aunt Laura. She's been persistent lately. I told myself I wouldn't listen to her guilt trips anymore. I couldn't. Not yet. This is the longest I've been away from my mother since I was eight, since the accident changed everything.

My father was instantly killed, but what happened to my mother was far worse. The doctors said she would slowly recover, or at least regain her motor skills. Wishful thinking. For fifteen years, she has been unable to walk or communicate coherently. Her mood swings are violent and unpredictable. My family insists she used to light up rooms. That she was this incredible musician and piano teacher. Now she's a sleepwalker, her days starting and ending in front of the television.

And then four months ago, I did the unthinkable. I abandoned her at my aunt's house, accepting this internship without a word to anyone. I left an envelope with all the money from the insurance payout, minus a few thousand dollars for a deposit on this overpriced five-hundred-square-foot apartment. I packed a duffel bag and moved to Los Angeles with dreams of becoming a writer. I should have been riddled with guilt. But as I drove away, I felt the happiest I'd been in a long, long time. I hate even admitting that. And I know what I'll do if I listen to those messages, I'll take the first flight back. I love my mother, I really do. But I came here for a reason. I need to see this internship out to the very end.

As I've done all summer, I delete every message from home. The remorse subsides as I breathe in my apartment. To the outside eye, this shithole, with its leaky sink and ripped shag carpet, is nothing to brag about. But to me, it's everything. It's something I've yearned for my entire life. A place of my own. A place filled with possibility and hope.

Before I fall asleep, I put my phone on the nightstand and grab my worn copy of *When the Lights Go Out*. I stare at the youthful face of Kohl Reynolds on the back cover. The only novel he ever wrote. He was only a few years older than me when he wrote it. Twenty-seven when he created a piece of literature that would be revered as a classic coming-of-age tale.

And now, he's at the center of my first big story.

I can't believe my luck.

* * *

When I arrive at work the next day, Tom Arnold is pacing in front of his office, preparing for his daily roundups—a barrage of shouting into a megaphone like he's on the floor of the stock exchange. He scans the room, hunting for his prey. "Where's that fucking intern?" His voice blasts through the office.

Before I can drop my messenger bag on the table, everyone is staring in my direction.

"How are you doing on the Kohl Reynolds story?" he bellows.

The fluorescent lights brighten.

"Working on it." I clear my throat. "Trying to set a meeting."

"A meeting?" Tom turns to Grace, hiding in the back. "Hey, hotshot. Are you helping this intern?"

She raises her porcelain coffee mug, which reads: *I don't get paid enough for your bullshit*. "Sure am, Tom," she says sarcastically.

"Well, c'mon, kids. Work together. I have a good feeling about this one."

Tom Arnold moves onto the next story. My gaze lingers on Grace, dressed in black leggings and a loose-fitting sweater, her sleeves rolled up to her elbows. She fixes the messy knot on top of her head, avoiding my pleading eyes. Why won't she offer me help?

When the meeting commences, I follow her to the cereal bar. Grace pours herself a cup of coffee from a cracked French press. Most of it leaks onto her sweater.

"Damn it!" She tosses her hands up before turning around. As soon as she sees me, she rolls her eyes and sighs. "I can't catch a *break* this morning."

"So you're not going to help me?"

"No." She accentuates the word, patting herself down with paper towels. She grabs her coffee and scoots past me.

I follow her out. "Why not?"

She stops dead in her tracks, whips around, the scent of lavender detergent wafting off her clothes. "Your name's Conner, right?" She taps her finger to her chin, squinting, feigning consideration. She continues. "Let me take a stab at this. You graduated from Kansas State, a degree in creative writing. Maybe you were tired of your small town and small ideas, so you think, 'hey let's try my luck in Hollywood, the city of dreams.'" Her mouth shifts. "But this isn't where you thought you'd end up when you came here, is it? Researching facts about celebrities' butt implants for zero dollars an hour. Not what you had in mind when mom told you to follow your heart."

For the first time since I set foot into this office, I don't find Grace attractive. I've only been in LA for less than a year, but that's long enough to spot a bitter artist when I see one. Maybe Grace is just like every other person in this soul sucking town.

"With all due respect," I say through gritted teeth, "You don't know me."

"Oh!" She stands back dramatically. "Did I strike a nerve?" Her face stiffens. "You're right. I don't. But I know you don't belong here," she whispers sharply. "You seem like a good guy. And this town eats nice guys alive." She puts her hand on my shoulder, and my body tenses. "There's no story here." Then she turns and strolls back to her desk.

"You don't know me!" I yell after her.

"Precisely, Jayhawk." She lifts her mug as she strolls to her desk.

I plop down at my desk in frustration, my mind reeling from the exchange. Who does she think she is? Just because I'm not some bitter, grumbling journalist doesn't mean I don't have what it takes. She doesn't know the sacrifices I made to be here.

"Going well with the girlfriend?" Allie mutters, eyes fixed on her monitor while shamelessly scrolling through job openings online. She shrugs. "What? Getting an early start. You should do the same."

I find myself staring at my own screen in defeat, not a single response in my inbox. But quitting isn't an option—not yet, not without a fight. I've spent years watching my friends move on with their lives, while I remained trapped in my town. Reading alone in the same small-town diner. Driving over the same potholes, day after day. I never went off to college like Grace speculated. I never did anything but work with my uncle, read books, and take care of my mom. I turn back to Grace, who is chewing on her pen. The charm of her quirks has all but faded. Her bulky headphones and the obnoxious sound of her typing annoy me.

I toggle back to my Google home screen. I've already tried everything, every combination between Savannah and Kohl to crack the code. Except one angle… Grace gave up on a story a while back: the friendship between Jacob Perry and Kohl.

It's worth a shot.

I enter a new search. An old picture populates on Google Images of three eager twentysomethings in snow jackets and beanies. The caption reads: *Jacob Perry, Kohl Reynolds and Jane Lacy in Sundance for the movie SHE'S COMPLICATED.* Jacob Perry's sandy blonde hair was much shorter then, but his familiar movie star face remains unchanged. Kohl Reynolds's hair was cropped shorter, too. A lot less wear and tear on his skin, fewer tattoos. So, they were friends in the beginning? They came up together. What story was Grace tracking?

I tap back to the search results.

A Yelp review catches my eye.

User: BigFish2092

REVIEW OF THE WHISTLING PIG

Beware. This is a piece of shit dive bar. Came here for its supposed Hollywood history. Rumor is that Jacob Perry and Kohl Reynolds wrote their first screenplay here. Not sure if it's true, but don't bother. The place reeks of piss. Only for the old drunks and lowlifes. I'm sure it will be torn down soon.

I look up from the computer, glancing over at Allie. She slumps deeper in her chair, sinking her knuckles into her cheek as she scrolls. A sigh of boredom escapes her lips.

"Wanna grab a drink?"

* * *

The Whistling Pig is a bar that didn't want to be found—a grimy hole in the wall hidden in a sea of high-rises and newly renovated restaurants. A place too stubborn to assimilate into its swanky new landscape. It took us twenty minutes to find the decrepit staircase outside a seedy parking structure that led to an alleyway and a chipped green door at the end, marked by a faded cartoon pig sticker.

Swinging the door open, sunlight pours into the vampire den, illuminating a handful of weathered patrons blending into the bartop. Big Fish2092 was right. The place smells like the bottom of a trash can. An unfelted pool table slouches in the back next to a battered jukebox and empty vending machine. The walls are covered with old pictures of downtown Los Angeles, a reminder of the glory days before corporations overran the city.

The bartender sports a faded polo shirt that fits snugly around his belly, transforming the shirt into a crop top. Fumbling with the TV remote, he grumbles. "Can I help you two?"

"We're looking for a guy named Kohl Reynolds."

"Who?" He smacks the remote in frustration, staring at the static-ridden television.

"The screenwriter. He used to frequent this place."

He takes a step toward us, his attention now on us. "Never heard of him."

A shudder ripples through me at the sight of his bloated, vein-covered face. At the bar's edge, an elderly patron winks at Allie, who clutches my arm tightly. "Can we *please* get out of here?" she pleads.

"We'll have two draft beers." I smile, settling onto the nearest barstool. The bartender rolls his eyes and cracks open two longneck bottles.

"Here's to our last week of work," I say, lifting up the bottle.

Allie reluctantly clinks before we both swig the warm beer.

She wipes her mouth, and sighs. "So, Conner. What's next?"

"I'm headed home." I sigh.

"Home? Like Kansas? C'mon. You just got here."

"I promised my aunt that if I didn't have a real writing job by the end of this internship, I would move back. My mom needs a lot of care."

"Shit. I'm sorry. What happened to her?"

I shrug. "Long story."

Allie nods, taking another swig.

"So what are you going to do?" I change the subject.

"Not sure," she pondered, peeling back the bottle label. "Maybe get a job as a barista at one of those pretentious coffee shops." She shrugs. "Maybe I'll start publishing my stuff online." She gulps the last of her beer. "Now can we please get out of here? It smells like shit."

"Yeah." I stand up, fumbling with my money clip in the low light. It falls to the sticky cement floor. *Shit.* I crouch down, trying not to inhale the stench simmering from the ground.

"Whoa," I say, scanning my phone's light underneath the bartop. Hundreds of jagged carvings etched into the hard oak, running up the bar rails—names, phrases, dates.

Infringement. 1999.

The Phantom. Mike and Rick. 2001.

More initials.

"Check this out," I say, scanning the names and dates.

Then something catches my gaze. A symbol. Roman numerals —XIIX. A dark chill prickles down my arms as I run my fingers along the carving. Next to it, I read, *We are going to be famous. Kohl and Jacob. 1999.*

"Holy shit. You've got to see this," I yell from under the bar. "Allie," I repeat.

No answer.

As I rise, a figure looms ominously at the bar. With his slicked-back hair and distinctive tattoos, Kohl Reynolds now stands before me.

3

CONNER

Far from the photo portrayed on his book jacket, Kohl Reynolds sported a thick, scraggily beard, glossy eyes, and a slight head sway. He was wearing a plain black shirt and blue jeans, with a cigarette dangling from his lips.

"Who the fuck are you?" Kohl slurs, inching his face toward me, the scent of bourbon heavy on his breath. Up close, the years seemed to have taken their toll, with deeply etched crow's feet framing hollow eyes. Streaks of gray glide through his slicked-back hair, and the tattoos covering his arms and neck are dull and faded.

"Take it easy, Kohl," the bartender intervenes. "The kid was just getting his wallet."

Kohl grunts then collapses onto a barstool. He lights the cigarette in his mouth and stares into oblivion. The bartender sets down a bourbon as Kohl takes a heavy drag from his cigarette, his eyes wilting downward. *What has become of one of the greatest writers of our time?*

Grace was right. He is a drunk.

Allie gives me an encouraging nod, and I take a seat next to him, my eyes drawn to the letters tattooed on his fingers, spelling out *DEATH*.

"Mr. Reynolds," I say. "My name is Conner. I'm from the InsideJuice.com."

His expression doesn't waver. He takes another heavy drag off the cigarette, the ash fizzling down like a fuse.

"You emailed us," I add, searching for any note of recognition.

He takes a sluggish sip of his bourbon.

"You said you had an important story to tell."

He groans and swivels his head toward me, exhaling a stale cloud of smoke in my face. "Who the fuck are you?"

"Conner from the—"

"No," he interrupts, thrusting his lit cigarette toward me, nearly slipping off the barstool. "*Who the fuck are* you? Why were you under the bar?"

"I was looking for my wallet."

"Bullshit," he snickers, stamping out his cigarette, leaving a burn mark on the filthy wooden bar.

"It's the truth, Mr. Reynolds."

Kohl's pupils dart erratically beneath cloudy whites. "I have a goddamn story that will destroy this shitty town, and they send some kid who looks like he's fresh off a bus from some fly-over state."

Allie snickers from the end of the bar.

I need to get a new wardrobe.

"What do you know about suffering, Conner?"

I turn away from his probing gaze.

"Ah, more than I know," he slurs. "Let me ask you something. When you looked under the bar, what caught your eye?"

"I don't understand."

"It's a simple question." He hiccuped. "What caught your eye?"

He leans forward, seething. "You were staring at that goddamn symbol, weren't you?" He tilts back on his barstool, mocking. "So what brought you to this town?" He asked. "Fame? Riches? Glory?" He lights another cigarette.

"I came here to write."

"A writer," he snickers. "Great fucking choice." He smacks his hand on the bar top, emphasizing his mockery. "So what was your book?"

"My book?"

"Your book," he repeats. "The book that inspired you to take on the most insufferable profession there is. Hemingway, Fitzgerald. . ." *hiccup*. . . "Kerouac. Every writer has a book."

"This isn't about me. So you and Jacob Perry used to—"

In an instant, Kohl leaps from his stool, clutching my shirt and shoving me against the bar top, my back colliding with the wood beams. A roaring pain sears through my ribcage as his forehead presses firmly into my temple, pinning me in place.

"Never mention that fucking name in this bar ever again," he froths. Then, as quick as he leapt up, he releases his grip, stumbling backward in confusion. He tosses a twenty-dollar bill on the bar's end and swings open the door to leave, letting sunlight sweep across the shadowy dive. I remain frozen against the bar top, my shirt undone, my ribs throbbing.

"Let me call you a cab, Kohl," the bartender yells. "Where the fuck are you going?"

"Oblivion," he yells as the door closes behind him.

* * *

Despite Allie's objection, I follow Kohl out of The Whistling Pig. I scan the busy intersection, clutching my aching sides. Blaring horns and screeching tires give away his position. He sways in the middle of the road, smacking the hood of a halted car before stumbling to the other side of the honking intersection. Between the passing cars, I watch him stare upward at a billboard, an advertisement for a movie starring none other than Jacob Perry. The ad displays a gymnast on a balance beam next to Perry's enormous silhouette faded into the background, *The Beam* across the top.

"You took everything from me, you asshole!" Kohl yells as he staggers back and forth, craning his neck up at the billboard. "Do you hear me, Jacob?" He laughs maniacally before tripping into the office building across the street.

The crosswalk turns green, and I follow him into the building's marble-floored lobby, trailing the lingering stench of stale cigarettes to the elevators. The light stops at floor fifteen.

I take the next available.

The elevator door opens to a stunning lobby, clean and modern, with leather couches and a large sign reading *The Artists Agency*. A young receptionist stares at me from behind a large computer display. I don't have a plan. But if I lose him, I lose this story. It's my one and only shot.

"Can I help you?" the receptionist asks.

Before I can answer, Kohl's voice booms from the back of the agency.

"Take that thing fucking down!"

I crane my neck past reception to see Kohl storming through the offices. The commotion has caused quite a scene; employees whisper and chat amongst themselves while suited agents poke their heads out of swanky glass offices. From my research, I recognize Kohl's agent, Brad Leibowitz, a heavyset man with a full head of gray hair. He shouts at the bystanders to return to work. The distraction is my chance.

I jet through the bustling office, shadowing the trail of Kohl's putrid body odor to the back exit into an empty vestibule with another elevator. The light on the panel indicates that someone just stopped at the top level. As I wait for the elevator to return, I hear the door slam shut behind me.

"Where did he go?" Kohl's agent, Brad, fumes toward me.

"Top floor," I mumble.

"And who the fuck are you?" Brad scrutinizes me with suspicion.

I avert my gaze, focusing on the elevator lights. "I'm his… intern," I reply, surprised how easily the lie leaves my mouth.

"An intern?" Brad scoffs, though he doesn't push further. "Maybe you can tell me where the fuck he's been the last few days?"

"What do you mean?"

"I haven't been able to reach him. The last time I talked to him, he was at Sav—" Brad cuts himself off, eyeing me with suspicion. "Then he shows up four days later drunk at my office. Ungrateful prick. I had a massive paycheck lined up for him, too." He angrily jabs the lit elevator button.

The steel door opens before I can respond. On the top floor, two cleaners stand in the middle of an abandoned office floor. They don't ask questions. They point to the staircase for roof access.

Blinding sunlight engulfs our vision as we step out into the scorching rooftop, with endless blue skies and city buildings stretching across the horizon. My gaze sweeps the roof, finding Kohl perched on the ledge, staring into oblivion.

"Look at that asshole." Kohl laughs, staring down at the billboard. "This is what I deserve."

"Get your ass down from there," Brad spews as he whisks past me.

"You've got to love the irony," Kohl snickers, one foot dangling off the ledge. "Jacob Perry will be the last face I see before I die. One last fuck you from God himself."

Brad reaches out his hand. "Whatever it is, we can make this right."

Kohl sways on the ledge, and my heartbeat skips. "No one's going to believe me."

"How long have I been your agent?"

"Please. You don't give a shit."

"Don't give a shit? Who's been cleaning up your messes this past decade?" Brad yells. "Who's been avoiding the cops all week? That detective has been all over my ass. And I know things about you and Savannah." Brad looks back at me, wondering if I can be trusted. He turns back to Kohl. "I know you've been staying at her place. And who did I tell? Who?"

"I fucked up," Kohl chokes out. "I fucked up—bad." He gazes out across the horizon.

"We will fix this." Brad inches even closer.

"Not even the greatest agent in Hollywood can fix this. It's over. They're all better off without me."

A heavy silence blankets the rooftop.

I turn to Brad, waiting for something, anything. He's frozen in his tracks. There is no objection to what comes next. I take a trembling step forward and scream, "It was you!"

Silence. Only the sound of the wind whistling across the rooftop.

I take another shaky step. "You asked me what book made me want to write. It was yours. I read *When the Lights Go Out* when I was in high school. My parents were in a car accident, too. My father died. My mother might as well be dead. And you—your book—gave me something to live for. It gave me hope that I could leave my town. That my tragedy didn't have to define my life. That I could escape and make my life a grand adventure. From the moment I read your book, I wanted to be a writer just like you."

"You don't want to be me," he whispers. "You have no idea what I've done."

"Tell me. That's why I came to find you."

He cackles, and I think I've pushed him too far. But then he turns around, his back facing the ledge. "You never should have found me, kid. You should have stayed in Kansas."

"Kansas?" I mumble. "How did you—"

He tosses my money clip through the air. "You never should have found that symbol."

4

CONNER

When I return to my desk, my encounter with Kohl feels like a distant memory. The dull ache in my ribs is the only evidence that it wasn't a dream. That, and an address of where Kohl is staying on a piece of paper in my pocket. I already checked the address in Google Maps six times to make sure it's real: a lackluster apartment complex in the Valley.

Grace is at her desk, plugged in. I want to tell her everything. She was wrong; there is a story here, and it might be bigger than anyone imagined. And I need her help. If she chased a story about Kohl and Jacob Perry, she might have information that could prepare me for the interview. Based on what I saw today, whatever happened to Kohl, Perry must be involved. But each time I glance her way, she leans closer to her computer screen.

"Jayhawk," Tom roars from his office.

When I enter, Tom's feet are perched on his mahogany desk, right next to a heap of diet soda cans and fast-food containers.

Senior reporter Lane Ferrell lounges casually on the red velvet couch in the back of the room, his legs crossed.

"Where have you been?" Tom snaps his fingers for me to take a seat.

"Chasing a lead." I sit.

"Listen." Tom smirks. "Lane's dug up some information."

I glance back at Lane.

Tom snaps again for my attention. "Seems like Savannah Beck's co-star, Tommy Sinclair, is finally talking. He mentioned that she was dating someone new. A screenwriter with a lot of tattoos."

I sit back, pretending to be shocked. But ever since Kohl and Brad's conversation on the roof, I had been wrestling with the same dark thought. Did Kohl have something to do with Savannah's disappearance? *I fucked up bad.* "Hold on, you think Kohl is a suspect?" I feign disbelief.

"Have you made contact?" Lane chimes in from the couch.

My mind veers straight to the piece of paper in my pocket. If I give up the address, my involvement with this story is done. Then again, what if I'm in over my head? Maybe someone like Lane or Grace *should* take the story. I peer out into the office at Grace's desk. She quickly averts her gaze, as if she had been watching our private meeting. Maybe she *is* interested in this story after all.

I shake my head. "He hasn't responded yet."

Tom exchanges a knowing glance with Lane, as if they had predicted my failure.

"Fine. But if he makes contact, let us know." Tom waves me out of the room. "Needless to say, we need the big guns on this one now."

When I walk out of the room, Grace is gone.

* * *

That night, I toss and turn, replaying the events of the day over and over. I dissect everything that transpired. The desperation in Kohl's voice. The image of him screaming at Jacob's billboard. What really happened to their friendship?

Eventually, I give up on sleep, flipping open my laptop. The clock reads three a.m. I research Jacob Perry and Kohl Reynolds, diving into their IMDb pages. They collaborated on three films: two romantic comedies early in their careers and the more recent gritty drama, *Impeachment*. But beyond that, there are no traces of their friendship or Perry's betrayal.

I click on Perry's Wikipedia page.

A string of quirky romantic comedies in the early '00s made him a heartthrob. Until he became a serious method actor. He starred in darker movies, embodying more villainous characters. A Roman general. A corrupt cop. An unhinged author. He finally won an Oscar for his portrayal of young Hitler in the movie *The Canvas*. I've never watched the film, but its climax, in which young Hitler finally faces the blank canvas, is touted as one of the most disturbing scenes in cinematic history.

I click away from the screen, desperate to keep searching.

Kohl mentioned that he did something bad . . . so bad that it would cause him to contemplate suicide. I think back to Savannah Beck. My cursor lands on an image from *The Offering* movie poster. In a provocative red gown, Savannah stands against a dark gradient backdrop subtly infused with stock market graphics. Her beauty is undeniable. Was Kohl really living with her? In every movie, TV show, and book about a missing person, the police always turn to the husband or boyfriend. What if he. . . No, I couldn't think like that. It couldn't be true.

As I browse, the symbol etched under the bar top flashes across my mind—XIIX.

Kohl had warned me about the symbol, as though it possessed some kind of magical power. I'm not superstitious, but ever since my encounter with it, I couldn't shake this sense of dread lingering within me. As if my subconscious was warning me. I jot down the Roman numerals on a blank piece of paper. Is it a year? A date? Staring at the symbol, Kohl's voice hisses in my ear. *You went straight to the symbol.*

I snap my laptop shut and reach for my timeworn copy of Kohl's book, *When the Lights Go Out*. I breathe a sigh of relief as I thumb through the familiar pages. The novel was gifted to me at a vulnerable time in my life. When I felt hopeless that I would ever escape my small-town fate. But reading this book, I knew . . . One day, I would go to Los Angeles just like the main character, Tommy. I would write stories, fall in love, and face my greatest fears. I would make my life an adventure.

And tomorrow, I would get to interview the author, my idol. I would get to ask how much of the book was real. What happened to his real parents? What happened to Laney, the love of his life in his book?

Deep in thought, I hardly notice the text alert that pops up on my phone from the *Huffington Post*: Savannah Beck Still Missing

I turn the paperback around, staring at Kohl's youthful face, wondering whether he's truly the person I thought he was. I glance back to the symbol in the notebook and another wave of fear crashes over me.

* * *

That night, memories of my childhood infiltrate my dreams. I see the day of my parents' accident, my mom humming about the kitchen with a bright smile. But something changes. The memory shifts, and dark shadows creep along the wall. It is late at night, and my mother is yelling, screaming at someone on the phone. When she sees me, she rushes toward me, tears in her eyes, kissing me on the forehead. She tells me to go back to bed. She promises to be back soon.

But she never returns.

The scene morphs.

I'm in a hospital lobby.

My aunt is pacing the linoleum floor, shouting at someone. Sitting alone, I feel a dark figure lurking in the corner by the vending machines—a shadowy presence with eyes as black as night. The dark figure is chanting something, beckoning me to follow them into darkness.

I wake in a panic, my shirt drenched in sweat.

The haunting images are gone, but a lingering dread clings to my chest. I haven't revisited the day of the accident in years, especially so detailed. As if the symbol unlocked something within me.

* * *

By half-past nine, I'm on the 405 heading north. As Kohl requested, I have an old school tape recorder along with seven blank tapes. The address Kohl gave me is thirty minutes outside of Los Angeles. Nearing the destination, my gut ties itself in angry knots. Who am I to be doing this interview? I'm just an intern. My first story should be some fluff piece about a former reality star. Not my idol. Not an Oscar-nominated screenwriter who claims to have the biggest story in Hollywood.

I can hardly breathe by the time I pull off the ramp at Topanga Canyon Boulevard. The address takes me to an unremarkable apartment complex with perfectly manicured trees and lawns. Sleepy residents walk their pets, plastic dog bags and iPhones in hand. This is a man who made millions of dollars selling scripts. One of the most coveted screenwriters in Hollywood. Was this really where he lived?

I knock gently on apartment 24C.

No answer.

I try the doorknob and find it unlocked.

"Hello." I creak the door open.

The apartment is mostly empty, minus a few cardboard boxes and two metal folding chairs in the living room, hedged by scattered books. A wooden desk holds a typewriter with a heap of cigarette butts in an ashtray.

"Anyone home?"

Kohl appears, wearing nothing but a towel. A fresh gauze wraps around his midsection, a slight stain of red seeping through. He is lean, almost too lean. Traditional tattoos of skulls, words, and animals stretch across his chest and arms. I spot the Roman numeral symbol on his forearm. As soon as I see it, every part of me wants to flee. To leave this apartment and never look back.

Kohl heads into the kitchen to grab a coffee pot. He glances up toward me as he pours. He looks better than he did the day before, his hair combed, his beard tamed. And though his eyes are still bloodshot, he appears lucid and alert. He motions toward one of the metal chairs in the living room. "Sit down. I'll just be a second."

He returns donning blue jeans and a simple black shirt, his hair still damp. He extends his coffee mug, raising it slightly. "Care for some?" he offers.

"I'm…" My voice falters, cracking. "I'm okay."

As he eases himself into the chair opposite me, I retrieve my notebook and the tape recorder. With a quick press of the record button, I flip open my notebook, pen in hand. "First question—"

"Hold on, hold on." Kohl waves his hand, smirking. He reaches for a pack of cigarettes from the table. "Relax." He pulls the ashtray closer, then lights up, inhales, and exhales. He examines me with suspicious eyes. "Shit. You're nervous."

I shake my head, trying to act casual, my eyes darting around the room.

"Not much to look at." Kohl follows my gaze. "Divorce is a motherfucker." He glances at the beads of sweat lining my forehead. "This isn't your first story, is it?"

Too embarrassed to admit the truth, I avoid his gaze.

"Fuck me." He shakes his head, blowing out smoke. "My name's really lost its luster, hasn't it? Can I see your copy of my book?"

I reach into my messenger bag and hand it to him.

He inspects the copy, thumbing through the pages, scanning the cover, the back. He smiles at the antiquated library card still stuck to the inside cover. "Where did you get this?"

"Some guy."

"Some guy?" He arches his eyebrow.

I take a deep breathe. "I was a bit of a loner in high school. I used to eat lunch by myself in the gym. One day I was reading a comic on the bleachers, when this mysterious man settled on the tier above me. Without uttering a single word, he placed your book beside me and departed. That was it. I never saw him again."

Kohl grins, shaking his head as he hands the book back. "So this is your first story," he says, as if mulling over the words. He gets up off the chair, gazing out the window. "Well, I hate to add pressure to this story, but I only have a few days to tell it, and we have a lot to get through."

"I'm ready." I crack back open my notebook.

"Are you?" Kohl stares intently. "By the time we're finished, the entire world will be clawing for this story."

"Does that mean you know something about Sa—"

Kohl's forehead furrows.

I stop talking.

"Kid. I'm going to teach you something. Your boss, like everyone in this town, treats people like commodities they can buy and sell. This story isn't some magazine article for clicks. This story requires more than a snappy headline and a three-line summary. Do you hear me?"

I gulp.

"If you stay, I need you to know everything. And when I'm done, you can do anything with the story you want. You can sell it to a publisher for a million fucking dollars. You can post it online on a goddamned blog for all I care. But you will not ask about Savannah Beck. Not yet. Not until it's time."

As I nod in agreement, my eyes gravitate back to the symbol on his forearm. Kohl catches me and takes a deep breath. "I've done horrible things. Things you couldn't imagine that young guy on that cover doing." He points to my copy of his book. "But in the end, everything will make sense. Who I am. What I have become. And most importantly, why you're here."

I flinch when he says it.

"Yes, Conner from Kansas. It's no accident that you sit in front of me. No accident that it's you who will tell my story."

Part One

THE ARTIST

"You can run from your shadow for a long time. But eventually, the reckoning will come. Hopefully, I'll be driving a Porsche in Malibu when mine catches me."

—Kohl Reynolds, *Rolling Stone* interview

5

KOHL

I was thirteen when the devil marked me on the chilly streets of San Francisco.

I was smoking with a few older kids under the awning of a charming bookstore called The Gate. The streets were enveloped in fog, leaving behind an enigmatic mist that clung to the pavement like thick smoke. I couldn't see five feet in front of me. But I remember the sound of boots clicking down the steep sidewalk.

A man's silhouette emerged from the haze; he was middle-aged, clean shaven, with closely cropped gray hair. He wore a beautifully tailored three-piece suit and a cabbie hat, a mahogany cane at his side. Lavish brown loafers to match.

The other boys paid him no mind, snickering amongst themselves. But not me. There was something so captivating, so mysterious about that man. As if he belonged to another era. I surveyed him through the window, conversing with the bookshop owner, opening a brown leather briefcase full of antique books.

The bell chimed softly as I entered the store, tiptoeing behind bookshelves, peering at the man from between stacks. I was entranced by his proper English accent. The scent of his Irish tweed and old leather briefcase. He handed over a stack of books to the owner and they shook hands. As the old man reached for the door handle to exit, he paused and glanced in my direction. I ducked behind the shelves. When I peered back, a playful grin stretched across his wrinkled face. He curled his index finger, summoning me out. He opened his briefcase full of books, scanning the contents, as if deciding which one I should receive.

Finally, the old man pulled out an unscathed hardback and placed it in my hands. And when I reached out to grab it, I felt something. A buzzing in my fingertips. A dormant power awakening within me. A deep inner knowing that this moment would define me.

The novel was newer than most of the books in his briefcase. It had a glossy yellow cover with an image of a diamond, *The Jeweler* written in red script across the stone. I flipped through the pages under his watchful eye, eventually landing on the back binding. That's when I saw it for the first time—the symbol. Those four ancient, enigmatic characters framed by an ancient skull. I was captivated in its presence, as if time stood still. The mark seemed both familiar and mysterious, both empowering and haunting. Little did I know, I had just been marked.

What does the symbol mean?

It won't be that easy.

The Jeweler. I've never heard of it.

Most people have never heard of this book. The author, Robert Drifter, only wrote one novel. That's it.

What's it about?

The story follows a young boy, Sal, whose father was a successful jeweler in the Diamond District of New York. He was a moral, hardworking man. So when he refused a local mobster's demand for a ring, his henchmen gunned down the store—killing everyone Sal ever loved. That started a twenty-five-year quest for revenge.

But I'm getting ahead of myself.

You should know why that was *my* book.

As you might have gleaned from my novel, I was orphaned at a young age. Our home was in a picturesque neighborhood in Berkeley, right across from a quaint park. The night of their death remains blurry, only fragments scattered across my subconscious. I remember faint voices luring me from my bed. I remember tiptoeing to the edge of the staircase, peering down at two police officers in my doorway, conversing with a woman. Perhaps a babysitter. Or a friend of my parents. I was never quite sure. But here's what I remember most about that night.

This will sound crazy, but I felt something, a shadow, a darkness, a foreign tongue calling out to me. When I looked across the street, I saw them: three cloaked shadows standing at the edge of the park, staring into my soul. Hissing foreign words I couldn't understand. I told myself several versions of this story through the years—that they were figments of my imagination, hallucinations. Stress under trauma. There were no shadows. But deep down, I wondered…

So what were they?

Next question.

Did your own parents die in a car accident like the characters in your novel?

That's what the police told me. That's what my grandma told me. I attended their funeral, but I never saw the bodies. My childhood imagination filled in the gaps. Growing up, I had distant memories of my parents. The smell of an aftershave. My mother writing in a diary with the sun dripping across her face. Trips to the bookstore. Good memories. I remember my father tapping away at the typewriter keys, a cigarette dangling from his mouth. On his hand, an ancient bronze ring with a hexagram gleaming between sacred geometry.

It's the only thing I have left of my father.

But there were other memories, too. Trapped memories. Visions locked inside a basement, desperately trying to escape. Images from that night that seeped into my dreams. A dark room. A door slamming shut. My father pounding a typewriter in a state of madness. Pages swirling about him. Bits and pieces. But never a full story.

What happened after your parents died?

Despite her reluctance, my grandmother took me in. She resided in San Francisco's Nob Hill, an antiquated Victorian home that hadn't been updated in decades. My grandma was a miserable widower. She lost my grandfather to a heart attack, and blamed my father for his death. For not accepting his place in the family business. For leaving my overworked grandfather to bear the burden. She blamed me for being his spawn.

My grandmother spent her days on a sofa, staring into a crackling fire, wearing glamorous dresses, jewelry adorning her neck and wrists. She drank vodka martinis and smoked two packs of cigarettes a day, an oxygen tank clinging to her side. Every so often, after god knows how many martinis, she'd manage to leave her sofa. With her twisted, hunched spine, she climbed the creaky wooden stairs, her oxygen tank pounding against the wood. *Thunk. Thunk. Thunk.*

She'd stand in my doorway, gasping for breath. Her blotchy, pale skin and deep wrinkles made her monstrous. Her irises were black and grotesque. She'd hiss: *You're no good like your father. He was a deserter. A degenerate. A drunk. He killed your mother, and he left you here with me.* I never responded. I never gave her the satisfaction. But that only made her angrier.

You have his no-good soul.

You are unlovable.

You are worthless like him.

In her rage, she banished me to the basement and locked the door. Leaving me in utter darkness. Much of my childhood was spent in that hole, letting my grandma's words trickle into my subconscious. Evil roots spreading across my soul, hardening my heart. It was a cold, concrete basement, with no furniture, no books. Nothing to pass the time except an old water-logged rug and a thick black rope.

Day after day, I unraveled the fibers of that rope, letting my imagination soar to distant worlds. Sandy beaches and ancient castles. Imaginary friends and characters. You could say storytelling was my way of surviving.

As I grew older, that basement became my refuge, just as much as it was my prison. Demons always are. I became an expert at losing myself in fantasies. I never cared about school. I liked being trapped in my own head, lost in my thoughts. The shit that motivated other kids—getting good grades, sports, popularity—none of it was for me. I was different.

But reading *The Jeweler*... That book offered me a roadmap for my life. I wanted to be like Sal in Drifter's novel. Leave everything behind and set off on a grand adventure. Sal was only sixteen in the novel when he became homeless on the streets of New York. Not a penny to his name. But he had something that eluded so many: a purpose. A will to survive. An unyielding thirst to make something of himself. To seek revenge on the people who took everything from him. I wanted that kind of purpose.

I wanted to go to Hollywood and become a writer.

As a fan of my novel, you might appreciate this—how I got the title for my book. My grandmother had plenty of money but wasn't capable of paying the bills. So every time the power went out, I'd conjure up all sorts of scenes: gangsters running in and shooting up the place, zombies tearing through the walls, vampires, mercenaries. In my fantasies, I always found a way to escape, just like Sal did.

When I turned seventeen, I made myself a pact. The next time the lights went out, I would run as far away from this evil house as possible. I didn't have to wait long. Six months before my high school graduation, the lights flickered out and I closed my eyes, imagining the scene.

The killer enters the house with a gun drawn, a shadowy figure, shooting through ceramic vases and glass windows. He sets fire to the curtains. I imagined my father protecting me, fending off the intruder, yelling for me and my mother to run. I watch my dad fall at the hands of the shadowy silhouette. My mother is next. I scream, and the murderer turns to me on the staircase. I can't see his face behind his dark, brimmed hat. But deep down, I know I have seen this man before. He is a ghost from my past. His shadow chases me through the burning house, but I crawl out through the fire escape, just in time. And I run as far away as I can.

Less than a block away from my grandma's house, I breathed in the cold San Francisco air and stared back at my prison. I pictured the imaginary flames engulfing the house, burning everything inside. All of it. Even that heavy black rope in the basement, searing down to its bitter end.

That night, I left it all behind.

I boarded a bus to Los Angeles, carrying only a bag of clothes and my treasured copy of *The Jeweler*, which I read for the hundredth time with a smile on my face.

6

CONNER

"Can I see the book?"

Kohl hands me a copy of *The Jeweler*. The cover is faded and worn with loose pages stuffed back into the binding. It reminds me of my copy of his book. Hundreds of nights reading into the wee hours, cramming it into backpacks and lockers, reading on my breaks at the construction site. His story feels like my story. I flip the book over to the back. But unlike Kohl's novel, there is no photo of Drifter. No contact information. Nothing.

"Did you ever find him?" I ask.

Kohl looks solemn. "When I was a kid, I used to write to his publisher every week, addressed to his editor. Hoping the letters got to him. I'd ask him for advice about my situation. I wrote those letters for years, but he never sent anything back..."

My eyes settle on the symbol at the back of the book, my fingers tracing the ink. Before I can ask another question, my phone rings. A call from the office.

"Take it," Kohl says. "I'll put on more coffee."

Stepping outside, I answer the phone.

"Where the fuck are you?" Tom Arnold barks in my ear.

"I told Allie. I'm sick," I reply, pacing anxiously.

"Have you seen the fucking news?"

"No. What's going on?"

"They found Savannah's car."

"Really?" I glance through the window; Kohl is changing out the coffee filter. I move farther away from the door.

"Totaled in the Malibu Canyon. Listen, kid, and listen good. Lane believes Kohl Reynolds will be arrested for the murder of Savannah Beck."

"Really?"

"Is that all you can say?" Tom screams. "I know you've made contact. Tell me where he is. I'm sending Lane right now—"

"Hang up." Kohl stands in the doorway. "Hang up," he commands.

I press the end button on my phone, cutting off my enraged boss. Fear floods my senses as I stare at my idol, struggling to contend with the truth. He may be a murderer. Perhaps this isn't his story . . . it's his confession.

"Come back in."

I hesitate.

"Look, things are going to get a lot harder from this point on. If you can't handle it, fuck off," he says, before walking back into the living room, leaving me alone with my swirling thoughts.

Despite the possible danger of being alone with a killer, or my boss's warning, there is something Kohl said that drowns the other voices out: *There's a reason you're here.*

When I re-enter, Kohl is seated, cigarette in hand. "Sit down," he orders. "We've only just begun."

7

KOHL

I SPENT my entire life savings on a nine-hour Greyhound. Taking a bus to Hollywood was a rite of passage, a pilgrimage to the city of angels. Stepping off, I was just another homeless kid on the streets. This town is no place for a wandering teenager, especially in the '80s. Bad drugs. Tough guys. The odds were stacked against me.

But I kept my wits.

On cold, rainy nights, tucked underneath the awnings of abandoned buildings, I'd read my copy of *The Jeweler* over and over, gripping my father's ring as I shivered through the darkness. I never got comfortable. I did what I needed to survive. Drifter's words gave me hope. Reading about Sal's displacement on the streets of New York. How he ate stale loaves of bread out of the dumpster. His loneliness. His story was my story. In the book, an owner of a deli eventually offered him a job.

As for me, a real estate tycoon named Arnie Dolowitz gave me my break. He found me sleeping in one of his vacant buildings. Instead of calling the police, he told me to meet him outside in five. He bought me coffee and gave me a place to stay, a tiny loft in one of his empty commercial buildings. The free rent came with a job. Once a month, I walked downtown, collecting rent from his tenants. It was the easiest gig I ever had. Aside from strolling through rough neighborhoods with a wad of cash. But I had everything I needed to pursue my dream. A used typewriter. A place to stay. Food in my belly and a roof over my head. There was only one problem—I couldn't write a damn thing.

I'd started drinking by then. Not because I was desperate to be like my grandmother. No, I was petrified of the blank page. I needed a distraction. I didn't know how to start. Or if I had anything to say. I feared what I'd find in my basement. I could only stare at the old typewriter, envisioning my fingertips pounding the smooth surface of the keys. After ten minutes, I'd leave my desk to go grab a drink at a nearby bar, The Whistling Pig—The Pig for short.

That's where I got my first lucky break…

Back then, The Pig was a mecca for aspiring artists drowning their Hollywood sorrows. Sulking at the bar, I caught a lively debate over classic films, whether *Citizen Kane* and *The Godfather* were overrated relics.

Suddenly, a self-assured voice sliced through the chatter. "You idiots wouldn't recognize a good story if it bashed you in the fucking head."

All eyes converged on a youthful incarnation of James Dean, sporting blonde locks, a chiseled jawline and bright blue eyes. He was drinking whisky by himself at the bar.

A burlier patron stepped forward. "Got something to say, pretty boy?"

The blonde-haired kid smirked, glancing casually down at his drink. "Not to a hack like you."

The Pig was known for a good bar fight, but this one... By the time I intervened, I was restraining the young rebel, blood streaming down his face, his eyes radiating fury.

So I borrowed a line from Michael Corelone in *The Godfather*.

"Keep your friends close, but your enemies closer."

A playful grin spread across the kid's bloodied lips.

"Name's Jacob Perry."

And that was it. For the next three months, we became drinking buddies. We both loved The Pig because it was right across the street from the biggest talent agency in the world. We used to dream about the pitch meetings we'd have in those offices. We'd talk about fame and women, good cocaine and red carpets. But it was more than that for us. We both wanted to make something real. Something as good as the works we idolized. For me, it was *The Jeweler*. For Jacob, it was a film called *The Scream*.

The Scream? Never heard of it.

It won an Academy Award for Best Picture in the '70s. It was about the painter Edvard Munch, known for the iconic painting "The Scream." You've seen the damn thing a hundred times. A marred man, holding his hands to his face, screaming in front of a wavy sunset. The actor who played Munch, Gary Vice, won an Academy Award for Best Actor for his portrayal, though he didn't show up to the ceremony to claim his statue. In fact, Vice never took another acting role again.

He fell off the face of the planet. Just like Drifter.

Jacob was obsessed with finding Vice in the same way I was obsessed with finding Drifter. We used to talk about those two pieces of art for hours, dissecting every chapter, every frame. I loaned Jacob my copy of *The Jeweler* to read. He loved it. He wanted us to adapt it into a movie together. He was also curious about the symbol in the book. He believed it was a symbol of the Great Muse, a mark of true artistry. We became infatuated with the symbol, a constant reminder to never compromise our artist integrity.

Jacob stayed true to that, at least initially. I admired that. He could have gotten an agent and booked commercials and smaller roles. But that's not how he wanted to make it. He wanted his Hollywood debut to be something good.

That's when I saw my opportunity. I proposed, "Let's write something together."

And thus, our creative partnership began.

We met up at the bar four times a week, notebooks in hand, spouting off ideas in a drunken haze. Mobster movies. Pulp crime movies. Noirs. Half-baked plots with surface-level characters.

In the midst of an all-nighter, I suggested mining our childhoods for raw material. Knowing he grew up as an army brat in Germany, I probed about his father. His reaction was visceral: jaw clenched, eyes darkening. "Don't ask me about that fucking man ever again."

I backed off. We were both young, cocky, and haunted by the monsters in our basement. Truly, if I hadn't met Jane, I'm not sure I would have made it out of that bar. Maybe I'd be another fixture at The Pig, slowly fading into the shadows, forsaking the dreams that brought me to Hollywood. And Jacob, well, he might have sold out, shooting TV pilots in the Valley. But I did meet Jane.

And one woman changed everything… for both of us.

8

CONNER

Kohl retrieves a framed Polaroid of Jane Lacy from a nearby box and hands it to me. She is stunning—a natural beauty with sandy-blonde hair and a freckly face. In the photo, she lies in bed, wrapped in hotel sheets, her gaze directed out the window, the turrets of a fairytale castle in the far distance.

"In Drifter's novel, Sal meets the love of his life while working at the deli. She becomes the one thing that he cares about more than his quest for revenge. In the end, he must make a choice. Will he follow the shadowy impulse to hunt down the men who killed his parents? Or does he choose to build a new life with the woman he loves?" Kohl smiles before tossing the photograph back in the box.

"Ever been in love, kid?" Kohl dangles a cigarette from his mouth, putting the flame to the tip.

I shrug.

"C'mon, there must be someone," he presses.

I can feel my cheeks redden.

Kohl exhales smoke across the room. "What's she like?"

"Smart. Ambitious."

He nods, intrigued. "And the first kiss?"

The blood rushes to my face in a fury.

"Jeez. No wonder you're so wet behind the ears," he teases, smiling. "At least you have something to look forward to. Who knows, she might even inspire you to write something life changing." He beckons for me to start the recorder.

9

KOHL

California has a way of luring you to sleep. With its perfect weather and good drugs, I managed to spend four years in Los Angeles without writing a goddamned thing. There was always tomorrow, always an excuse. Dreams don't always have a quick death in Hollywood. Sometimes it's a slow burn.

Jacob and I agreed to take a week-long hiatus from our brainstorm sessions. By then we were both dead broke, our poise fading. You start to wonder—what if you're not one of the few who make it? There's not enough room in this town for every bright-eyed artist. Even the talented ones don't always get their lucky break.

On a laid-back Sunday, I found myself in Venice Beach with a few buddies. Baked on both sun and weed, I wandered off by myself, stumbling upon an art exhibit in an abandoned warehouse. There was no guest list or security, so I slipped in unnoticed, dressed in a casual T-shirt and ripped jeans. I made a beeline for the nearest waitress holding champagne flutes.

Most of the crowd had congregated around one painting, a chilling portrait of Marilyn Monroe, painted three days before her tragic death—an Isaias Everett masterpiece. Maybe it was the haze of weed, but I felt this deep connection to the work. Like I could sense the painter and the subject's vibrational energy merging, the sorrow, the pain, the hope, as if they were tethered by the same mysterious bond.

Just as I was sinking into the painting, a mumbling woman broke my trance. "You'd be lucky to have a night with me."

Distracted, I knocked into a tray filled with champagne.

"Shit," the mumbling woman cursed, frantically patting me down with cocktail napkins.

The moment I laid eyes on Jane Lacy, my world tilted on its axis. Her freckled-face was framed by strawberry-blonde hair tangled in a messy bun. She had big full lips and dark blue eyes. She was dressed in the catering staff uniform, a white collared shirt and black pants.

After a few feeble pats, she handed me the napkin and went back to mumbling to herself. "You'd be lucky to have a night with me," she repeated.

I stood there, baffled.

She finally acknowledged my presence. "I'm getting ready for an audition." She gestured to a man across the room. "See that guy? He's directing a new movie, and I'm about to persuade him to cast me instead of the talentless model he's going to pick."

She glanced dismissively at my clothes and then at the painting before me. "Why are you staring at this overpriced crap?"

Before I could respond, she darted off toward the director. I watched in awe as she auditioned in her catering outfit, gesturing wildly with her hands, animating the scene. When the exchange was over, the woman returned to her rounds, champagne tray in hand.

From then on, I couldn't stare at another piece of art; I only stared at Jane. She had no business working that party. She dropped two trays. Never lingered long enough for anyone to take a drink. Still, there was something so refreshing about her. It was the way she moved about the world. This effortlessness. This ability to not give a shit what people thought. Finally, the night was winding down, and my buzz was wearing off. It was my last chance to make a move. As soon as her tray was empty, I followed her into the kitchen.

"I need to know how it went."

"Bombed," she said, filling her tray with skewered chicken. "He said my tits weren't big enough."

"Fuck off, he did not."

She finished loading the tray. "No, but I know that's what he was thinking," she said, glancing up at me. "Who are you? Why are you back here?"

I took a step closer. "I just had a feeling that you and I were supposed to meet."

"You watch too many movies," she said, rolling her eyes and attempting to step past me.

"I'm a writer."

"Of course you are," she cackled.

We entered the gallery, and I kept following.

"What's that mean?"

She stopped. "Any books or movies I would have heard of?"

"Well . . ."

"Precisely," she said, turning her back and gliding down the hall.

"Wait a second." I grabbed her hand. "You don't think I'm going to make it?" I asked.

"I'm sure you will," she responded, rolling her eyes once more.

"Actually," I interjected, blocking her path, "I'm researching a script right now."

She took a deep breath, tolerating my resolve. "Oh really?"

"An aspiring writer meets an up-and-coming actress."

"How original." She started to walk off. I stopped her again.

"You haven't even gotten to the big montage."

That earned me a smirk. She looked me up and down. "What do you want?"

"A date."

"Do you have a real job?"

"Kind of."

"Come from money?"

"No."

She shoved past me.

"What about fate?" I yelled, and that made her stop.

"Imagine the odds," I added. "Out of millions of people in this city, our paths intersected at this exact moment." I came closer. "Something led me to this warehouse. You spilling that drink on me wasn't an accident."

"You weren't my first tonight, you won't be the last," she said, her back still turned.

"I'd like to be."

She turned to face me.

"You'd like to be what?"

"Your last."

She sneered. "Are you for fucking real?" Then she sniffed the air, her eyebrows raising. "You have any more of that weed?"

I pulled out a joint from my pocket

"Then as fate would have it." She smirked. "My name is Jane Lacy."

* * *

After her shift, we strolled the boardwalk as the sun set over Venice Beach. She was still wearing her stained catering outfit, now covered by an oversized fleece sweatshirt. We got high and strolled the city for hours. She told me her life was a hustle between waiting tables and going on auditions. Doing her best to keep afloat. But she didn't complain about it. Just the opposite. She loved her tiny apartment, the thrill of the chase. Staying up every night studying the greats. Bette Davis. Audrey Hepburn. Elizabeth Taylor was her favorite. Fame wasn't her end goal. She wanted full expression and mastery. I admired that about her.

We went to a bar.

She downed three martinis; I matched her with three whiskys. We talked about literature and music and Hollywood. She probed me about my writing. I spat out several far-out plots, dystopias, alien invasions, dismal scribblings from my notebook. She tried to restrain laughter.

"What?" Heat ran up my cheeks.

"Maybe try writing something you know about." Her eyes flickered to the bronze ring on my finger. "What about that? You religious?"

"It's the only thing left of my father," I said, avoiding her gaze. "I use it to keep the darkness away."

"I could use one of those," she mused, grinning.

"What do you mean?"

"I attract bad people." Her voice tapered off.

I didn't press further.

I walked her ten blocks back to her apartment. When I asked her for her number, her mouth shifted to the side. She said, "It's complicated."

When I asked why, she said, "Tomorrow I'll be someone else."

"Then I'd like to remember tonight's version."

She rolled her eyes, but I leaned in nonetheless, and our lips collided, my entire world shifting in a split second.

You think I'm being dramatic, but I'll say this: our existence—light, heat—it's all reliant on atoms colliding. Energy vibrating through us. Infinite potential. Every inch of my body felt that connection. Like a tuning fork struck inside my chest. An outpouring of her vitality flowed into my veins, giving me waves of new life and divine inspiration. No amount of cocaine and booze in the world could ever capture that feeling. Trust me, I tried.

As soon as she walked into her apartment, my inner voice spoke for the first time: "Go write."

If you ever hear that voice, you run. I mean, *run*. I'm so thankful my pea-sized brain didn't sabotage the muse. I sprinted to my tiny loft, bolting up the ladder. I pounded the keys, the vibrations of our encounter still coursing through my veins. I typed like the devil was chasing me toward the finish line. Scenes came to me in a brilliant flash. I wrote about things I was years from understanding. Love. Heartbreak. Jane's face, her smile, her laugh. They were the driving force that granted me access to an ocean of higher consciousness.

I wrote my first script in under two days.

The title: *She's Complicated*.

All from one kiss?

That's the power of a muse, kid. When I finished, I sat back, dumbfounded. I hadn't slept. I barely ate. But I felt more alive than ever. I wasn't sure where half the words came from. It was written by a higher authority; I was merely the conduit. A vessel for something bigger than myself.

But even as a naïve kid, I did know one thing. I'd been given a gift. That type of shit doesn't just happen; there's a process for people chasing the Hollywood dream. You gotta fight and claw and scrap your way through this town. You gotta show the universe how bad you want it. And I swear, if I hadn't met

Jane, it would have taken years to write something good. Maybe decades, if ever. Don't you see? She was a miracle. My miracle. Something that few writers ever get in their careers. A muse that could move mountains.

As soon as I finished, I ripped the last page out of the typewriter carriage and brought the stack down to The Pig. Jacob sat there and read the script while smoking cigarettes in the back, pacing. As soon as he finished, he walked over to me in silence. I held my breath, waiting for him to bring me back down to earth. But after a long pause, he said: "You fucking did it."

I repeated: "I fucking did it."

Imagine the farce. Two kids holding a first draft of a script, jumping up and down in celebration. As if we had accomplished anything. Everyone in Hollywood has a goddamn script to sell. Janitors. Baristas. You know how many stacks of unread scripts line the mailrooms in this town?

But it didn't matter to us. We toasted to inevitable fame. High on delusional hope. We carved our names below the bar top, which became a tradition for other artists who frequented the place. And if it were up to me, I would have spent another year hiding the damn thing. Loving it. Hating it. Probably tossing it away in some desk or dumpster. But I had something else that none of them had.

What's that?

The drive and ambition of Jacob Perry.

10

CONNER

Kohl blows out a puff of smoke and stares out at the gray concrete patio beyond the window. Shadows sweep across the unlit apartment as the sun sets on the Valley.

I turn the audio recorder off. "You want to stop for the day?"

He doesn't acknowledge me.

"Kohl," I repeat, and he snaps out of his daze.

"Give me an hour," he mutters.

I pull into a strip mall to grab fast food. While eating, I scroll through all my missed calls. Six from the office and two from my aunt. I ignore them all. Instead, I google "Robert Drifter author."

As expected, only one novel, *The Jeweler,* populates on the search results. There are two thousand reviews on Amazon but nothing on the actual author. He had no profile picture. No link or website or social media. He was a ghost.

I google *The Scream*. An old movie poster displays, a recreation of Munch's famous painting with actor Gary Vice's silhouette in the background. I find Vice's name on Wikipedia. Kohl was right. After winning an Oscar, he disappeared, never to be seen again. *So strange.* I stare out the window, recapping everything that Kohl has told me thus far. There is something that connects it all, a common thread running through everything.

It was the symbol.

A notification appears from my Breaking News app: *Inside-Juice.com Names Kohl Reynolds as Possible Suspect in Murder of Savannah Beck.*

I hold my breath as I read through the article.

Co-star Tommy Sinclair discusses his relationship with Savannah and her final days before the disappearance.

I skim the rest of the article. Sinclair states that Savannah came to the set with a bruise on her face. That she was living with her boyfriend, screenwriter Kohl Reynolds. Sinclair had met Reynolds days prior at a cast party. According to him, Kohl was untethered and out of sorts. It was clear he was using drugs. Reynolds left the party in a hurry, which upset Savannah. The couple had been fighting.

My phone rings; an unfamiliar local number.

"Conner," a voice crackles.

"Who is this?"

"Grace."

"Grace." My heart skips. "What's going on?"

"I don't know, but Tom is piss—"

Static.

I step out of the car. "Grace, are you there?"

"Yes. Listen, Conner." Her voice returns. "I didn't tell you everything about that story I was digging up."

Every muscle in my body tenses.

She continues "Kohl and Jacob were part of something. Something dark and evil. I don't know what it is. But I know it's some twisted shit. Has he shown you the symbol?"

"What is it?"

The signal cuts out.

"Grace?"

"He is dan . . . ger . . . Conner," she chokes out through the static.

"Do you think he did it?"

Silence.

The phone goes dead.

I dial her back, straight to voicemail.

* * *

It takes me thirty minutes to wrestle the courage to start the car. I'm not sure what's motivating me anymore. Curiosity? Loyalty?

When I arrive at Kohl's apartment, the door is ajar. Kohl is sitting at the fold-up table, rifling through a box of memorabilia. I can't help but wonder if I'm in the home of a murderer. Does he have a gun? Kohl glances up from the box, a puzzled look on his face.

"You went online," Kohl observes, lighting up a cigarette.

I timidly sit down in the chair across from him.

"Ask me." He exhales a cloud of smoke.

"Do you know where Savannah is?" I ask.

He nods.

I swallow hard.

"What about the symbol?"

My phone vibrates. It's Tom Arnold from the office.

"You need to take that." Kohl smirks.

"No," I say, letting the call go to voicemail.

Kohl folds his arms, snickers to himself. "Most careers in this town aren't built on talent; they're built on opportunities. Finding them and then having the guts to seize it. You took initiative by coming down to that bar. You took initiative on that rooftop. And here's your reward," he says, staring down at the new voicemail notification on my screen. "Unless you're too scared to claim it."

I don't respond.

Kohl continues. "Right now, your boss sees a story that could make his magazine a few more bucks. What about you? What do you see?"

The answer comes to me in a flash. It isn't about advancing my career. Or my ticket out of Kansas. It is so much more than that. There's a part of me that truly believes Kohl has the answers to my life. Why I was drawn to his book. Why since I saw that symbol, I can't stop thinking about the night of my parents' accident. I need to know my place in all this.

Kohl examines my reaction. "Now that you know what you want, what are you going to do about it?"

I grab my notebook.

Kohl smashes his cigarette in the tray. "You might just make it after all," he says, then gestures to the tape recorder.

11

KOHL

Where was I?

You had just written the script and shown it to Jacob.

I'm sure you're wondering how two un-agented first-time writers sold a script in Hollywood. Jacob understood the cardinal rule of selling a movie—all it takes is one yes. He flooded the goddamn town with our script, showing up at every swanky restaurant, fancy gala and red-carpet event. He even pretended to be bathroom attendant at Morton's Steakhouse so he could slide it underneath a stall when Spielberg was taking a shit.

But our yes came at a Hollywood networking event.

I was busy pointing out agents and producers, and Jacob locked in on a nervous young woman clutching a cocktail glass. "That's the one," he said.

He moved in like a serpent, slowly slithering around his prey, his hands sweeping through his golden locks. With a flirtatious grin and pleading blue eyes, he delivered his pitch—a goddamn love story for the ages.

The next morning, the assistant showed up at her boss's office with tears in her eyes, the script in her hand.

Our first Hollywood meeting was set.

Baymore Studios was a small shop with a few indie hits. They had an office in Burbank, a dingy commercial building with fluorescent lighting and cubicles. Far from the grandeur I had in mind when I pictured selling my first script. I had this absurd expectation of what my Hollywood experience should be. Driving onto a huge studio lot to meet with powerful executives in swanky offices. Walking down corridors lined with posters of blockbuster movies.

So when we sat down with the head of the studio, Lyle Patrick, I acted like a petulant child. No B-rated studio could possibly do my script justice. I told him that the budget needed to be ten million. Imagine that. What did I know about budgets? I was a cocky little shit. I thought my script was special. I thought I was special. Because I didn't spend a decade toiling away in LA coffee shops like most screenwriters. This cruel town had yet to humble me. Lyle should have kicked my ass out of his office.

After the meeting, Jacob and I went to the bar. He was fuming. I'd almost sabotaged this movie after six months of schmoozing and scheming. After a dozen drinks or so, we had our first fight. Two idiots wrestling on the grimy floor, exchanging headlocks and wheezing in exhaustion. Not a single person intervened or even cared. When we were done, we sat back at the bar, and Jacob gave me the words I needed to hear.

"This is not the best shit you are going to write. So let's get ourselves in the fucking arena so we can start playing the game."

He handed me the phone, and I called Lyle and apologized.

We took the first offer. Thirty thousand for the script, two and a half percent of the net profits. But I asked for one condition, which they conceded: Jacob and I would be executive producers, giving us input on who they cast.

They also paired us up with a director, Vick Tuttle. The same director who later won an Oscar for Best Director in *The Canvas*. Back then, he was just a young director with big ideas.

Our first meeting with Vick was at the Beverly Wilshire. He blew in twenty minutes late and ordered a scotch and a stack of pancakes from the hotel bar. I thought he looked like a sleazy hustler, dressed in his signature red velour tracksuit, with a thin gold chain buried beneath a pile of chest hair. Jacob thought the guy was a fucking genius. I wasn't so easily sold.

Before the meeting ended, I told him about Jane. "She's the perfect actress," I insisted. The inspiration behind the screenplay.

Vick immediately dismissed the idea, waving his hand with a wad of pancakes oozing out of his mouth. "We need to reset the creative energy."

"You don't understand. You just need to see her."

"Fine." He waved me off. "Let her audition."

* * *

Finding Jane was the only producer responsibility I took seriously. And that was no walk in the park. Her apartment complex proved to be a dead end. I knocked on every single door in that building, but not a single tenant knew of her. Talent agencies, casting directors—they all drew a blank. I was on the verge of losing hope when my phone rang.

"If you don't stop stalking me," Jane seethed on the other end of the line, "I swear, I'll—

"No, wait," I hastily interjected. "I have an audition."

A long pause.

"It's real, I swear," I assured her. "I wrote it, and we're casting."

Another long pause.

"I'm sorry I showed up at your building," I added. "You're a hard person to get a hold of."

"I have to be right now." She finally broke her silence.

I didn't push further. "Just be at the studio at two p.m. tomorrow."

"What's the film about?" she asked before getting off the line.

"Something I know about."

The next morning, Jane tiptoed into the casting room wearing a plain white shirt and blue jeans, her strawberry-blonde hair in a springy ponytail. We both took a deep breath. I knew this movie needed Jane. She was Claire McIntosh. The stunning, enigmatic female lead. Without her, there was no movie.

The audition was the toughest scene in the film. A monologue in which Claire converses with all seven of her personalities in a mirror. I was so smitten that I didn't notice what happened in that room. Her voice cracked every time she transitioned between personalities. She revealed her nervous tic, her jaw shifting back and forth between pauses. I thought it was endearing. It was only years later that I could watch it with objective eyes.

When it was over, I asked Vick what he thought.

He said, "Are you fucking kidding me?"

That should have been the end of it. He gave her a chance, and there were a dozen good actresses up for the part. But I wouldn't give up so easily. I pestered Vick for weeks, begging him to give her another shot. He was adamant that she wasn't good enough. Not enough experience. Not the look he wanted.

So what did you do?

I pulled a petty stunt. I called the studio head and told him that Vick was ruining the film, casting all the wrong people. The studio set a lunch meeting to hash it out, and Vick lost his shit. When he showed, his face was as red as his tracksuit. He told everyone that I was just some wannabe writer trying to fuck some talentless actress. He had creative control. He would walk if they didn't take me off as a producer. Jacob was infuriated with me. He demanded I apologize to Vick and let this Jane thing go.

Did you?

I called Vick and extended an olive branch. I invited him to the Del Mar horse track to apologize. Vick never turned down a day at the track. We spent the afternoon betting on horses while I bought him round after round. He didn't give two shits about the apology, as long as I fell in line. We were nearing the final race, and Vick had just put a thousand bucks on a local favorite named Portlander.

"Why not up the stakes," I proposed. "I'll bet you Lucky Strike beats Portlander."

Vick downed his seventh scotch. "Lucky Strike is a sixteen to one underdog."

"Then you have nothing to lose," I reassured him.

"The terms?"

"If I win, you cast Jane."

He tensed. "And if I win?"

"I walk off the movie and hand you the thirty grand I made for writing it."

"All for a fucking girl?" He fumed.

We shook hands.

When Lucky Strike ousted Portlander by a few yards, Vick smashed his plastic cup and stormed off. Unknown to Vick, I spent three weeks studying the horses. I knew that Lucky Strike was a horse on the rise. Still, it was a gamble. I'd bet everything on Jane... I always did.

I delivered the news to Jane at The Dayton, an old Hollywood lounge downtown. She was effortlessly cool, dressed in a vintage Ramones shirt, her hair cascading down in waves. Her deep blue eyes and freckled skin glowing in the dim pendant lights.

"I got the part?" she screamed, drawing attention from the entire restaurant. "But I bombed that audition."

I told her, "That part was written for you. That line you said after we kissed . . . 'I'm complicated.'"

She laughed. "I don't even remember saying that."

Classic Jane. We toasted and celebrated with expensive steaks and top-shelf whisky, while belting out '80s anthems from a live band. Her obnoxious laugh and horrible singing were infectious. We were making a movie, our entire careers ahead of us. On the cusp of our wildest dreams.

After our buzz kicked in, I asked her what she meant about being hard to find.

"My father just got out of prison," she confessed. "He's been looking for me." She paused, then met my gaze. "I'm tired of letting bad men into my life."

She changed the subject, raising her glass. "Here's to a working writer and actress."

"To the real Claire McIntosh," I added, clinking glasses.

I could have stared at her smile all night.

I wanted to write movies for her until the end of time.

I walked her back to her cousin's apartment, and when we kissed at her doorstep, our spark reignited. In my mind, there was no one else for me. I could have married her right then and there. But a few seconds into the kiss, she pulled away. "I wasn't kidding when I said I'm complicated."

"I know," I said, leaning in for another kiss, but she turned.

"I have to go away for a little while." She backed up even farther.

And then she left. Always mysterious. Always leaving me wanting more.

When I got home, I wrote fifty pages of my second script.

* * *

We had seven months until production. I called Jane every week, but she disappeared yet again. To pass the time, I partied with Jacob. It was nice having a little bit of money in our pockets. We were young, dumb and pumped full of cocaine. Thanks to Vick, we started mingling with famous people. Vick introduced Jacob as an actor on the rise… That shit went straight to his head. He started wearing leather jackets and slicking back his hair. He pursued women like it was a sport. Champagne in hand, arm slung around my shoulder, he'd declare that Hollywood was ours for the taking. That we were on the precipice of greatness. But every so often, after a long night of drinking, a different Jacob emerged…

There was this one evening at a studio executive's mansion in the Hills. I found him brooding in a leather sofa beside a crackling fire, his usual glass of scotch in his hand. The fiery glow illuminating those piercing blue eyes. As soon as I sat across from him, an evil grin stretched across his face.

"Did I ever tell you why I loved Gary Vice and that movie, *The Scream*, so much?" he asked.

I shook my head.

He swirled his glass. "When I was a boy growing up in Germany, my father used to go on hunting trips in the Black Forest. I'd beg him to let me tag along.

"Then, one morning I got my wish. I awoke to his stern face staring over me, the smell of whisky on his breath. He didn't say a word. He ripped me out of bed, handed me a gun and hurled me outside in my pajamas.

"We must have walked for hours, wading through the trees' ghostly mist, my feet nearly frostbitten from the icy grounds. At last, we stepped into a clearing, a radiant field with sunlight dripping through the canopy.

"That's when I saw it—a single red elk grazing in a lush field. The most stunning thing I had ever laid eyes on. This field of divine light and energy. Even as a child, I knew that this creature was everything good and right in this world. But when I turned to my father to share this moment, he pointed at my gun, and he ordered me to kill it.

"I tried to obey, raising the gun, but for the life of me, I couldn't pull the trigger. I couldn't destroy something so pure, so good. In response, my father called me pathetic and shot the elk with his own rifle. Then he put the gun to my head and marched me to the dying animal. He commanded me to stare into the animal's eyes, to see its pain and fear. When I flinched, his rifle struck me in the head.

"With the blood dripping down my face, I relented. I stared into the terrified black eyes of that magnificent creature. And right before he died, he made one final scream, a piercing screech that reverberated with me forever.

Jacob continued. "There's a single line in *The Scream* when Munch sits in the darkness of his room with that young woman, and she asks him how he could paint something so horrifying. And Munch says, 'When I heard the screams of mother nature echo through the night, I wasn't scared. I was comforted. Finally, a sound that matched my tormented mind.

"The way Gary Vice delivered that line—that was a man who knew real suffering. Who understood a tormented mind. A man who took his own anguish and made it into something beautiful. True alchemy. That line made me want to be an actor."

I didn't say a word.

He got up, then glanced at the tattoo on my forearm.

"Sometimes I wonder if I'll ever turn my shadows into something that beautiful. That's all I fucking want."

And then he walked away.

Shooting for *She's Complicated* kicked off that summer on the Universal backlot. I was given my own parking space and a personalized chair on set—it felt like a dream. From homeless on the streets to smack-dab in the heart of Tinsel Town making a movie that I wrote.

I've always loved the first day of production—this buzz in the air. The smell of freshly painted sets and curated props. Golf carts whipping back and forth. I loved watching my creation brought to life on sound stages and backlots. All these people working together to turn my ideas into reality.

The first scene was shot on one of the most famous sets on the lot, an urban landscape that sitcoms dressed up and down for years. I sat in my chair and watched the scene unfold. I hadn't seen Jane in months, and there she was, the perfect Claire McIntosh, adorned in a green coffee apron, thick-framed glasses, her hair tied back.

Vick yelled, "Action," and the world I penned came alive.

On set, a jogger bumped into Claire, spilling her tray of coffee samples every direction. This triggered one of her seven personalities—the malicious one. She turned and screamed in a dark, menacing voice, "You cocksucker! I'll gut you like a pig."

Everyone on set restrained laughter.

Sam, Jacob's character, stood there with whipped cream and coffee all over his shirt. When Claire turned and noticed him, her posture shifted, a slight head tilt, eyes narrowed. The spunky, charming Claire materialized. The personality that Sam fell in love with. The one I fell in love with.

As soon as Vick yelled, "Cut," applause filled the set. The entire staff knew we were making something special. But I wasn't clapping. My attention was drawn to the palpable tension between Jane and Jacob.

I followed Jane back to her trailer. She seemed on edge, her fingers nervously playing with her apron. When she finally broke the silence, her words sound practiced, almost scripted. "I don't want to be the girl who slept with the screenwriter to get the role."

"You didn't," I reassured her. "You inspired this whole fucking movie."

"You don't know me," she argued. "You're in love with Claire McIntosh. Not the real thing. Believe me, I'm sparing you."

I attempted to grab her hand, to tell her she was wrong. But she pulled away, and my pride overwhelmed me. I didn't fight for her. I slammed the door in anger.

That night, I met up with Jacob at The Pig, questioning that moment on set. He brushed it off. *You're being paranoid. It's just acting.* He told me I had nothing to worry about. He gave me his word. *Who am I to get in the way of a writer's muse?*

As the weeks passed, I stomached their intimate scenes. Off camera, they were always rehearsing, practicing their craft. I was jealous of the passion they shared. Jacob kept reassuring me that it was strictly professional. Maybe I didn't want to believe it.

I busied myself by rewriting and tweaking scenes with Vick. We'd sit up for hours, poring over notes in his trailer, drinking good scotch. In between our sessions, he gave me career advice. He told me that screenwriters are the lowest on the Hollywood pecking order. They always get shit on first. *But if you keep standing up for what you believe in, people will respect that.* He saw the way I looked at Jane and told me to let her go. He was on his second marriage, the first one was to an actress. I didn't listen to him. My story with Jane was different. I just needed to wait it out—as soon as the movie wrapped.

Then came the day of the big sex scene.

It was a pivotal part of the movie. An intimate scene between Sam and all of Claire's seven personalities. When I wrote it, I fantasized about the faces of seven different women. But when Jane's beautiful face emerged, I imagined myself putting my hand up to hers, squeezing her tightly, as if saying, "I choose you." I want you. No one else. And when Sam does this in the movie, Claire breaks free from all her personalities. As if Sam's touch could liberate her from all her alter egos.

I decided to tell Jane the truth that morning—why I wrote that scene. Maybe I didn't know her, but I knew the feeling. I wasn't religious, but our connection was bigger than us.

An hour before call time, I approached her trailer, the sound of loud music blasting through the thin walls. I knocked repeatedly. No response. With a sense of dread, I opened the door and—shit—even to this day…

You caught them?

Jane's shirt and pants were off. They were kissing with their scripts tossed to the side. Did I react poorly… Yeah. I tackled Jacob, nosediving into the makeup chair. We grappled on the trailer floor, tossing each other out of the door and exchanging blows on the asphalt. When crew members pulled us apart, Jane was nowhere to be seen.

Three weeks later, the wrap party was in full swing at a dive near the backlot. Putting my feelings aside, I knew that we made a great movie on a shoestring budget. It would go on to be Baymore's biggest hit. Everyone was in good spirits, except me. My eyes were fixated on Jacob. As soon as he went out to smoke a cigarette, I followed.

"I told you how I felt," I seethed, trying to pick a fight.

He blew smoke in my face. "And I told you there's nothing between us."

"Fuck you."

"What did I tell you when I met you?" he said calmly, slicking his hair back. "The art comes before anything. My relationship with Jane was strictly for the performance."

I walked forward, fists clenched.

"Oh, c'mon. You're going to make me say it?" He grinned.

Silence.

"We didn't fuck," he said.

My entire body exhaled, and suddenly everything would be okay. Because I was young and immature, and in my pea-sized brain, the physical act was more important than the emotional connection they had. "You should have talked to me," I said.

"I know," he replied, lighting a cigarette. "But fuck. You were so emotional about the whole thing, acting all bat-shit crazy with Vick. But the performance required chemistry. It had to be real to make your script work."

I softened even more.

"But you're done?"

He nodded. "Of course. The movie's over. She isn't my type," he said, just so I knew it was *his* choice. He couldn't stand losing.

I smashed out my cigarette, willing to let it all go. Because I was scared of losing him as an ally. He was going to be a movie star, and I knew it. Everyone knew it. "So what's next?" I asked. "Should we talk to Vick about adapting *The Jeweler*? He could be the perfect—"

"I already took my next project," he interrupted, then paused, the tension swelling back. "You're a writer; I'm an actor. The team's got to break up eventually." A cruel smirk stretched across his face.

That was when I truly understood Jacob. He no longer needed me. He'd gotten what he needed out of our relationship. Just like he'd gotten what he needed out of Jane. Or so I thought.

"So what's *your* project?" I scoffed, feeling the treachery in the back of my throat.

"A story about a guy, a girl, and...

"A romantic comedy," I interjected, laughing. "I didn't think you'd sell out that quickly."

He snapped, grabbing me by the throat, squeezing until the purple veins in his neck bulged. I grinned as he choked me. I couldn't help it. It was too easy. He was too fragile. He might grasp everything he wanted out of this town, but he'd never be satisfied. When he let go, he didn't look remorseful for laying hands on me—only for letting me see a chink in his armor. Then he walked away.

I went back in the bar, and I found Jane talking to Vick. Without a second thought, I kissed her in front of everyone. She kissed me back, because Jacob was watching. Because she wanted to make him jealous; she had feelings. I knew that. Fuck. I hate this part of our story. But that night, I grabbed her hand, and I led her out of the bar, feeling Jacob's eyes on us the entire time. It felt so good in the moment. Spite and revenge always do.

Did you two sleep together?

Yes. But that spark and energy between us... It was different. The emotional vibration had been corrupted. Not that the sex wasn't great. But our love story was better than that. It should have been about us. Not Jacob.

Afterward, she rolled to the side of the bed, her voice filling the space. "Was that script really written about me?"

"Of course."

"Then you got something wrong."

I said nothing.

"The scene where Sam saves Claire by touching her face, freeing her from her tormenters."

"What about it?"

"You're not the hero in my story. I don't need you to save me."

And that was it.

When I woke up the next morning, she was gone. I wouldn't see her again until Sundance.

12

CONNER

KOHL'S HAND trembles as he puts a cigarette to his mouth, lighting the tip. I glance at the clock. It's ten p.m. We have been talking for hours.

"We can pick this up tomorrow." Kohl winces, his fingers reaching for the bandaged wound beneath his shirt. "Be here bright and early." He stares uneasily at the clock as if every tick is precious.

I nod. "I can be here at seven."

"Good," he replies, gingerly walking into his room and leaving me alone.

The freeway is jam-packed, even at this hour. I don't bother with the radio; my mind is a whirlwind of thoughts. Like Kohl, I've grown accustomed to being alone with my imagination. It was easier not having friends to bring home. Not having to explain my mom's condition. Why she sat in front of the television in her wheelchair. Why I had to clean the drool off her face. Why I had to change her clothes and help her dress every day. My home became a prison just like the basement was for Kohl.

And just like him, I'd imagine faraway worlds with grand adventures and new friends. I envisioned writing stories and creating worlds. But every time I'd sit in front of the computer, the words never came. I'd stare at the blank screen for hours, struggling to bring my fantasies to life. Like they were trapped in my subconscious.

Maybe I needed divine inspiration like Kohl did. Maybe that's why I came to Hollywood.

By the time I pull into my run-down apartment complex, it's almost midnight. The adrenaline has all but faded, and fatigue settles into my muscles. I drag my heavy body up the stairs. Nearing the door, I notice a figure lurking in the darkness.

"Who is it?" My voice shakes.

The shadow moves closer. I crouch, holding my breath, my heart pounding as the shadow grows larger. Grace steps into the light, and I exhale a sigh of relief.

"Someone's a little jumpy," she observes.

We linger in silence.

"May I come in?"

"Of course," I snap out of my daze, fumbling with my keys to unlock my door. The place is a mess. My futon is littered with books and clothes, the kitchenette filled with dirty pans. Grace scans the tiny apartment with indifference. She's wearing a fleece jacket and jeans, her arms folded together. As she lingers in the doorway, the reality kicks in. Grace is in my apartment.

"Do you want a beer?" I ask.

She nods. "Why didn't you answer your phone?"

"Sorry, it was on silent." I retrieve the last two cans of cheap beer. "What's going on?"

Grace sits on the chair next to my futon, her body tense.

"They found her."

"Savannah?"

"Yeah . . . Dead."

Grace pulls out her laptop and sets it on the coffee table. Her browser is open to a photo of police officers in front of the Roosevelt hotel. There's another image open in a window. The marred body of Savannah Beck. I grimace at the sight: her beautiful, tanned body riddled with bullet holes and knife wounds, crimson blood stains saturating the floor beneath.

"How did you get this?"

"I have a source in the LAPD." Grace zooms in on another picture. "And look at the room number." She leans back, pointing to the police report on the screen.

I read the number: "Eleven... So what?"

She tears an overdue bill on a coffee table. She writes "XI" on one piece and repeats the same letters on the other. "That's the Roman numeral for eleven," she explains, flipping one piece to connect the "IIs" in the middle. "And this is the bond between the subject and the one who marks you, the creator."

The realization sends a dark chill down my spine. Have I been marked? What the hell am I involved in? I turn to Grace, our faces somber. "Tell me what you know."

She gets up from the sofa, pacing the room. "Like I said, Kohl and Jacob were obsessed with that symbol. They both chased it, and lost their souls in the process. Whatever is at the end of those numbers, it's evil."

"Like an Illuminati thing?"

She shrugs. I can't tell if she's lying.

"How was Savannah involved?"

Grace sits back down. "Don't know. Has he mentioned her?"

"Sort of." I don't make eye contact.

"Sort of?" Grace asks expectantly.

I'm embarrassed to admit the truth. That I've been so wrapped up in his story that I haven't gotten a single question about Savannah answered. Or maybe I didn't want the answers. I didn't want the image of my idol shattered. Could he really be a killer? *I've done horrible things.*

"Don't beat yourself up." Grace's tone softens. "This is what he does. He tells stories."

I take a long, slow swig of beer, trying to process.

She touches my arm. "You good?"

"Yeah." I snap out of my daze. "How are *you* doing?"

"Fine," she says, avoiding my gaze. "It's just been a long day." She lets out a heavy sigh. "Fucking Tom. What an asshole."

She stretches her neck, running her hand through her long black hair.

I can't help but stare with longing. The way Kohl described his first meeting with Jane, that's how I felt when I first saw Grace. She was standing over a cubicle, chatting with a coworker, a mug that read: *No one cares, work harder* in tow. I love her smile, this light and warmth that lights up everything in her presence. And yet, you could tell she keeps sides of herself hidden. Like you had to earn those pieces of her.

"You know, I've wanted to talk to you ever since I started working at the magazine."

Her eyebrows rise.

I can feel the blood rush to my face. "I mean . . . I love your articles."

She smirks, teasing back strands of hair behind her ear. "My articles," she laughs. "Every kid's dream… To write celebrity articles that get refreshed every minute."

"So what *do* you want to write?"

"When I was younger, I wanted to write novels," she snickers.

"So what happened?"

She avoids my probing gaze. "Life, I guess."

"Will you come with me tomorrow to the interview?" I blurt. "I could use your help."

"I can't," she replies, draining the last of her beer. "And something tells me that you're the right person for this anyway."

Grace is refusing to be part of what might be one of the biggest stories in the magazine's history. Nothing about this made sense.

Before I can ask, she stands up. "I'm sorry for being such an asshole. It wasn't you; I promise."

"Thanks."

She lingers at the doorway. "I'll do what I can to help. But you have to do this interview alone. The fewer people who know, the better. Got it? Tom is doing everything in his power to find you."

I nod.

Just before she passes through the door, she turns. "Don't let him use you, Conner."

* * *

I'm exhausted, but my mind is still racing. I flip open my computer to the Google home screen. I should be investigating Savannah Beck. I should be making a list of probing questions for tomorrow. But I can't stop thinking about Kohl's tale—his feud with Jacob, his love for Jane, and the mysterious symbol that connects everything.

I pull up the trailer for *She's Complicated*. From the opening sequence, I can tell how dated the movie is. A youthful Jacob and Jane strolling down a generic New York neighborhood street, arms linked. A deep voiceover cuts in: "They had one magical night, and then she disappears. But when he tracks her down, Claire McIntosh is not the same person. She is seven different people."

Seven faces of Jane flicker across the screen.

I smile, relishing the outdated trailer. When the trailer zooms in on Jane, I pause it. Kohl's right—she's stunning. Her freckly face is so refreshingly unique. I can't help but wonder what happened to them.

It's past three when sleep finally overtakes me.

I dream about Jane and Kohl kissing on the doorstep, thunder flashing through the night sky. The scene changes, and I'm in a hospital. As my aunt anxiously paces the lobby, my gaze falls on a cloaked figure staring at me from the corner of the room. When I turn, the shadow is gone.

I walk toward it—fluorescent lights buzzing down a sterile hospital hallway, into a blinding white room. My mother is in a bed with a neck brace, her eyes swollen shut.

She lifts her hand out.

Does she want me to hold it? No. She is pointing to something behind me. When I turn, I see the symbol carved into the wall. The cloaked figure materializes, lifting the hood from his head. I can't fully see their face, but I know it's familiar. Is it my father? Is it Kohl? How do I know this person?

The scene changes.

I am running through the darkness.

I hear my father sobbing.

My mother's heart monitor beeping.

I see Kohl falling off the edge of the building.

I jolt awake, staring at my tiny apartment. I sigh in relief as I fall back on the pillow. The nightmare is over, but a nervous energy scampers through me.

* * *

I dress and hit the road with a renewed sense of purpose. Today will be different. I'll steer the conversation. I will ask the hard questions about Savannah Beck, even when he tries to avoid them.

When I arrive at Kohl's apartment, the door is ajar. I'm in shock at the sight of his apartment. Framed photographs are busted, boxes of memorabilia overturned, books scattered across the floor. Glass shards from shattered posters crunch underfoot.

"Kohl," I shout.

No response.

His copy of *The Jeweler* lies amidst the debris.

I grab the book, quickly flipping through the pages until I land on the dark symbol and skull inked on the final page. The dark energy from last night's nightmare returns, and I see the silhouette of the cloaked figure standing before me in my dream. Who is this man? I can see him slowly lifting off his hood…

I snap the book shut as Kohl enters the living room. He rubs his tired eyes, sinking into the chair and lighting a cigarette. "Apologies for the mess. I had a rough night."

I set the book down and sit across from him. I change my posture, straightening my back, gazing at Kohl with intensity.

"I want to know about Savannah Beck."

Kohl chuckles, sipping a fresh cup of coffee from the table. "C'mon, Conner. Did you really come here to talk about that?"

"I need answers."

He nods, clearly amused. "Fine, Conner. If that's what you want. I'll give you everything you need in a few hours. You can get some clicks for your fucking magazine."

I don't respond.

"But you and I both know this story is bigger than that. It's bigger than all of us." He gestures toward *The Jeweler*. "When you stare at the symbol, you feel it. It calls to you, doesn't it? It calls to something deep inside of you. Just like it called to me. And you need to know more. You need to know why."

I refuse to meet his gaze.

"Your next question decides it all," Kohl says, smirking.

My mind drifts to the book, then back to my nightmare. To the images that I've buried deep inside of me. I can't deny it. There is a shadow inside me that is trying to surface. But there's another part of me that doesn't want to face it. Whatever this evil is. But if I get the statement, if I find out what happened to Savannah, this will make my career. I can picture everyone at the magazine standing up and clapping when I enter the office. Grace would be up front, beaming proudly. This story would make my career. I may never have to go back to Kansas. I will never have to relive my past.

"So what's it going to be, Conner?"

It nearly slips out of my mouth. "What happened after you slept with Jane?"

13

KOHL

You see all these tattoos? Most of them were inked in the lead-up to the Sundance Film Festival. I had enough money to rent my own place, and I settled for a nice neighborhood in North Hollywood. I had an agent, a computer, and money to blow. Life was quiet. Too quiet. I spent most of my days obsessing about Jane, who had once again vanished without a trace. I did my best to get out and meet other women, but none of them compared.

So I quenched my loneliness in a tattoo parlor.

I got the serpent to remind me of snakes slithering through Hollywood. The quill, self-explanatory. The eye. The diamond. The pyramid. All ancient symbols that I thought represented truth. And this—the symbol I first discovered in Drifter's book. The only symbol that really mattered. Right on my forearm. Right where I can see it. By that point, the symbol had taken on a life of its own for me. It gave me purpose. As if Drifter himself had branded me. I was carrying on his legacy.

I wanted to write something as good as Drifter.

I sat in front of the computer, waiting for inspiration to strike.

But the longer I sat there, the more the blank cursor taunted me.

I was still terrified of writing something real. Terrified of facing the shit inside me. Instead, I finished the romantic comedy I started months earlier. It was clever, I suppose. A classic enemies-to-lovers romance. But it was as deep as a puddle. A young hotshot consultant slowly falls for a reporter on a plane. Both spend their life traveling, in and out of airport terminals. It follows their love story over the course of ten years. All they had were little moments. Layovers. Connecting flights. Meeting in strange countries. War zones. I called it "Connecting Flight." I pictured Jane as the lead.

I sent it to my agent.

I sent it to Vick.

* * *

The call that *She's Complicated* got into Sundance came at the perfect time. Living out of bars and tattoo parlors is a recipe for disaster. Solitude has never been my forte. I was drinking more than ever, starting earlier and earlier each day. I began using harder drugs. And I usually did them alone.

The studio paid for seven of us to fly out to the festival, Jane included. A buzz was circulating around our film, but I didn't give a shit. Seeing Jane was the only thing that brought me to Utah. I drank three shots on the plane just to steady my nerves. I was a mess. I made up my mind. The past was in the past. *I wasn't leaving that festival without her.*

As soon as I landed, Vick called. He wanted to meet the team at a coffee shop in downtown Park City.

Through the cafe window, I spotted Jane in a neon snow parka and beanie. She sat sipping her coffee, her eyes lost in a faraway place. As I stepped inside, our gaze met, and she greeted me with a radiant smile, casting away all the darkness inside me. All the nerves. All the worries and fears and feelings of inadequacy. With Jane, reality always matched the fantasy.

"Looks like you found a tattoo parlor?" She examined my arms. "I like it."

I ordered a beer, my foot nervously tapping against the wood floor.

After a brief silence, I blurted out, "Why did you leave that night?"

She avoided my gaze.

"I love you, Jane."

Maybe I was coming on too strong. Erratic, half-drunk in the middle of the day. But I didn't give a shit. I couldn't bear to be apart any longer.

"I love being your muse," she said. "But it's going to take more than that to make this work."

Before I could speak, she reached out her hand.

"I'm not the person you think I am. "

"Jane—"

"I'm fucked up," she added.

"Good." I squeezed her hand. "My basement is no paradise either..."

She grinned briefly before her gaze returned to the window.

The shop's bell chimed as Jacob strolled in. The movie star had arrived. I heard through the grapevine that his next film had been scrapped by the studio, but that didn't tarnish his confidence. He wore a black coat with black sunglasses, short stubble and longer hair. When I turned back to Jane, her rosy cheeks drained of its color. Her smile dissolving into a scowl. Jacob sat down, the tension unbearable between them. My gaze drifted back and forth. For better or worse, their connection ran deep. That's what hurt the most.

I got up and left before Vick came.

It should have been the greatest moment of my life—seeing my first screenplay come alive on the big screen. But I couldn't focus on the film. I kept sneaking glances of Jane in the glow of the screen. I was proud of her. This was her dream, too. The audience laughed, cried, and applauded our small-budget indie movie. It was a great film. When it was over, we all got on the stage for a Q and A.

While Jacob and Vick reveled in the attention, I couldn't enjoy it. I was an absolute wreck. I hated lying. I couldn't admit that the true inspiration behind the movie was the girl two seats down from me on stage.

"And we have an announcement," Vick said as the Q and A ended. "Jane and Jacob have signed on to do my next movie together, with a script by Kohl Reynolds, the writer of *She's Complicated*."

Applause.

The movie is called *Love at First Flight*.

I nearly fell out of my seat.

They changed the name of my script.

Worse than that, Jane and Jacob were doing another movie together—my movie.

I craned my head down the stage. There was a deep sadness blanketing Jane's face. Despite her better judgment, she loved him. She was drawn to his malice and rage. That's the funny thing about broken people: we find things that keep our wounds intact. She took a deep breath and forced a smile as the crowd applauded.

I had lost her.

I knew I couldn't survive another movie with the two of them. I couldn't watch her and Jacob kiss on camera. I couldn't watch the sex scenes I wrote. In an airplane bathroom. In a rundown hotel in Italy. The scripted scenes replayed over and over in my head, now perverse and tormenting with their faces attached.

Vick cornered me after the screening. He apologized for springing this on me, but he had tried to explain things at the coffee shop. They had been scrambling to get a deal inked, and the announcement was all part of the plan. I stood to make a lot of money. But I didn't give a shit about the money. I told Vick to do whatever he wanted.

I watched Jane exit the theater with Jacob.

I staggered through the cold streets of Park City until I found the first dive bar. I laid roots there for the next three days of the festival, while Jane and Jacob schmoozed with studios and stars, solidifying their partnership. I drank until the bar closed. Until everything was numb.

On the final night, Vick walked into the bar, shaking off snow from his boots. He wore a turtleneck and coat, his puffy cheeks bright red from the cold. He took a seat next to me, pulling off his beanie and gloves, blowing on his hands.

"So this is where you've been hiding out?" He waved to the bartender. "Well, I thought I'd come deliver the good news, since no one can get a hold of you." He held up his beer.

"You just made two hundred and fifty thousand dollars on your script."

I didn't react. I didn't care.

Vick laughed. "I'll take that as 'I accept.'"

I raised my glass and threw it down the hatch.

He continued. "You know, when we first met, I fucking hated you. Seriously. This punk kid writer gets his first ever screenplay green lit. Then he has the *balls* to go behind my back." He chuckled. "But you know, I've grown fond of you. You got this bullshit code of conduct about you. Like you actually believe the shit you write about. You actually believe in love. I guess that's why you write good scripts." He laughed again.

"But let me give you a piece of advice." His tone darkened. I glanced at him out of the corner of my eye. "Hollywood is nothing but a fantasy." He pointed at me. "A place we all come to suspend reality. Fall in love with a project, and then move onto the next one. Fall in love with a girl, and then move onto the next one. Don't get lost in that fantasy."

I lit my cigarette, letting the words sink in.

"Don't look so goddamned glum. You just became an in-demand Hollywood writer." He got up from the bar. "So go find yourself a new muse."

"Jacob's not a good person," I said.

He nodded. "You're probably right. He's got something dark inside of him, doesn't he? But he's also the most ambitious actor I've ever seen. And you? I suggest you find a way to make your career last and not throw it down the shithole for a girl." Vick threw a twenty down on the table. "Or drink your life away…What do I care?"

* * *

It was three a.m., and I roamed the empty streets, haunted by Vick's words. I had gotten exactly what I wanted. I had made something of myself despite my grandmother's best efforts. I earned a quarter million dollars on a fucking script. My entire career ahead of me. But I couldn't enjoy it. Why couldn't I enjoy it?

Then, I saw her.

Jane stood across the street, wearing an oversized sweatshirt and sweatpants, her hair matted, mascara running from her swollen, puffy eyes. She shivered in the frosty air. I didn't ask what happened. I didn't need to. Jacob would never stop hurting her—that's who he was. I held her in the middle of the road, rubbing my hands on her arms. I never asked questions. Maybe I should have.

"What's wrong with me?" she sobbed.

"Nothing." I held her tightly.

She cried harder.

We stood there for a few minutes, her head digging deeper into my chest.

"Don't do the movie," I pleaded. "Let's go somewhere. You and me."

She snickered softly, lifting her head. "Where?"

"As far away as we can."

"I've always wanted to go to London," she joked.

"Then that's where we'll go."

"And our careers?"

I paused, Vick's words echoing in my mind. *Don't live in the fantasy.* But if reality was making money writing skin-deep screenplays for Hollywood assholes like Jacob and Vick, then I no longer wanted any part of it. I'd take the fantasy. At least the hope of something more. I'd have plenty of time to sell out later. I wrapped my hands tighter around Jane. "Are you happy?"

She didn't respond.

"If you stay here, there will always be something missing. Something that all the money and fame won't be able to buy. But if we leave here tomorrow, at least we have a chance."

Her eyes scanned the horizon, weighing her options.

I placed my hands on her cheeks, just as I'd written in the script for *She's Complicated,* as if to say, "I choose you. I want you. No one else. This version of you. The one that believes in love and all that is good. I will always bet on this version of you." Then I kissed her.

When we pulled away, she beamed from ear to ear, our connection reignited.

"You think we can really overcome all the shit inside of us?" she asked.

I shrugged. "There's only one way to find out."

14

CONNER

Kohl grabs a framed movie poster for *Love at First Flight* from an overturned box, its glass shattered into pieces. Jacob and the lead actress are sitting in the first row in an airplane. Sandwiched between them is a sizable man, resting and drooling on Jacob. In the bottom right corner, the words "Congratulations on your success. –Kohl Reynolds."

The symbol is scrawled in sharpie underneath Kohl's name.

Kohl holds the poster up with pride. "The studio hired another writer to rewrite my script. They made that shit so over the top that Jacob tried walking off set. It wasn't the kind of art he wanted to make. So I sent him the poster as a nice middle finger, a reminder that he had sold out. His manager returned it back to me with his fist through it." He shrugs. "I thought that was worth keeping."

"The movie was a big hit though, right?" I ask.

"Highest grossing romantic comedy of its time. It made Jacob a movie star." Kohl smiles and puts the poster back in the box. "But don't you see? That's how Jacob made it. He sold out."

"And what about you? You didn't sell out?"

Kohl's eyebrows raise, pointing his lit cigarette toward my bag, where my copy of *When the Lights Go Out* pokes out. "I like to think that's how I made it. The first time my photo and my name were front and center. The first time I wrote something special." Kohl inhales his cigarette, eyes narrowing. "You written anything yet, kid?"

I shake my head.

"Let me ask you a question," he continues. "You said on the roof your parents died in an accident. What's your earliest memory of them?"

The question startles me. "Maybe we should continue the interview."

He maintains his gaze. "Humor me."

"There's not much I remember before the accident," I say. And for some reason, I don't want to tell him about the vivid dreams that have appeared the last few days. Maybe I just don't want to admit it to myself.

Kohl nods, as if anticipating my response. "I was like you once. But then I started looking behind the veil. For better or worse, writing that novel was the spark that unlocked everything."

15

KOHL

THERE'S NO BETTER city to fall in love in than London. Don't let anyone tell you otherwise. Jane and I got lost in our own little world.

We rambled down cobblestone streets and narrow alleyways with no agenda or destination. Rode the Underground to any stop that piqued our interest. We explored every museum, every pub, every nook of that ancient city. The night wasn't over until we drank, danced, and collapsed onto the floor.

In the London fog, the venomous spirit of Hollywood dissipated. We sang songs with locals we didn't know. Celebrated football matches for teams we didn't care about. With the buzz from cheap ale, we talked for hours. About small stuff, important stuff, and everything in between.

Jane opened up about her father, Ricky, a proud Irishman grappling with manic depression. He was in prison for a list of felonies. As a child, Jane would take refuge in her closet during the bad episodes. He never harmed Jane; he was always gentle with her. But he took his rage out on her mother, who resented Jane for it.

"My home was a mix of rage and passion, love and hate. So when I met Jacob… there was a part of me that felt home. I was drawn to whatever chaos that lives inside him. This—"

"Darkness," I interjected, and she nodded.

Jane pressed me about my parents.

She'd run her fingers along the engraving on my father's ring, pleading with me to divulge details. I wanted to remember. I really did. But the memory of my parents seemed just beyond reach. I recited the bits and pieces I knew. My dad on the typewriter. The frequent trips to to the bookstore.

"Was he a writer?"

"I think so."

"Did he publish anything?"

"Not that I know of."

She kept trying to solicit memories.

Eventually I'd shut down. I didn't want to talk about my past. I wanted to talk about our future. The family we would create together. The adventures on the horizon. Some days we spent all day in our tiny hotel room, making love, beaming as we rolled around in the sheets. She pointed to the skull and Roman numerals on my arm.

"What does it mean?" she asked.

"I found the symbol in a book." I pulled out the copy of *The Jeweler*.

She flipped through the pages. "What's it about?"

I told her about my favorite story. About Sal and his great adventure. About the choice he had to make between revenge or love. I told her about the strange way the book came to me. How the symbol took on a life of its own for Jacob and me.

"Did you ever find the author?" she asked.

"No. I wrote to him, his editors, his publisher. Never got a response."

"Wait." She leapt up in bed, her eyes widening. "You said the bookseller who gave you this had an English accent? What if he's from here? What if he knows how to locate Drifter?"

"Are you saying we should go to every bookseller in London and ask about him?"

"Why not?"

I couldn't help but smile.

And that's what we did.

We must have visited fifty booksellers. Every large and quaint bookshop in London, a few on the outskirts of the city. I humored her, but I never imagined we would find anything. Until one of the book custodians grabbed a UV light and shined it on the inner cover. "Invisible ink," he said, smiling, and when he turned the book around, we saw the image of a small oar and the words *The Ferry Bookseller*.

"It's in Castle Combe," said the bookseller. "The owner calls himself Charron."

I stumbled backward when he said it. I couldn't believe it.

That night, on the cusp of discovering the truth, Jane and I had a huge fight.

About what?

I got angry with her for meddling in my business. Of course that wasn't the real reason. I was terrified of the fucking truth. What if there was more to my encounter with the bookseller in San Francisco? What if it revealed the truth about who I was? Why that book really came to me. Maybe the symbol was better left a mystery.

Jane saw past my fear.

"What if the symbol holds the answer to your past?" she pleaded. "What if that's why we're here."

It was a three-hour train to Castle Combe, a storybook village with cobblestone roads and old stone buildings. The address took us across a charming bridge to a quiet lane where ivy clusters covered ancient stonework. An old wooden sign dangled on a rusty chain, an image of an oar and the words *The Ferry* written in Old English below. Three pints on the train couldn't prevent my body from shaking with nerves.

That moment between me and the bookseller had defined my life.

The chime of the bell echoed the sound from my childhood, putting me back in that bookstore in San Francisco. I tiptoed across the creaky wooden floorboards, marveling at the rows upon rows of bookshelves bursting at the seams. At the far end of the shop, a man stood behind a counter, inspecting the binding of an old leather book.

It was him.

"Charron?" I asked.

I swear, he hadn't aged a day, that perfectly groomed hair and a manicured white beard. Even his deep wrinkles seemed straight and orderly. He wore a well-fitted suit with a vest and pocket square. He grinned, and I was thirteen again, mystified by the enchantment and possibility. The greatness of it all.

"Can I help you with something?"

Jane urged me forward.

"You gave me a book a long time ago." My voice wavered. "That book changed my life."

"Is that so?" He put aside the tome he'd been examining and reached for another.

"How did you know that I needed that book?" I asked.

He held the magnifying glass to the next book. "I have become somewhat of an expert at giving people the right book. Some say it's my job." He chuckled.

"That book made me want to be a writer."

Finally, he looked up. "And what have you written?"

"Two screenplays that were made into films," I boasted, and for some reason I wanted his approval. He offered a slight head tilt.

"But now," I blurted, "I want to write a novel—something as good as the book you gave me." I stepped closer to the counter, my heart pounding. "Do you know him? Robert Drifter, the author?"

He placed his hand to his chin in thought. "Name doesn't ring a bell. But may I give you some advice?"

"Of course."

"The masterpiece you aspire to write isn't out there; it's within. You, my friend, are both the quarry and the sculptor, slowly finding the raw materials and whittling away, until the book reveals its true form. To do this, you must simply sit at the typewriter and start carving."

"I've tried that," I pleaded.

A playful grin appeared on his face. "May I suggest you start with the places in your heart that frighten you the most." He fumbled with a drawer beneath the counter, emerging with a thick coin. "A long time ago, I came across this." He rolled the coin along his finger. "I was told that a few great authors used it to create their literary masterpieces." He handed it over to me.

As I reached for the coin, a wave of confidence anchored me. I stood straighter. My legs felt stronger. Maybe it was the mystery and excitement of it all, but a tingly sensation buzzed in my fingertips. This sense of power. This craving to be at my desk writing. I read the inscription:

"In the middle of the journey of our life I found myself within a dark wood where the straight way was lost."

"I've heard that quote before."

"Dante's *Inferno*." The man smiled. "A reminder that everything good comes out of fire."

I inspected the heavy bronze piece.

"Keep it," the man said.

"Oh no." I held the coin out. "I couldn't."

He waved me off. "Consider it another loan. Perhaps one day I will read your masterpiece."

Then he turned his attention again to his work as if our interaction was complete.

"Do you know about the symbol?" I tried to sound casual, as if the question hadn't tortured me my entire life. As if my heart wasn't pounding in anticipation. He stayed silent. I continued: "It was in the back of the book you gave me."

A mixture of irritation and remorse brushed across his face. "I know of no such things . . . Now if you excuse me, I have work to do."

"But—"

"Please go," he said.

* * *

That night, I settled my computer on the tiny hotel desk, placing the coin and my father's ring beside me. I glanced over to Jane's stunning body, wrapped in the soft white hotel sheets, her breathing rhythmic and peaceful. I turned back to the screen. Suddenly, a piece of the inscription hissed in my mind. *I found myself within a dark wood where the straight way was lost.*

I stared at the blank screen for five minutes, ten minutes, an hour.

But then three words came to me.

Enter the woods.

A memory ignited.

My father, lost in madness, typing furiously on the night of the accident. Pages floating softly around the room. A cigarette dangling from his mouth. I slowly entered the room, but the door betrayed me with a creak. When my father turned to face me, his eyes... They were voids—dark and evil.

Just as quickly as it had come, the memory faded. But in its wake, fear and panic lingered in my veins, grief seeping into my chest, leaving me gasping for air. Something had been released. A small fragment of darkness breaking off from a greater mass, an evil that prowled inside me.

In its shade, my hands started to move. It was slow at first, but I found a rhythm. I wrote about a young boy witnessing his parents' murder by a faceless figure, a silhouette that would haunt him the rest of his life.

I wrote and I wrote.

For hours and hours.

When the words started to blur, I crawled into bed with Jane, a satisfied smile on my face.

I had written fifty pages of something real.

For the next month, Jane and I traveled England by train. We made love in cheap hotel rooms. In the quiet of the night, with the city lights shining through the window, my ritual began. Beside me, I placed the gold coin and my father's ring, alongside an ash tray. Then I took a deep breath and hovered my hands above the keyboard. I let the dark images of my past rise to the surface. My parents' grave. The three black-cloaked men standing at the edge of the sidewalk. I saw the evil eyes of my grandmother. Passed down to my father. Passed down to me.

And then I began.

Sometimes, when the writing was done, and I closed my eyes in bed, the symbol flashed across my mind. But this time, I welcomed it. I took it as a sign—that I was finally writing something meaningful.

You make this symbol sound magical.

I can hear the disbelief in your voice. While in London, I became obsessed with it. I scribbled it down in notebooks. I dreamed about it. I'd see it flash across walls, on tunnels in the tube. It unlocked mysterious parts of me. It inspired me, frightened me. Like you, I was skeptical. I blamed it on my active imagination. But its presence was inspiring. I leaned into its ancient power.

One day, I stumbled across the real thing.

You saw the symbol somewhere else?

Yes. By then, London's charm began to wane. The drinking felt repetitive. The tours and sights lost their mystique. The adrenaline of new love began to settle.

Thankfully, the writing was going well. I submerged myself deeper into the story. I'd run into a pub to finish a scene, scribbling my thoughts down on receipts and journals. I started to feel an overwhelming pressure, this obsession. It was all I could think about. One rainy day, I had finished a writing session in a pub and went to find Jane at the National Gallery.

I wandered from gallery to gallery, looking for her. I didn't stop to stare at a single painting. Not a Van Gogh. Not a

Monet. I couldn't care less. But then I entered a dimly lit hall, and a sudden chill bristled on my arms. A shadowy hand directed my gaze to a single painting: *Saint John the Evangelist on the Island of Patmos* by Diego Velázquez.

Saint John was sitting with a book, scribbling notes, as if receiving divine inspiration from God himself. In this case, a vision of a woman and a dragon, just like in the Book of Revelations.

But that wasn't what caught my eye. In the lower right-hand corner, the symbol was calling. The average spectator might not see it…but for me, the symbol projected out of the canvas. The "X" and "I" painted on a book in the lower right corner. The other "I" and "X" flashed from behind the first layer of paint, as if it showed itself only to me. And for the first time, the symbol frightened me.

I was bonded to something evil. Like I had sold my soul by using its inspiration. Deep in thought, I hardly noticed Jane beside me.

"I want you to see this one," she said, pulling me into the next room. I was relieved to leave. I wanted to forget I ever saw it. I just needed sleep and to slow down on the booze.

So was it true? Was it really the symbol on the painting?

Even when I pored over photos of the painting, I thought, *it isn't that clear*. It was just a coincidence. A few missed brush strokes that gave off the impression. It was the alcohol, my obsession with the symbol. But I was lying to myself. I knew the truth. That symbol was painted with intention. I wasn't going mad.

You don't need to say anything. I know you don't understand. Not yet.

Just let me keep going.

* * *

By then, we had been in London for seven months. I had completed the first draft of *When the Lights Go Out*. It was raw and overwritten, but I was proud of the work. I love the final scene where my main character, RJ, pulls a gun on the shadow man, his parents' killer. It was just like Sal in *The Jeweler*. RJ had that same decision. Which path to follow? Light or dark? Revenge or love? Drifter's story was *my* story.

Jane and I arrived at LAX nearly broke. We promised ourselves that we weren't going to get side jobs. She was an actress; I was a writer. We were determined to make that work. But Hollywood is a vindictive overlord. It scorned Jane for departing to London. She went on audition after audition, but the competition was stiff. *She's Complicated* had great reviews, but no major release. It was still a year away from getting the cult following it deserved. Till then, Jane was an unknown actress who had passed on a studio movie.

And me . . . I had nothing to sell. Just a few half-finished scripts and an unpolished novel. My first agent stopped returning my calls. Jane moved in with me out of necessity. Each day, the last of our money dripped out of my account like sand in an hourglass. I spent my time working on my book. Jane kept going out on auditions. Months went by. At night, I would hold her and tell her that everything would be all right. *You won't have to wait tables again. You won't have to move back home*. That was her biggest fear.

We were three days late on rent when we saw a billboard for *Love at First Flight*. Jacob and his co-star, Natasha Littleton, were perched on either side of the airplane wings towering over Wilshire Boulevard. That asshole was larger than life. The tension in the car swelled as we passed the billboard.

Jane resented me for convincing her to go to London. She was angry at herself for accepting. Being a working actress was her lifelong dream, following in the footsteps of Judy Garland and Bette Davis. And right when it was within reach, I'd swept her away.

For me, the billboard brought up other things. What had really happened between her and Jacob on that night at Sundance? It shouldn't have mattered. But it ate away at my insides. Jealousy rooted its dark claws in the pit of my stomach. Had he had her first? In the silence of the car, the bitterness churned and churned until I could taste its poison in the back of my throat.

"Did you sleep with him?" It slipped out.

There was a moment of silence before she screamed, "Pull over." Her voice grew more frantic. "Pull over now."

I skidded into a run-down gas station.

She got out of the car, pacing in her jean shorts and white tank top.

"Get back in the car," I yelled out the window.

Her eyes welled up with tears. "Do you love me?" she yelled. "Do you really love me?"

"Of course I do," I said.

Bystanders were starting to stare.

"Then you need to do two things," she said. "First, never ask about that night again."

"And the second?"

"Reach out to him," she said. "Get us back on our feet."

"Jacob?" I threw my hands up. "Fuck no!"

She stood resolute, her arms crossed. It was an ultimatum.

I dropped my head onto the steering wheel in defeat. She climbed back in the passenger seat, her next words seared into my memory: "Get us back, Kohl." She put her hand on mine. "Or I fucking will."

So you called him?

Jacob agreed to a lunch, likely out of curiosity. He chose the Ivy, an extravagant restaurant where A-list celebrities hold court. Since my departure, he had grown more Hollywood. Long tousled blonde locks with an ugly brown beard to match. Trendy dark sunglasses and a distressed T-shirt completed his look. He kept slicking back his hair as we sat on the patio in plain view of everyone.

"Saw the movie poster." I smiled.

He grinned, unfazed. "Corporate fucking pigs. How's Jane?" he asked.

Hearing her name come out of his mouth sounded like knives on a glass table. Every fiber of me wanted to leap over the table and choke him. But if this was what Jane needed from me…

"She's good." I grabbed a cigarette as the waiter came over.

"I'm sorry, sir. You can't—" The waiter did a double take when he spotted Jacob. Then he glanced up at a new billboard towering above the restaurant. A new movie he was starring in. *Of course he chose this table.* That asshole wanted me to stare at his movie star face on a giant billboard. I put the cigarette away.

"So what can I do for you?" Jacob leaned back.

I threw down twenty pages of something I had written before London. I made my pitch: "It's about a cocky baseball player who ends up falling in love with his female agent."

He leafed through the pages, smirking. "Is it good?"

"Better than the shit your agent's giving you."

He raised his eyebrow. "I've been getting pretty good scripts lately," he said, tossing the screenplay back to me. "Not sure I want another Kohl Reynolds rom-com."

He was going to make me beg.

"Let me ask you a question." He removed his glasses, his blue eyes shining behind the tan skin and beard. "Was she worth it?"

"Worth what?" My jaw clenched.

"Ruining our partnership."

"You're blaming me?" I frothed. "You took that fucking movie without asking me."

He chuckled dismissively. "You left me no choice. You broke the cardinal rule."

"And what's that?"

"Putting your emotions ahead of the art."

I sneered.

He leaned in. "Admit it. You got caught up in your feelings. You forgot our objective."

"And what's that?"

He pointed to the tattoo on my arm. "To be the fucking best."

Taking a deep breath, I managed. "Look, we need a favor. Can you get this movie sold?"

His self-satisfied grin said it all. After a heavy pause, he took the screenplay. "I'll read it. But no promises."

When I got in the car, I punched the steering wheel and screamed until my throat was hoarse. I'd done a lot of things to sell my soul in Hollywood, but that...That was the worst of it. In the car, I promised myself that I would never grovel to Jacob again. I had a new goal that burned like a furnace in my soul. A monstrous flame that burned for a decade, stoking my rise and guided my fall.

I would be bigger and better than Jacob Perry.

16

CONNER

The tea kettle boils, whistling across the room. Kohl glances up at the clock before heading to the kitchen. I glance at my phone: six missed calls and an unsettling text from Allie: *Are you ok?*

I reply: *Yeah, why?*

Three dots type.

You need to get out of there.

A link follows.

I angle my phone away from the kitchen and click the link. A video reveals a stern police captain at the podium.

"Kohl Reynolds is formally being charged for the murder of Savannah Beck. As of right now, Mr. Reynolds is still at large. We ask that anyone who has information about the whereabouts of Kohl Reynolds come forward."

"Tea or coffee?" Kohl asks casually.

Frantically, I close the video, the realization leaving me in shock. The most wanted man in America is standing in front of me. A man who brutally murdered a woman. The image of Savannah Beck's mutilated body flashes across my mind. Multiple stab wounds and gun shots riddled across her flesh.

"You look like you've seen a ghost," Kohl observes. He sighs, a knowing look in his eyes. "It's funny—good attention, bad attention, there's a mystique about it. Fame." The words hiss out of his mouth. "Perhaps I'll die even more famous than ever. In this shithole of an apartment." He looks around. "You should have seen my first house." He smirks. "I was a king in this fucking town."

Silence lingers between us.

I glance at my phone and then back to the recorder.

There's nothing but adrenaline running through my veins. A vigor and excitement that bolsters my nerves. I made up my mind a long time ago.

I start the recorder and settle in.

17

KOHL

Six months after my meeting with Jacob, the tide turned for Jane and me. Three cherries lined up on my Hollywood slot machine.

First, *Love at First Flight* became the biggest-grossing romantic comedy of its time. Then, thanks to Jacob's success, *She's Complicated* sprouted a huge following. More importantly, I got an agent who could sell anything to anyone. You've already met him—Brad Leibowitz of the Artists Agency. A ruthless son of a bitch. Back then he was thirty pounds lighter with a full head of hair. While sucking down ribs at a shabby barbecue joint, he posed the question: "What do you want from this town?"

It was simple: Out-earn and outshine Jacob Perry.

He grinned, his face covered in sauce. "Consider it done."

Within days, my name hit every studio watercooler in Hollywood. The writer behind a hundred-million-dollar rom com and an indie smash hit. Brad brokered fifteen meetings with studio heads and directors.

He set my screenplay quota at four hundred thousand dollars a pop.

To me, that number was comical. But that's the thing about this town: it's only ridiculous until it's not. If one studio thinks you're worth it, they all fall in line.

My first meeting was with the renowned director Joseph Palowitz. He had this wild film idea; small-town farmers uncover local cops colluding with the Mexican drug cartel. After a string of overdoses, the citizen squad bands together to bring down the police. I told Joseph that I loved the idea, but I needed to do some research. He said, "Forget that. I want this movie to be outrageous, pure fiction. Use your imagination."

Best piece of screenwriting advice I ever got. I wrote *Cops & Vigilantes*, a comic-book style movie with a protagonist that made Rambo look tame. A ninety-minute blood bath with sawed-off shotguns and piles of cocaine. Joseph thought it was the greatest script ever written. He said it moved him to tears.

I've never heard of that movie.

It never got made. The script had so many dead cops that the studio demanded a rewrite. But Joseph—his dedication to the script was unwavering. He wouldn't let the studio change a single word. So when the studio refused to greenlight the movie, he marched into the studio head's office and spit in his face. He was promptly fired, and the script got shelved. I still made my money.

And my name became larger than life.

I was the writer who had written a screenplay so good that Joseph Palowitz risked his entire career. After that, the universe was mine for the taking. Doors opened without knocking. Even my novel became a hot commodity. Publishers lined up to buy *When the Lights Go Out*. My agent presented all the offers, but I only took one seriously. Bravado Publishing.

When I flew out to New York, the company gave me the VIP treatment. Steak dinners. Over the top marketing meetings. They promised to make me the next literary sensation. Of course, none of that mattered. I was there to see one editor.

Stanley Davis was a lean man with short gray hair and colorful eyeglasses, with a bow tie to match. He gave me his pitch while I paced around his high-rise New York office, running my hands along his illustrious bookshelf. As he talked, I pulled out a novel and dropped it on his desk. *The Jeweler*.

"Who is he?" I asked.

Stanley shifted nervously in his seat.

"You edited his book. You must know who he is."

Stanley picked up the book, staring down at the yellow cover. "Robert Drifter is true to his name. Elusive. An enigma. A writer who refuses praise for his work."

"You've never met him?"

Stanley sighed. "The manuscript was a referral. I was informed that the author had no interest in publicity or recognition."

I sat down in my chair, dumbfounded. "Do you have any way to get a hold of him?"

Stanley shook his head. "He's a ghost, son."

"And what about this?" I pointed to the symbol on my arm.

Stanley shook his head.

Was he lying?

Of course. He knew more than he let on. But if I'm being honest…I was content with the lie. As long as Drifter's editor was my editor. It connected me to my idol without shattering the dream. I didn't want the truth. I wanted fame, money, and drugs. Hollywood had finally given me access to all its riches, and I wanted everything.

Jane and I bought a house.

We bought furniture, new cars.

The best drugs money could buy. I started relying on them to write.

I began wearing trendy clothes and ripped jeans. I got tattoos on my hands and neck. I appeared in magazines. I traveled to New York for book events. I was on top of the fucking world.

Meanwhile, I kept signing contracts. I kept promising studios that I would deliver screenplays. At one point, I had six scripts in my queue. To fulfill my obligations, I holed up in the Beverly Wilshire with a bagful of drugs. All I did was drink, write and do drugs for an entire month. Some of the scripts I wrote were decent. Only one of them made it to the big screen.

Jane was also busy. She landed an acting role as a handmaiden in an adaptation of Rick Mullins's series, *Gods of War*. It wasn't the starring role, but the character had enough depth for her to sink her teeth into. We were both living our dream, untouchable and rich. But in the quiet of the night, I felt a restlessness, a dark stirring from deep within. The faint rumbling of a demon trapped in my soul.

My reckoning was coming.

It was only a matter of time.

A trip to Salem, Massachusetts, was the catalyst. I was in the town doing research with the director Taylor Andrews. She was obsessed with seance and witch trial folklore and wanted to incorporate them into a vampire film. She demanded that we spend three days visiting landmarks in the town.

Most of my trip was spent in a drug-induced haze, stumbling through gravestones, half-listening to tour guides ramble on. I dismissed it all as bullshit. Until the final night.

Taylor arranged an underground night tour, only known by a select few—rumored to be hosted by actual descendants of Salem witches. At midnight, we stumbled down an old alleyway, our entrance marked by a discreet black door with a crow and pentacross. I was half drunk already and didn't give it a second thought.

In a small, candle-lit room, a handful of spectators huddled around a cloaked woman. As soon as I reached for my flask, her watchful eyes shifted in my direction. Like she could sense the demon that lurked inside me. Raising her gaze beneath the hood, she curled her crooked finger in my direction.

Taylor shoved me forward.

The woman told me to sit at the table, which was set with worn ivory tiles and tarot cards.

Up close, the dim light carved hollows on her leathery face. She took my hands, tracing her aged fingers over my palms. The alcohol and drugs evaporated from my body. She lifted a tile from her table.

A skull.

"You seek something." She glanced at the symbol on my arm. You seek something that lures you into darkness." When she spoke, I saw the three cloaked figures standing across from my childhood house. Then I felt it, a rush of dark energy trapped within me. I heard it, screaming through my bones. The voice of a demon locked in my basement, pounding on the door. Chained to the floor. Begging to be freed. Pulling at its restraints.

She lifted the next tile.

A snake.

"You will meet a woman with eyes as clear as the water, and she will bring tragedy upon you."

Then she pulled up a third tile.

Fire.

"She will drag you into an inferno, revealing a truth you've been running from your entire life. And it will cost you everything."

As soon as she finished, an overwhelming sense of dread consumed me. I scrambled out of my chair, desperately shoving myself through the crowd. I found a hole-in-the-wall bar, and I drank until my flight the next day.

Was the girl she referred to Savannah Beck?

Next question.

Did you write Taylor's script?

Not a fucking chance. As soon as I got home, I told the studio I wouldn't write that witchcraft trash. I wanted no part in it. Instead, I spent two days writing another script that would set the psychic's foretelling in motion. It was called *The Offering*, and it was the best thing I'd written in years. My encounter with the psychic inspired me. Run-ins with my demons always did.

Brad shopped the script around and started a bidding war with every major studio. He sold it in three days to Warner Brothers for three and a half million dollars. The highest amount anyone had ever paid for a single screenplay at the time.

You familiar with the film?

I've seen it.

Two founders of a revolutionary drug company are manipulated by a cunning broker, who covertly works for a shadow corporation. By seducing both founders, she pit them against each other, unraveling the company on the eve of its public offering.

Like most of my screenplays, I imagined three people when I wrote it. Jane was the broker. Jacob and I were the founders who'd lost everything.

On the night I got the check, I made Jane dress up and recreate the boardroom scene in which Erin Brooks spreads her legs to distract my character during an investor meeting. It was the best sex of our lives. I was the creator of my own destiny. Not some fortune teller.

After we were done, Jane and I sat up and watched *Love at First Flight* for the first time. Jane smiled and said it was a shit movie. My original screenplay was better. She was glad she didn't take the part. Vick and Jacob were sellouts.

That night, with Jane sleeping beside me in bed, I should have slept like a baby. Instead, I had this lingering dread I couldn't shake. I knew the truth. That darkness inside me had awakened. No amount of money or fame would quench its hunger. Its shrill scream echoing through my body. Thrashing against its restraints. The words of the witch: *She will drag you into a fiery hell.*

And yes, that woman was Savannah Beck.

* * *

The year that followed was an absolute whirlwind.

Jane's series got picked up for another season, and they moved the entire production to Oslo, Norway. Jane pleaded for me to go with her, saying it would do us some good to leave Hollywood. She knew what was happening to us.

I should have listened.

I stayed in Hollywood out of fear. Fear that the offers would dry up, and Jacob would pull ahead. I had been following his career closely. He was taking more complex roles. A vigilante police officer. Mark Antony in a modern-day retelling of *Antony and Cleopatra*. A ruthless tyrant. A murderous lawyer. He had begun to hit his stride, embracing his shadow self. Making allies with his rage and anger. He was slicing off pieces of his soul to make better art.

But who was I kidding? So was I.

Jane was in Oslo for nearly seven months, and I hated sleeping at the house alone. I booked my usual suite at the Beverly Wilshire. That's how I spent my birthday that year, drinking and snorting drugs by myself.

During that period, I wrote one decent script. *Impeachment.* I was watching *Access Hollywood* when they ran a piece on the set of Jacob's new movie, *Finding Gatsby*, a film about the origin of F. Scott Fitzgerald's classic novel. When I saw a clip of him filming, rage boiled in my veins. They were already projecting it as an Oscar contender.

He was pulling ahead.

I flipped the channel to a presidential announcement about the war in the Middle East. I snorted a line of coke, and then I closed my eyes, letting my anger and hatred for Jacob simmer to the surface. A vision struck me: Jacob's charm and evil manifesting itself as the leader of the free world.

With a cigarette dangling from my mouth, I started typing, pounding the keys in anger. I wrote the script about the rise and fall of a corrupt politician, his dark deeds culminating in a dramatic Senate trial. Once the movie was a success, a lot of people asked about my inspiration. Nixon. Taft. Bush. I never told a soul this, but I wrote it only about one person: Jacob fucking Perry.

That year of my life was a turning point. I was rich, yes. But I became a full-blown addict.

My demise was inevitable.

Jane returned to Los Angeles before Christmas. I cried when she walked through the gate at LAX. I held her tightly. She was the only thing left that fastened me to the light. And I knew that if she left me, I would have nothing left to push the devil away.

* * *

After changing directorial hands for years, *The Offering* got the green light that spring. It landed with director Javier Santino, who had enough juice to get Warner Brothers to fast track production. Santino was a revolutionary director who was reinventing the thriller genre. He was also a champion of screenwriters. We had a great meeting about the script, and he asked me to come on board as producer. I would be involved in every part of the project, including casting. To him, this was still my story.

On a beautiful day on the Warner lot, a striking young woman walked in the room. A woman whose eyes were as clear as the pristine waters of Bora Bora.

Her name was Savannah Beck.

18

CONNER

As soon as I mention Savannah's name, a loud knocking reverberates through the apartment. Kohl glances nervously at the door, then puts his finger to his mouth. Silently, he rifles through a box, producing a black metal gun. Every muscle in my body seizes in panic. I slowly set down my coffee, my hands raised in disbelief.

"Kohl Reynolds." A loud voice booms through the apartment. "This is InsideJuice.com. Can we have a second of your time?"

Kohl studies my colorless face. "You told them?"

I shake my head, my eyes glued to the weapon.

"InsideJuice.com. This will only take a minute."

Another knock.

"I can talk to them," I blurt.

Kohl paces with his head down. After a few drawn-out seconds, he nods, waving the gun toward the door. I unlock the deadbolt. The door catches on the golden chain.

"Tom?" I whisper. "How did you find me?"

Tom's eager face appears in the narrow opening. "You researched this address on our network. I need this story. Let me in or I'm calling the police."

I gulp, turning back to Kohl. He's still transfixed in his own thoughts. Would he use the gun on Tom? Is he really a killer?

"Did you kill Savannah Beck?" Tom hollers through the crack in the door.

I flinch as cold metal grazes my shoulder. Turning, I find Kohl, his expression hard and resolute. He motions for me to step aside. When I do, he flings the door open and aims the gun at Tom. The camera man behind Tom stumbles back, tripping on his own feet. The heavy equipment smashes to the ground.

"Whoa there." Tom's voice wavers as he backs up. "Let's not do anything rash."

"Follow us and you're dead."

Tom and his cameraman do what they're told. Kohl motions for me to follow him into the parking lot. I'm too stunned, too terrified to object. He uses a key fob to unlock an old Lexus in a carport, beckoning me to get in. I sit down, trying to calm my breath. Trying to process what just happened. Have I become a hostage? Should I make a run for it?

Before I can do anything, Kohl starts the ignition, the gun resting on the steering wheel. The vehicle moves through the complex and onto the main road. As soon as I get on the freeway ramp, he turns to me. "Give me your phone."

I do what he asks.

He throws it out the window as he steps on the pedal.

Once we reach the highway, the gravity of the situation hits me like a ton of bricks. I don't really know this person. I don't know what he's capable of. I've been blinded by my infatuation. He's a killer, a dangerous man. Grace warned me…We drive in silence, heading east out of Los Angeles. Kohl turns on the radio.

"If you're just hearing this, screenwriter Kohl Reynolds is wanted for the brutal murd—"

He changes the station to an oldies rock-and-roll station.

I panic, scrambling for the door handle. I can hardly breathe. It's locked. I need to get out of here. I rip the seat belt restraints off, lowering my shoulder into the car door, desperate.

The gun presses firmly against my temple.

"Relax," Kohl says. "Take a deep breath."

"Where are you taking me?"

"I'm giving us time."

Kohl removes the gun from my head. Then he sets it on the dashboard.

"You killed her, didn't you?" I scream through panic breaths. "You killed Savannah Beck."

He takes a long sigh, unwilling to give me an answer.

I sit back in disbelief. It was true.

"Listen. You're down the rabbit hole now. You want to know what happened? You want to know what the symbol means? You want to know why *you* were the one who showed up at that bar looking for me?" He shoves the tape recorder into my chest. "Then finish this."

19

KOHL

SAVANNAH BECK WASN'T your typical Hollywood actress. She wasn't driven by fame, attention and money, even if her beauty had other objectives. Her heritage was a blend of half Canadian, half Native American. Her mother lived on the Fort Mojave reservation and waitressed at a nearby casino. Her father was a deadbeat truck driver passing through. As you can imagine, her childhood was unmistakably harsh.

She was famous for her eyes, an enchanting shade of light green, almost teal. A fantasy you want to be swept away in. When she walked into the audition room for *The Offering*, every asshole looked up from their phone, including me. There was something so familiar about her. Maybe I'd seen her in another casting reel or headshot. Staring at her, a dark memory rose to the surface. Three tiles lay in front of me. The skull. The snake. The fire. I knew right then and there. She was the one that would drag me to hell.

Her audition went smoothly. She had that thing that every director looks for. Hollywood magnetism. The star factor. But as soon as she left the room, I made the decision.

She wasn't right for the movie.

I wrote the character Erin Brooks to be Jane. Late twenties, early thirties. Proficient and powerful. Sexy, sure. But I needed something more subtle. Someone who could pull off a pantsuit. Someone with a little more experience. After Savannah's auditions, Javier asked me what I thought of her. After I told him, he looked at me and said, "I've been asked nicely to cast her."

"By who?"

"People we don't want to disappoint," he said.

That shit didn't fly with me. Not when I produced my first movie and certainly not when I thought I was hot shit. No higher-up was going to tell me who to cast. I told Javier she wasn't getting the part. Final decision. We cast Josie Paulson, a seasoned actress that fit the budget. No one would have a problem with her.

But someone did.

Three weeks before filming, Javier called me to the set. I arrived on the Universal lot after a long night of partying. I imagined it was some pre-production meeting, some snag with the script or shot list. They called him Virgil. Even then, I knew it wasn't his real name. He didn't come to the set in a golf cart. He came in a Rolls Royce with a driver. Javier was terrified of this guy. No one knew who he was. But even without a title, the studio made it very clear—he was someone you didn't fuck with.

Virgil got out of the car in a sharp black suit, matching gloves and low-brimmed hat. He was tall and angular, an elegant cane complementing his stride. His face bore deep lines, and a prominent, hooked scar stretched from cheek to chin. His eyes were the darkest I've ever seen. He walked straight toward us: "I heard we have a problem," he said in a dark and raspy voice.

Javier didn't say a word, forcing me to answer.

"Not really. The woman you'd like us to cast wasn't a fit."

He stepped closer, and a wave of dread overcame me. Like the devil himself was standing in my presence, staring into my soul. And he found something he liked.

His gaze fell to the mark on my arm, a wicked grin stretching across his face.

"I'd think twice before defying me."

Then, he was gone.

His departure left me stunned. Javier went ballistic. "What should we do? Who the fuck is this guy?"

I didn't respond. The life had drained from my face, my hands shaking like a leaf. There was an unsettling familiarity. He knew things about me. Secrets that haunted me. I ignored Javier and left to get high.

I didn't return to set until he made the decision without me.

Savannah Beck became Erin Brooks.

And I tried my best to forget that encounter.

* * *

Savannah Beck arrived on set four weeks later for a table read. The lead actors couldn't resist a double take when she walked by in her jean shorts. This was a movie about a woman manipulating two successful men. You gotta love the irony.

The shot schedule for the movie would be tight, starting with our first two weeks in New York. The urban landscape and the iconic Wall Street backdrop were essential to the film. Of course, the weather didn't give a shit about our schedule.

We spent the first few days waiting in trailers and hotels. On the few shoots we had, it was clear we'd run into a major problem. Savannah was changing the movie. Even the cameraman couldn't contain himself. I swear, the first cuts felt like a montage of Savannah. After watching the reels, Javier and I were in agreement. The character had to be rewritten. A different backstory and personality. She needed to be mysterious, edgy. Less dialogue and more dramatic tension. It would significantly change the script. But it could work.

Savannah came to my hotel room to discuss the changes. When I opened the door, all I saw was her bright eyes staring back at me. A reflection of my fear and insecurities. She was a snake on a tile, a prophecy that I was running from. I let her in, but I was cold and distant.

She confessed that she read my book multiple times, and I fought the urge to lower my guard. I gave her a few notes on the script that night. That was all. When she left, the smell of her floral shampoo lingered. I dreamt about her.

I saw the tile being flipped over.

The snake emerging from the ivory, onto the table.

The scene changed. I was in a cold, dark house. I heard Savannah laughing, giggling, skipping across creaky floors. I followed her down wooden stairs, into a cement basement.

Suddenly, the door shut, and I screamed in absolute dread. I was in my childhood prison. Savannah was still laughing, smiling in the corner. I shoved her against the wall, but she kept laughing. I tied the waterlogged rope around her neck. Tighter and tighter around her throat. Still laughing. Her eyes shifted to a shadow sweeping across the wall. A large beast emerged from the depths, shackled at the wrist. Eyes black. Fangs exposed. It lunged forward. I awoke drenched in sweat.

The sun was shining through the windows.

And our production began.

I still can't believe we pulled it off.

I wrote completely new scenes the night before we shot them, sneaking in lines of coke every ten minutes to stay sharp. For inspiration, Javier recommended that Savannah and I run lines together. It helped. Her quirks began to shape the character of Erin Brooks. The way Savannah pulled at her earlobes when she was concentrating. Her addiction to sugary cereal. Her all-pervading gaze. Her mysterious smile. Her presence. I wrote entire scenes while she sat cross-legged on my bed, pajama shorts and a white T-shirt. I loved the way she stared at me. As if she admired my craft. The way Jane used to stare at me from our bed.

My ego craved the validation.

After I finished a scene, Savannah would read the lines while I tweaked the dialogue on the computer. In one scene, Erin needs to steal a flash drive from one of the founders. As she read, I could feel her body moving toward me. I stayed focused on the computer.

She was next to me at the desk.

She stopped reading the lines.

"So wait, sorry, may I?" she asked, leaning into me. "Are you saying she distracts him like this?"

Her soft lips breathed up and down my neck.

I could see the lace of her black underwear just beneath her shorts.

Her scent, her warmth, her full lips. My jaw locked in restraint. I wanted to tear her clothes off. I was no longer thinking with my brain. She was influencing me. Getting into character. She was the perfect Erin Brooks.

I told her that she needed to go.

I dreamt about the basement again that night.

Two weeks later, we headed back to Hollywood. With Jane back on set in Norway, I continued my friendship with Savannah, texting late into the night. I told myself it was innocent. Bullshit. It was a welcome distraction from fixing my relationship, from dealing with my shit.

At the Warner lot, our relationship stayed professional. I kept my distance, finding solace in a nearby office. But an unexpected issue on set changed everything.

Javier rang me from my office. They were filming an intimate scene, where Michael catches Erin changing in a private office. They share a kiss, and he proceeds to go down on her. Savannah was refusing to leave the trailer to shoot the scene. He needed me to handle it.

I knocked on her door.

"Go away."

"It's me."

The door to her trailer swung open, revealing Savannah in a state of angst. She paced back and forth, wearing a sleek black robe, her hair and makeup styled for the scene.

"What's wrong?"

"I don't want to do it." She chewed on her lip.

"We can make it a closed set?"

"It's not that. It's fucking Dan."

Our lead actor.

"He's been hitting on me all movie. Telling me how excited he is for our kiss."

"I'll talk to him," I assured, seething.

"No," she pleaded. "It's just—" She sat down on the couch, a tear falling down her cheek. "It's not just that."

She took a deep breath. "I've always had men assume they can take from me. But becoming Erin Brooks, I finally feel my own power. Like I can control my destiny."

I sat down beside her.

"But being fully vulnerable in that scene, with him? It's a disservice to the character you created."

"Savannah." I brushed away a tear. "I didn't create this character. You did. I captured *you* on paper. That power you feel, it comes from there." I pointed to her heart.

A blissful laugh broke through the tears.

"But whatever you need, I'll do it," I added.

She played with her earlobe nervously, steadying her nerves. "It's just a shot of the back of Michael's head, right?"

I nodded.

"You could pass for him."

"Me?" I said, staring into Savannah's pleading eyes.

"You're the same height, build," she repeated. "I want this scene as authentic as possible."

My heartbeat pounded, the scene running through my head. I wanted to kiss her. That's the truth. And if it was on camera, I could get away with it. I claimed it was for the movie. As a producer, it was my job. But that was a lie. Maybe it was all those scenes I stomached between Jane and Jacob. It was my turn. I wanted to do it.

It was my film debut.

They cut my hair shorter. They covered the tattoos on the back of my neck. I stood there nervously in a white business shirt as Javier directed me to my mark. Savannah grinned, her blouse undone, reaching for my hand.

ACTION. I stepped forward, grabbed her face, and our bodies crashed together. I ran my hands along her jaw, to her mouth, to her soft lips. It was carnal. Fiction and reality blurring together.

She shoved my head down.

Savannah hiked up her pencil skirt, spreading her legs as I hunkered below the desk. With my head in her crotch, I took a deep breath, sealing my eyes shut. I told myself I wouldn't breathe, smell, or do anything until I heard Javier yell, "Cut."

But then I felt her legs move, writhe, squirm. She moaned, louder and louder. She was acting. I knew that. But the heat between her legs was real. The ache inside me was real. I squeezed my eyes shut so hard that my head hurt.

"Get into it," yelled Javier. "C'mon."

Savannah's body lurched forward, and I felt her legs wrap my face. She softly moaned, "I want you."

I smelled the sweet aroma radiating off her body, and a deep craving ran through me. I wanted to taste her. She moaned again, and my jaw clenched with hunger. I inhaled the heat between her legs, and it was as sweet as I'd imagined. *Stay professional.* The snake tile flashed across my vision, but I brushed it aside. I opened my eyes. She wasn't wearing underwear. Her bareness, beautiful, flawless, imprinted in my mind.

I was so thankful when Javier finally yelled, "Cut!"

Savannah kissed my forehead and whispered, "Thank you."

I went back to the Beverly Wilshire, and I drank the guilt away. I called Jane in Norway, and I told her that I missed her. I loved her. But as soon as I hung up the phone, all I could think about was Savannah.

I made myself scarce on set the final few weeks of production, until Javier begged me to come watch the final scene. He wanted to make sure he got it right. An hour before filming, Savannah came to see me in my office. She tapped lightly at the door, and I knew it was her. My heart pounded with excitement. She wore a white robe, and I knew what lay beneath it. It was written in the script. What I imagined her wearing the first time we had sex.

"I just wanted to thank you for everything."

She locked the office door, and a mischievous smile swept across her face. She opened her robe to reveal her black thong and white tank.

"How do I look?"

She spun around, skulking closer. She ran her hands through my hair, and I pulled her into my body. A low growl droned from my mouth. I put my head into her soft, glowing skin, breathing in her scent. She arched her neck, and I closed my eyes. I ran my hands over the soft fat on the side of her hips, then gripped her bare cheeks. And for a moment, I wondered what my life would be like with her. If she was the answer I was looking for. But when I reached my hand for her underwear, Jane's face projected in my mind.

"I can't," I said, my hands still gripping her body.

Her chin rested on my head.

"I can't," I repeated.

I wanted her to keep pushing.

I wanted her to ignore me.

She pulled away, closing her robe. "She's a lucky woman," she whispered.

Then she opened the trailer door and left.

I came to the soundstage to watch the finale unfold. It was one of my favorite scenes. Erin Brooks is in a hotel room with two million dollars sprawled out on her bed, her fee for sabotaging the IPO. She eats cereal in her underwear and dances to dark, orchestral thriller music. Then Michael comes in and blows her brains out.

When I wrote it, it was supposed to be a satisfying moment for the audience. The founders lost everything because of this woman. Their entire life's work destroyed. And yet the movie had changed with Savannah as the lead. The audience was going to fall for Erin Brooks. She was a deity, a goddess. Untouchable to us mere mortals. She had outsmarted these weak-willed men. She was above the law. Michael and Jeff were the fools who had risked everything. No one would give a shit about his redemption.

And when I saw Michael's character enter the hotel room with the gun, I waved my hands, yelling for production to stop.

"What the fuck, Kohl?" Javier yelled from behind the camera.

"You can't kill her," I said, pointing to Savannah.

"Why?"

"Erin Brooks needs to walk away with the money."

"What the fuck are you talking about?" Javier paced behind the camera, his hand on his chin. "This is the ending you wrote. What about Michael and Jeff?"

The whole crew stared on, watching our debate.

"They aren't the heroes of this story."

Jacob and I were never the heroes.

We were the weak men.

Savannah stood there, arms crossed, grinning in her underwear.

"So what do you suggest?" Javier threw his hands up. "We don't have time for a fucking rewrite."

I walked onto the hotel room set. "On the first day they met her, both Michael and Jeff give her a business card, correct?"

"Yeah?" Javier sighed. "So what?"

"That's our ending." I pace. "She takes the business cards and pins them on a wall, and as the camera pans out, we see hundreds of business cards from all the men she's conned. It's her kill list. It's dark and seductive, but it's cool. And you realize that Erin isn't just a weapon of some sinister patriarch capitalist. No. She's the orchestrator. A trained assassin. She makes her own rules."

I pace across the set, thinking. "And then—"

"And then?" Javier bellows.

Yes. And then the man who hired her, the old pharmaceutical billionaire, walks out in his underwear. Thinking he's going to get lucky. And Savannah seductively walks over, wraps her arms around him. And then when the man's back is turned, she stares right at the camera, as if she knew the audience was watching the entire time.

Javier scoffed. "We break the fourth wall."

I continued. "She says, 'Powerful men all share the same weakness. They never think it can happen to them. I wield the power.' And then we hear the billionaire choking, panicking.

Finally, we see the needle sticking out of his neck as he falls to the ground."

Javier paced the set for at least five minutes before looking up, eyes wide. "I fucking love it."

I glanced over at Savannah. She was beaming with pride. She didn't get what she wanted earlier. But this was Hollywood, and I gave her something even better.

* * *

The Offering went on to be the highest grossing movie of the summer, catapulting me to the top of the Hollywood Mountain. Critics called it *sexy, provocative, powerful*. They called me a screenwriter with real juice. My stock doubled overnight. Within days, I got calls from dozens of actors and directors, all begging me to write them something similar. I attended their parties. I did their drugs. I agreed to write their screenplays. I accepted their big checks.

Rolling Stone did a story on me. As if my ego needed the feature and photoshoot. I exposed my tattooed chest, slicked back my hair. The interview made me out to be a gritty artist living a fast Hollywood life. One of the last American authors. I liked that. They asked me about Jane. I told them she was the love of my life, my muse, my everything. But truthfully, Jane and I were growing apart. We went out together. We made love. But I lost track of what was important.

During that time, Jane's father showed up at our house. As soon as I opened the door, I recognized him from the pictures —a short, burly man with a rugged, freckly face. Anger simmered in my veins as I stared at Jane's haunted past. I ordered him to leave immediately, or I'd shoot him dead on my doorstep. He didn't leave. His eyes fixated on Jane frozen behind me in the foyer.

"Janey," he whispered, taking off his cabbie hat and rubbing his hands over his bald head. "I just wanted to see your face and let you know I'm sober... And I'm sorry. I'm trying to do better. When you're ready. I'll be around."

As soon as he left, I convinced Jane to keep her distance. She didn't need that kind of distraction with her career taking off. She agreed. But I could see it in her eyes. She wanted to heal. And me...All I cared about was one thing.

What was that?

Being more famous, more sought after than Jacob.

Jacob's new movie *99 Bullets* did eighty million.

The Offering did one hundred twenty million.

Jacob was offered a role in some over-casted heist movie.

I wrote and sold a script called *Band of Thieves* for a million dollars.

Jacob signed on to do Oscar-winning director Rusty Trujillo's new biopic about psychedelic legend Timothy Leary called *Tune In*.

I read the news in *Variety* at Morton's steakhouse with Javier, and I told him our next project needed to be a biopic. We both were Deadheads and fans of Jerry Garcia. We did a bump of coke, and I took out a kids' menu to write on. With a blue crayon, we sketched a rough outline for a wild, fictionalized script based on the band's origins.

"Let's go pitch this," I said.

"Right now?" Javier asked.

I called my agent, who called every studio, and an hour later, the head of Paramount let us walk right into his office.

Did you sell it?

Of course. My agent planted a rumor that we had meetings all over town. With one single pitch, we sold that napkin for a million dollars. When we sobered up, I didn't want to write the damn thing. Javier didn't want to direct it. We never got the check.

I went to more parties.

I did more drugs.

The next two years were nothing but a blur of drugs and parties. There was no growth or healing. Only chaos and consumption. New cars and toys. More drugs and more distractions. I took Jane on shopping sprees at Rodeo Drive. I spent my money as fast as I could make it. During that time, I wrote one shitty screenplay after the next.

Jane's show got picked up for another season.

Her character became the sovereign ruler.

She was headed back to Norway to film for another four months. On the night before she left, we sifted through an old shoe box of photos. Memories from the set of *She's Complicated*. Our time in London. Our first apartment together. Staring at the Polaroids only made us miserable. We were happier back then. Back when we had nothing to lose, and it was just us against the world. Halfway through the stack of pictures, Jane rushed to the patio, clearly distraught. She leaned against the railing and stared out at the ocean.

I joined her.

"My dad wants to visit me on set."

I didn't say anything.

"I want a relationship with him."

I scoffed, and she grabbed my hand.

"I'm scared for you," Jane said, her mouth twitching back and forth.

"What do you mean?"

"What you're becoming. What's happening to us."

A tear rolled down her cheek.

"We're slipping."

I hated seeing her in pain.

"I'll fix this." I put my thumb to her falling tear. She leaned into my hand, and the world stopped spinning so out of control, just for a second. I saw the woman I fell in love with. Before the drugs. Before my ego poisoned my mind. The way I first saw her. That clumsy waitress in that art gallery.

I kissed her that night, desperate to rekindle our spark. That mysterious energy that set everything in motion. But even with her lips on mine, nothing ignited. It was like trying to strike a flame in a snowstorm. I just wanted my next fix. I should have gone to Norway with her to try to rebuild what we'd had. I should have gotten sober.

Maybe I was too far gone by then.

I was too scared of losing to Jacob.

The next morning, I checked into the Beverly Wilshire with my computer and enough drugs to kill me. I stayed holed up for the entire four months Jane was gone. Every night, I paced my hotel room, snorting, sitting in front of a typewriter, my lucky coin next to me at the desk. Hoping for a miracle from the gods.

I turned the television to an interview of Jacob Perry on *Inside the Actor's Studio*. He was about to embark on a new film, one he referred to as the most challenging role of his life.

"This script came to me in a mysterious way. As if the Great Muse, the Hollywood Gods, knew my time had arrived. This role will define me. I am ready to risk everything."

My entire body went numb. Great Muse? Hollywood Gods? Had he found out about the symbol? No he couldn't have.

Then Jacob smiled, his gaze slightly turning toward the camera, as if he was talking to me. "I believe when you're ready for the truth, it will find you."

I smashed the television with a bottle of booze.

I left the hotel a few times to get more drugs and attend more parties.

I woke up in strange places.

The list of scripts I agreed to write piled up.

One night, I was completely loaded when Robert Drifter's book fell to the floor. I hadn't read it in years, but packing it was second nature. I tore through the familiar chapters, rereading Sal's plight, his pursuit for the truth. I thought about my own life. My own pursuits. My own destruction. What was I searching for? More importantly, what was I running from?

As I had done a million times, I went straight to the back of the book, staring at the symbol. Had Jacob really discovered its meaning? On that night, a dark vision returned. It was clearer than ever: my father smacking the typewriter in a fit of madness. Pages whirling about the room. Me, as a child, tiptoeing in to pick up a single sheet. The image was blurry at first, but then it sharpened; the symbol leaping off the page. And it struck me . . . I had seen that symbol as a child. Had my father known about it? Was he obsessed with it as well?

I slammed Drifter's book shut.

But the damage was done.

The floodgates opened.

The shadows began leaking out of me.

The drugs no longer kept them at bay.

The more I snorted and drank, the more the symbol haunted me, its edges burned into my vision. I saw it in the hotel shower. In the liquor store. In my dreams at night.

The devil was coming for me.

Jane called to tell me she was returning early.

Just for a few weeks.

I cried when she told me.

I was so broken.

I still held out hope that she could save me. The way she always saved me. I flushed the last of the drugs down the toilet, and I checked out of the hotel. I would get sober. I searched a newspaper and found the most expensive house on the market. A last-ditch effort. A new house would save us.

The next day, I picked Jane up from the airport with flowers. I blindfolded her, and we drove to the Mount Olympus of Hollywood. The new place had a giant black iron gate, seven bedrooms, concrete counters and floors, vaulted, industrial ceilings, a home theater, and a sauna—a fortress for my queen. Somewhere no one could get us. Not my demons. Not her father. No one.

I took off the blindfold and studied Jane's reaction. She was quiet as she tiptoed around, taking it all in. She walked outside, gazing at the infinity pool that overlooked the entire city. The sun was setting, and a beautiful orange light glowed behind a filter of grime and smog. I wanted to believe we were Hollywood legends staring at the city we'd conquered.

"What do you think?"

She burst into tears.

My heart sank.

"You hate it."

"No" she cried.

"So what is it?"

She took a deep breath, flaring her arms. She was confessing something. She was leaving me. Was she leaving me for Jacob? No amount of money or fame could destroy that insecurity. Then she said the words that changed my life forever.

"I'm pregnant."

20

CONNER

I'VE BECOME SO ENGROSSED in the story that I hardly realize Kohl has pulled into a gas station. It's almost eight o'clock, and the California skyline has faded to darkness. We've been driving for nearly two hours. Kohl stops at a gas pump, glancing around suspiciously before reaching for his wallet on the dash. He hands me a fifty. "Better if you pay?"

I stagger into the gas station, shielding my eyes from the fluorescent lighting. The clerk is engrossed in a tabloid. When I approach the counter, I see my face on the television alongside Kohl's. The volume is muted, but the chyron reads: Suspect is armed and dangerous. He is accompanied by a 24-year-old male who he took hostage this afternoon. A shaky video of our encounter with Tom plays over the screen. The attendant takes my money without looking up from her magazine.

Exiting the store, I watch Kohl pumping gas with an old baseball hat pulled low over his face. Am I crazy for willingly getting into his car? For riding with a possible murderer. This was my chance—I could tip off the gas station clerk to call the police. And yet I can't deny what I've known all along: I need to finish this. And he knows that.

Back in the car, Kohl sighs, starting the engine. His eyes are droopy, his shoulders slumped. He pulls back on the road. After ten minutes, he finally breaks the silence.

"Kid . . . I need you to know something." He looks like he's about to reveal a secret, but then he shakes his head, changing his mind. "Let me ask you a question."

I stay silent.

"Do you remember anything about your parents?"

I shake my head. "Just like you, only bits and pieces . . . She made the best pancakes. I remember watching her play piano. I loved the way her hands moved gracefully over the keys. I'd sit and listen to her for hours."

"And your father?"

"He was gone a lot, I think. When he was home . . . They fought a lot."

"And still nothing about the day of the accident?" Kohl asks.

Images from my dreams surface again. Sitting in that hospital lobby, my aunt shouting at someone, a shadow in the corner of the room, my mom's black and blue face. Ever since I started this journey with Kohl, I can't shake the feeling that my childhood memories have become misplaced.

"Nothing."

Kohl nods, letting me off the hook. "Why don't you tell me about that girl you like so much?"

The tension in my shoulders eases as I think about Grace. "She's amazing—smart, beautiful. But it's more than that. I love how passionate she is. I love the way she types too fast for her own good. I always laugh when I hear her smacking the delete button, fixing all her mistakes. It's almost like she's too excited and it all just overflows out of her."

I pause, staring at Kohl. "You know, she was working on a story about you before this . . . About you and Jacob."

Suddenly, Kohl's face looks ashen.

I've struck a nerve.

He says nothing.

"Do you know anything about that?" I ask.

His jaw clenches, his hands gripping the steering wheel.

"Kohl?"

Finally, he leans over, seething. "Just hit the damn record button."

21

KOHL

Jane and I got married ten days after she returned. Our wedding was a small affair in the backyard of my agent's house in Malibu, the Pacific Ocean our backdrop. Jane looked absolutely beautiful in her simple cotton dress, crowned with a wreath of flowers. I read my vows. I told her that I had given her my heart and soul a long time ago. She was my muse, my love, my everything. Jane was too emotional to say anything. She crumpled up her speech and said, "I will love you forever."

That was enough for me.

After the ceremony, Jane's father approached me. We had been cordial since he returned to Jane's life, but I still didn't trust him.

"Congratulations." He smiled.

I feigned friendless.

"You know—you and I are cut from the same cloth." He winked.

That set me off. "You're an ex-con that beat his fucking wife."

"No." He pointed at Jane. "We need her. We need Jane to tether us to the light. Can I give you some advice?"

I scoffed.

"Don't lose her. Or this is what you'll become." He gave me a toothless grin. "An ex-convict that beat his wife."

I'm embarrassed to say that even after that exchange, I still went to the bathroom and did coke on my wedding day.

In the coming months, Jane's belly started to show. She fell madly in love with our unborn child, spending hours gazing at and rubbing her belly. It was different for me. I felt no connection. Not even when I heard the heartbeat. All I felt was fear—fear of the unknown, fear of passing down my own brokenness. Jane sensed that fear and laid down an ultimatum: never return home high.

That was most of the time.

I spent the first months of our married life away from home. Attending parties, passing out in hotel rooms. I signed on to write a few more movies, though my name was starting to lose its weight. I was hired to write a political thriller, an alien western, an apocalyptic movie. I can't even remember the rest. I did anything to avoid looking at Jane. I hated staring at my future. I could hear my grandma's words hissing in my ear. That old sack of bones screaming, *You're no good like your father.*

Jane was five months pregnant when I got a lifeline. My agent asked if I wanted to write the autobiography for Blitz Cab, the legendary rock band. It was a good project. They weren't just a band… They sang about politics and war and still made Top 40 hits. Lead singer, Shawn Conway, was a rock god. I was humbled that the band requested me for the job. They wanted to meet up in person in New York to discuss. Jane couldn't believe I was willing to take the meeting.

I told her I would turn it down.

I went to New York, and I partied with the band. They were easy to get along with. Shawn, Billy, and Eric. They were all six feet tall with skeleton-like frames. Colorful mohawks and scattered track marks on their arms. They didn't give two shits about critics or money or fame. They only cared about their music and their fans. They saw me as one of them. A true artist. I wasn't one of them.

I cared about critics, money, and fame.

I wrote mind-numbing stories to entertain the masses.

The only thing we had in common were drugs.

They asked me to come on the US tour, to party with them from city to city. The truth was—I needed them. Not only to escape my responsibilities, but more importantly, to write something good again. Here was this group with real fire and passion, and I wanted to borrow what made them special. I wanted to use them the way I used Jane. After a long night of partying, I agreed to write their story. When I returned home, Jane and I fought for hours, days, weeks...

In the end, I left my pregnant wife so I could live like a rock star. The concerts were outrageous, filled with rejects and misfits like Shawn. Every concert was a full-blown riot. Shawn gave his fans everything, screaming until the veins bulged out of his neck. He leapt into the crowd, into the eye of a storm. Every show left him bruised and bloodied.

The afterparties were an extension of his show, filled with all the drugs and booze an addict could wish for. All the groupies you could fit into a hotel room. It was a dream escape. I followed Shawn into the madness. I idolized the way he didn't give a shit about anything. His heart was wild and untamed. We all tried to keep up, trashing hotel rooms, setting fire to the drapes. Consuming more drugs and booze than humanely possible. Shawn screamed with rage, and we all shouted like madmen back at him.

It was animalistic, and it felt good.

We were in Orlando when a teaser for Jacob's new movie flickered on the television. Slow, haunting piano keys introduced an ominous figure perched atop a blank canvas. When the camera zoomed in, I almost didn't recognize him. Jacob's face was pale and hollow, with haunting eyes, lost in a state of madness. The film was called *The Canvas*.

I knew Jacob had done it . . . He had unearthed the worst parts of his soul, the root of the evil that lived inside him. He would win an Oscar for playing the most despicable man in history.

Shawn handed me a bottle of whisky, then a bat. I smashed the big-screen television and the glass coffee table. Exhilarated, I screamed with all the rage and anger and unanswered questions that were rotting inside me. When I realized that I had knocked over the last of our coke, I plummeted to the floor and sucked up the drugs like a vacuum cleaner. Rock bottom was near.

The parties ended when the sun rose, and light poured through the hotel windows. Our bodies collapsed into the nearest furniture or bed. We'd lie on the tour bus and spend the afternoon sobering up. It was the only time I'd ask the band questions, though I didn't record any of it.

But there was one moment I do remember.

I asked Shawn, "Do you ever think of death?"

As his eyes closed, he said, "Mate. I'm already dead." He pulled out a crumpled photo of him and a red-headed girl with more freckles than Jane. "Killed by the needle." Shawn's face was so sunken that his tears couldn't traverse the slope of his eye socket.

"There's nothing left to fear, because there's nothing left to lose."

Then he looked at me and said, "Go home, mate. You don't belong here."

* * *

Blitz Cab's final date of the tour was in Los Angeles. Jane was nearing the end of her pregnancy, and there was nowhere left to hide. This was it. One last hurrah. I took a handful of pills and snorted a table full of lines. Clutching a whisky bottle, I wandered backstage. Los Angeles was different than the rest of the shows. Celebrities were in attendance. They gathered backstage for a meet-and-greet with the band, including Jacob Perry.

The drugs couldn't dull the fury that stewed within. I hated him with such passion. From a distance, he appeared unchanged: disheveled hair, biker jacket, mala beads around his wrist. But as I stumbled closer, I spotted the change. He had lost significant weight, his face drained of its color. His once sparkling blue eyes were murky and distant. His recent film had taken its toll.

Watching him interact with Shawn, I felt another surge of anger, my knuckles and jaw clenching. I smashed a whisky bottle against the concrete wall and lunged toward him. With one hand gripping his jacket, I shoved him against the wall, pressing the broken glass bottle to his throat. The glass pierced his stubbly cheek, drawing blood. I screamed the way Shawn taught me to scream.

Two muscly bodyguards quickly subdued me, pinning me against the wall and prying the bottle from my grip. Shawn yelled at the gathering crowd to disperse. "Nothing to see here. Move along." Then he turned to me. "Get your shit together, mate."

I sat back, gasping for air.

The adrenaline fading.

Jacob fixed his jacket and offered me a hand. "Jesus, you look like shit."

"So do you." I got to my feet, both of us unsure how to proceed.

"You know…" I broke the silence. "I've thought about this moment for years. What I would do if we crossed paths."

"And?"

"You're still breathing."

He chuckled, and it disarmed me. He grabbed two beers from a nearby table and handed me one.

"To our success." He smiled, holding up the bottle.

I reluctantly clinked.

"I saw *The Offering*." He took a sip.

I hung on his next words.

"It was commendable," he admitted. "My agent sent over the script, but I didn't think you were ready to work with me."

"And you were?" I fired back.

"For me, the art always comes first."

I took a swig. "What about you? This new role... *The Canvas*?"

Mentioning the name caused a flicker of discomfort in his eyes. "So what are *you* working on?" He deflected.

"I'm writing a memoir for Blitz Cab," I declared, expecting approval.

He gave a slight nod.

"What?" My tone sharpened. "You have something to fucking say?"

"Nothing."

"Don't hold back now."

"You can do better."

"Fuck off." I threw my hands up.

"Look at you. You're strung out, and the show hasn't even started."

"And?"

"You're scared."

"Of what?"

"Only you know that."

I scoffed, downing the last of my beer. "It's been a pleasure as always," I said, and then turned to walk away.

"I found them," he said, stopping me cold.

I knew exactly what he was talking about.

He had found the source of the symbol.

"When you're ready for answers, come find me."

I was about to press further, but Jane's call interrupted.

Jacob glanced at the photo of Jane displayed on my phone, his expression softening. His eyes filled with regret. Did he actually miss her? Did he truly care about her? There were secrets buried. Maybe I was being paranoid. No. There was something I was missing.

I ignored Jane's call.

"What happened that night in Park City?" The rage had returned with a vengeance. "What did you do to her?"

He avoided my gaze.

"What happened?" I pushed, frothing with rage.

Jane called again.

I turned, picking up her call. "What, Jane?"

There were tears on the other end.

"They're killing me," she cried.

I scrambled to find a quieter spot backstage. "What's happening?"

"My show."

"Your show?" I repeated.

"They're killing my character," she said.

"So you're fine?" I sneered. "The baby's fine."

"No, I'm not fine," she cried. "I need you home."

"I'm working."

"Please," she mocked. "You're off doing drugs."

She'd been holding that one in.

"I don't come to your fucking set and say you're not working."

"You're such a cliché," she cackled on the other end. "Loaded fucking writer."

"Fuck you," I screamed.

"Don't come home, asshole."

"Fine."

I turned around and Jacob was gone. Savannah Beck stood in his place.

***

I was weak that night. That's what I told myself. But the truth was…Savannah was better than any drug I could have ingested. Those things had lost their euphoria long ago. But not Savannah, with those beautiful oceanic eyes, jet black hair. She wore tight black jeans, a white crop top, and black denim jacket. I remember how she smelled when my head was between her legs.

"I heard you were doing TV," I said, snorting a line of coke as we sat together on a couch. The concert hummed in the background. It was just the two of us backstage.

"Lesson learned." She smirked, grabbing the straw. "Don't bite the hand that feeds you."

"You mean that asshole who came to the set? Who was he?"

She snorted a bump. "You don't want to know."

"So what's next?"

"Screw Hollywood," she sneered. "They'll never make anything as good as *The Offering*. Or write anything as good as your book."

I needed to hear it. I needed her validation.

We sat in silence, a veil of tension building between us…. Then our bodies crashed together. Years of pent-up sexual energy roared to the surface. I raced to get her pants off. She raced to pull mine down. She straddled her half-naked body on top of me, and I quickly slipped inside of her. The high and the warmth crashed over me. I gripped her hips and pushed as deep as I could go inside her.

She whispered in my ear. *I've wanted this for so long.* Suddenly, the serpent tile flashed across my mind, and I switched positions, picking her up and pinning her against the wall. She bit down on my fingers as I thrust from behind. Burying my head into her neck, I released inside her, our heartbeats and breath holding on for dear life.

That was the last thing I remember.

I woke up in the hotel room.

Savannah wasn't there.

I ran to the toilet and threw up.

I heard a knock at the door.

Jane stood there, holding her swollen belly.

My pregnant wife had to come and find me.

I cheated on my pregnant wife.

It doesn't get much more despicable than that.

On the car ride home, I took a deep breath, preparing to come clean. Even if it destroyed our marriage. She needed to know. She needed to know who I was. What kind of dad I would be.

"Jane. I need to tell—"

"Listen." She grabbed my hand before I could finish. "If you clean up. . . If you become the man I need you to become, you can keep your secrets."

"I'm so sorry," I cried.

She knew what I'd done.

And she was giving me a pass.

At the time, I held her on the highest pedestal. She was a better human than me. How could she forgive just like that? But there was more to it.

She had her secrets, too.

22

CONNER

After a three-hour drive into the mountains, we arrive at our destination—a deserted cabin buried in a sea of pine trees and shadows. Kohl parks the car, the engine rumbling softly as he turns off the ignition.

I follow him out of the car.

On the side of the house, Kohl removes a key from a water heater covered in cobwebs. I take in the surroundings. The porch is filled with covered patio furniture. Broken children's toys are scattered across decaying wood floorboards, some floating in a plastic pool of murky water. Kohl opens the door, and a wave of stale air wafts over me. The place is spacious and cold, everything blanketed in a thick layer of dust. Family portraits of Jane, Kohl, and their baby daughter decorate the wall.

"Make yourself at home," Kohl suggests. "I'll go get the heater going."

I trail my fingertips along dusty shelves brimming with photo albums and old books.

As I browse, I find myself face to face with a trophy case displaying awards and other Hollywood accolades. A giant space on the shelf is empty, as if someone stole the most prized award.

"Heater's out." Kohl enters the room with a few wood pieces. "I'll sort it out in the morning."

"I'm fine," I say, still staring at the blank space. "What was here?"

Kohl chuckles. "I was reserving it for my Oscar. I never did get one. Got close."

He kneels next to the woodstove. In no time, the fire swells, and warmth flows through the house. Settling into a leather armchair, Kohl lights up a cigarette.

"So what is this place?" I ask.

"A relic of my old life." He exhales. "The only thing Jane didn't sell in the divorce. She knew how much it meant to our daughter." His gaze sweeps across the room, lost in thought.

I reach to start recording, but he motions for me to stop.

"Not yet," he says. "Let's just talk off the record."

He takes a long drag off his cigarette. "The night my daughter arrived, I was in the Malibu Hills partying, and I couldn't get reception. When I did, the voicemails from Jane flooded in... I still don't know how I made it through the canyon in one piece. By the time I got to the hospital, she was already born. My beautiful daughter. Jane had her swaddled in a blanket, pressed against her chest. She passed her over to me, and when I looked into those innocent eyes... She changed me. When those tiny hands wrapped around my fingers, I just started sobbing, rocking her back and forth. I told myself I would be better. If she couldn't get me to stop using, nothing could."

"After she was born, I bought this little cabin. I knew we needed to get out of the city. This was our lifeline." He looks around, remembering. "I can still picture our daughter crawling on these floors." He points to the kitchen. "She said 'dadda' for the first time right there. It was hard at first, getting clean. But I loved the pride on Jane's face, seeing me as a father. The way Pips curled up in my lap on the rocker."

"Pips?"

"Her real name is Penelope. But I called her Pips."

"Why?"

"She always loved books. I read them all to her: classics like *Oliver Twist*, *To Kill a Mockingbird*. But *Pippi Longstocking* was her absolute favorite. Always made her stop crying as a baby." Kohl smashes out his cigarette. "Hence, Pips."

"Living here, Jane and I got our spark back. We used to dance as a family, Pips in my arms, old music playing from the radio." He points to a dusty record player on a rolling cart. "Maybe we should have stayed here, things might've been different…"

He beckons to the record button.

23

KOHL

THAT YEAR in the cabin was the best of my life. No reception, no calls from my agent. Far away from the smog and congestion of the city. Nobody to buy drugs from. It took a while for the withdrawals to settle, but I had my family . . . That was enough. Maybe I thought we could live like that forever, just the three of us. Avoiding all the problems that nearly tore our marriage apart.

But the truth lingered like a pending storm on the horizon.

At some point, we'd have to return.

Jane was the first to get restless. I'd catch her watching old episodes of her show, sifting through recent pictures of her co-stars. Soon, scripts began arriving at the house from her agent. She tried her best to hide them, but I'd find them stashed in random places—the pantry, beneath the bed. She needed to get back to doing what she loved.

Things were different for me. I wasn't writing anymore. Not even the Blitz Cab book. The truth was . . . I couldn't write without the drugs. And for the first time, I didn't give a shit. I wasn't trying to line up paychecks and chase success. I was no longer trying to beat Jacob Perry.

Then one night, I overheard Jane talking to her agent on the phone outside. She had an offer for a TV pilot. She told her agent that she couldn't leave. She didn't think I was strong enough to return to the city. She was choosing me over her career.

When she came back in, I lied to her. I told her that I was ready to get back to work. A smile spread across her face. "You're sure you'll be okay?"

I stared at our daughter, crawling on the floor.

If she couldn't save me, no one could.

We returned to Los Angeles just in time to celebrate Pips's first birthday. We hosted an extravagant celebration at our new house in the hills. It was a star-studded affair with Jane's former co-stars, Javier's family, even my agent was in attendance. Both Pips and Jane wore pink dresses with fluffy unicorn horns. Halfway through the party, Jane's father made a surprise appearance, pulling out a flask and offering it to me. He had fallen off the wagon.

I caught a glimpse of Jane watching from afar. She saw me refuse the flask, but it still stung. The two most important men in her life were addicts.

I knew the tests would keep on coming.

I started to despise Los Angeles, the noise, the chaos, the incessant calls. I never left the house. Jane and I watched the

Oscars together from the couch. When it was time for Best Actor, Jane left the room, but I needed to watch. Everyone knew he would win. When the camera panned to Jacob in his seat, I was stunned. The crisp black tux couldn't mask his complete physical demise. His face was sunken in, his collar cinching closely around his slender neck. I hadn't seen the movie he was nominated for, *The Canvas*. But it was everywhere. No one could stop talking about the final scene in which his character, the young artist, finally faces the blank canvas after a bone-chilling murder, revealing that the character was a portrayal of the most notorious villain of our time. Adolf Hitler.

It was controversial, and it would win him a gold statue.

When they announced his name, my entire body prickled with jealousy. I hated that he had pulled ahead. We were supposed to conquer Hollywood together. But he had done it without me. I hated that I cared. I hated that my family and my daughter weren't enough.

Jacob stepped to the podium; his gaunt cheeks more expressed under the stage lights. It was eerie. He didn't thank a single soul in his speech. He spoke of the power of true artistry and sacrifice. That it is an artist's job to go places others won't. That Hitler himself might have been a great artist had he confronted his shadows. But look what he became…Then Jacob stared straight into the camera, staring into my soul.

"It is our duty to seek the truth, even when the path is filled with evil. Even if the evil is you."

Suddenly, I had an urge to throw up. To find as much blow as I could. To drink myself into oblivion. My hands trembled as I leaned over the bathroom sink, staring in the mirror. Within that reflection, the haunting shadows from my childhood hovered over me, breathing down my neck.

They knew their time was coming.

I turned my father's ring around my finger, begging for the darkness to retreat.

Then I went to my daughter's room and held her.

I prayed that her light could push back whatever evil lay inside me.

The following week, I got a call from Vick Tuttle, who had also won an Oscar with Jacob for directing *The Canvas*. He wasn't wasting any time on his next project. He asked if we could meet for coffee. My script *Impeachment* had been shelved at Universal for years, unable to find a producer or director with a clear vision. Until it fell in the hands of Vick.

I knew what "taking a meeting" implied. It meant stepping into the lion's den. My recovery was still fragile. But that night, Jane showed me our bank statements. I was bad with money. I'd made millions and spent millions. We didn't have a choice. She encouraged me to take the meeting.

I met for coffee on the Universal lot.

It was an ambush.

I had barely taken a seat when Jacob Perry strolled over. All I could see was red. Rising from my chair, I squared my shoulders, ready to brawl in the middle of the shop.

Vick grabbed me by the shoulders, shoving me back down. "Relax."

Jacob Perry took the seat opposite of me. I scowled at him. He looked worse in person, his shrunken frame swimming in a black shirt. Deep bags pulled the attention away from his blue eyes. Whatever drastic method it took to enter that role, it had destroyed him. I turned to Vick. "What the fuck is this?"

"*Impeachment* is going to be our next movie."

I scoffed. "And you want Jacob to play President McNealy?" I retorted.

"That's the idea."

I sneered.

"Don't bullshit us. You wrote that role for Jacob."

"He's too young," I shot back. "McNealy is in his sixties."

"He's middle-aged in half the movie," Vick countered. "Makeup will fix the rest."

"Congratulations on your daughter," Jacob interjected. "How old is she now?"

"Don't talk about my daughter."

Jacob sighed, addressing Vick. "I told you. This isn't going to work."

Vick snapped his fingers. "Kohl. Take the fucking job. The script needs work. You know Jacob. You know this character. You need the money," he said, and then flinched.

"How do you—"

It was a hard blow to my already-wounded ego. My mind raced. Had Jane spoken to Vick? Or had she spoken to Jacob? I couldn't imagine they still had contact. Paranoia ate at my insides.

* * *

Production moved quickly, with the soundstage constructed in just a few weeks. The Senate chambers. The hotel room where McNealy carried out his illicit affairs. His childhood home. The Oval Office. I worked for three weeks on the backlot doing rewrites as the set came together. It was good to be a working writer again.

One afternoon, Jane stopped by the set with Pips. Truthfully, I didn't like my daughter spending time on the backlot. I didn't want her anywhere near show business, not even as a baby. I didn't want the grime of this town to corrupt her. But Jane had the opposite view. She loved showing our daughter where Mommy and Daddy worked. That her parents were part of something special. Part of Hollywood history.

"Look at Daddy's words come to life," Jane said, holding our daughter's hand as we strolled across the soundstage.

We let Pips crawl on the carpet of the Oval Office, a real Hollywood Kennedy. We were laughing and smiling, chatting about the movie, when Jane's face suddenly froze. Following her gaze, I saw Jacob standing there with the same expression.

He wasn't supposed to be there.

The look between them held a four-hundred-page novel. It made me so fucking sad and angry. After all these years, after everything Jane and I had been through…She would never get over him. He left before a confrontation, but Jane and I didn't speak to each other at dinner that night. We ate in silence. After she put Pips down, I waited for her at the dining table.

This time, I couldn't shake it.

I needed to know.

She sat down across from me.

"It's time," I said, bracing myself.

She pulled out her final card. "Are you going to tell me what happened after the Blitz Cab concert?" she asked.

"I fucked Savannah Beck."

My heartbeat pounded.

"What the fuck do you want me to do with that?" She stood up, pacing.

"Your turn," I pressed.

She wouldn't look me in the eye, and I knew that it was bad. It would hurt. Did she love him? Had she slept with him? I just needed the words to come out of her mouth. Then I could process it. Then I could move on. Because in the end, she chose me. We made a life together. Neither Savannah nor Jacob were strong enough to destroy that.

She sat down on the couch, tears running down her cheeks.

I couldn't comfort her. Not yet. Not until I knew.

"It was a mistake," she whispered.

"What was?"

"It was a night shoot, and he came to the set."

"To the set? What set?"

"Norway. He was doing research for his movie, and he came to visit."

Bile leaked into the back of my throat. It was recent. I rose to my feet, shaking with rage and jealousy.

"And I was vulnerable," she continued. "My father had just come to visit. And I just . . ."

"When did this happen?" I screamed.

She put her head into her hands. "Jacob was different. He was going through something. And I fell for his bullshit again."

"Stop," I screamed.

But she didn't. "He brings out this horrible side of me, Kohl. I'm another person when I'm with him. And there's a sick part of me that craves it—"

"Stop," I yelled.

"But there's a reason I chose you."

I ignored her, pacing. I was physically sick.

"I hate who I become when I'm with him."

"Stop talking," I scream. "Give me a second…How long ago?" I glanced up to Pips's room. "Give me a date."

"No," she cried. "Don't go there. She's yours."

"How do you know?" I choked up. "How could you know?"

The side of her mouth twisted. Her silence spoke louder than words.

She didn't know if Pips was mine.

* * *

I packed a bag and left our house that night. I didn't even say goodbye to my daughter. I'm so ashamed of that. She reminded me of my deepest fear. If she wasn't mine, then she was his. And I couldn't face that hard truth. I checked into the Beverly Wilshire armed with a week's worth of narcotics.

I broke my sobriety without a second thought.

Jane and Pips could no longer save me. I stopped going to work.

I stayed in isolation, letting the darkness consume me. I stared at the symbol in the back of the book for hours, letting my childhood nightmares resurface. I replayed the images in my mind: the figures standing on the edge of the park, their dark eyes staring into my soul. The figures skulked closer, crossing the street, standing before me, reaching out to me, latching onto my soul.

Six months into my stay, I was drinking heavily in the hotel room, when *The Canvas* came on the television. I had to watch…

A young artist named Aden falls madly in love with Clara. She was played by an actress with sandy-brown hair and scattered freckles, a striking resemblance to Jane. But Clara's heart belongs to a poet named Milo, Aden's best friend. Throughout the movie, Aden agonizes over the blank canvas, unable to paint, unable to express himself.

Aden's resentment for Milo fuels his demise.

He hates how effortless it is for Milo to create his poetry.

How easily he can express his affection to Clara.

Aden sits for hours in front of the blank canvas, slowly descending into madness. In a horrific climax, Aden succumbs to his demons and brutally murders his best friend. When the deed is done, he sits in front of the canvas one last time. He runs the paintbrush bristles over the wet blood on his skin. Then he paints for the first time the entire movie. A symbol that would come to define true evil.

When the film finished, the truth struck me. Jacob had always loved Jane. He was jealous of me.

I pictured him entering Jane's trailer. I pictured him holding my daughter. I threw the bottle at the television, shattering the screen before the credits rolled. I took my father's ring off my finger. I wrote a letter. I said goodbye.

As I wrote, visions of Jane and Pips overwhelmed me. The only things in my life worth a damn. If I couldn't be with them, there was nothing left for me in this world. I know it was selfish. But when you're in that place...I...I couldn't see beyond the pain. There was no other way out. I took down a bottle of Vicodin. I closed my eyes.

If Jane hadn't come to check on me, I would have died that night. She discovered me keeled over on the side of the bed with a pool of vomit on the floor. She called the ambulance, and medics rushed me to the hospital. When I came to, Jane was sobbing at my bedside.

She handed me a piece of paper.

"What's this?"

"A paternity test," she said through the tears.

"She's yours."

I crumpled the paper to my chest, sobbing in my brokenness. Jane's father led my daughter into the room, and Pips climbed up on top of me, and I kissed and hugged her. I closed my eyes, and I held onto her for dear life. Her father smiled at me from the corner of the room. His words rang true. The only two things that tethered me to the light.

I checked into rehab a day later.

24

CONNER

Kohl smashes out a cigarette, glancing down at his watch with weary eyes. This last session had visibly taken a toll on him

"I'm just going to close my eyes for a few minutes," he murmurs, sinking further into his leather chair.

My stomach grumbles. I head to the kitchen, rifling through the empty cabinets for food. Only a few expired cans remain. Opening the fridge, I find a six-pack of non-alcoholic beers. I grab one and settle on the kitchen table.

Kohl's laptop is sitting out. I peer into the other room to make sure he is asleep. There was something that's been gnawing at me... There's no Wi-Fi, but I connect to a password-free network from a nearby cabin. Navigating to Gmail, Kohl's inbox comes into view, revealing at least a hundred unread messages. Scrolling, I spot my own email sitting there. *He did read it.* It seems like a lifetime ago that I sent him that. Why didn't he respond? He was the one who reached out to the magazine. Then I see another familiar name.

Grace had reached out to him as well.

I read the thread.

To: kohlreynolds@me.com

From: grace@theinsidejuice.com

I'm running the story. The world should know the whole truth.

To: grace@theinsidejuice.com

From: kohlreynolds@me.com

Please call me.

My mind spins. Grace must have already linked Kohl to this mysterious cult. Why didn't she tell me at the start of this? Had she discovered more about the symbol? Did she already know that Kohl was a suspect when I took the story?

I walk back into the living room to find Kohl stirring. He has turned on the television to a news station broadcasting from his old apartment. Kohl pours himself a glass of whisky. His gun rests on the coffee table. Noticing me in the reflection of the TV screen, he quickly tucks his gun into his jacket, turning off the television. "We're running out of time."

I don't believe a word he says.

I'm not sure I'll make it out of here alive.

25

KOHL

Getting clean at this cabin was a whole lot easier than rehab. Here, I had Pips. I was learning how to be a new father. Both my girls were relying on me to step up. But in rehab, there was nothing but idle time. I had to confront my past. I had a therapist, and we talked about my parents, and the night of their death.

Under hypnosis, I revisited that chilling memory.

She led me back down that dark corridor of my parents' home. The light in my father's office was on, the distinct click of a typewriter echoing, the draft from the window swaying the curtains. My father typing in a fit of rage, mumbling something under his breath, tears streaming down his face.

"What was he mumbling?" my therapist asked.

"Undecim. Undecim."

Eleven in Latin.

The symbol flashed before me.

When I opened my eyes, I found myself on the therapist's floor, rocking back and forth, mumbling the numbers. She gazed down at me with horror. She never put me under hypnosis again.

Jane and Pips visited every week. We'd sit outside on a picnic table, under the shade of the blue jacaranda trees. While Jane and I talked, Pips drew pictures, painting our family beneath the blue flowers and rays of light. She was pure and innocent, and I was terrified of passing these demons onto her.

Jane and I never discussed what happened with Savannah or Jacob. We just wanted to forgive and move on.

I didn't write in rehab.

It had been over a year since I wrote anything new.

And truthfully, I was terrified that I would never write again. That I needed booze and drugs to write anything at all. I told myself that once I was out of rehab, once I had ideal conditions, then I would get back to my career.

I got out of rehab that winter, just in time for the holidays. Our family spent a cheerful Christmas at the cabin, watching movies, eating cookies. We took long family walks through the snow-filled forest. We shared laughter again, and I held out hope that we could make it work.

But in the silence of night, I found myself confronting the blank screen. Every time I tried putting words to the page, the symbol flashed across my vision, and I withdrew my shaky hands from the keyboard. I tried using my love for Jane as inspiration. But I couldn't stop picturing Jacob's hands all over her. Their bodies intertwined as Jane closed her eyes in pleasure.

I recoiled every time she touched me.

I was slowly slipping, and she knew it.

She looked at me with sadness.

Five months out of rehab, Jane and I still hadn't had sex.

The pressure from the outside world was mounting. The tabloids had covered my stint in rehab, and Hollywood seemed to have moved on. I needed a comeback. I needed to prove that I wasn't washed up. There was still some juice left. I was desperate to feel something, anything, to bleed black onto the page again.

One night, I sat at my computer, waiting for inspiration, when her text came.

Savannah Beck.

And I felt something.

An eagerness that I mistook for passion. Images of our night together swirled through my mind. Those captivating eyes, her rhythmic motions on top of me.

I arranged for us to meet at the Beverly Wilshire. I told Jane I needed to get away and write. Savannah showed up wearing the same outfit from the final scene of *The Offering*. When she removed her robe, my body and mind awakened. I didn't hesitate. I tore into her body, tasting every part of her. After we finished, I started writing.

As the words finally flowed, my ego rebuilt from the rubble.

I would climb back to the top of the Hollywood mountain.

I would surpass Jacob.

I would write something spectacular.

And Savannah would be my inspiration.

We met in hotel rooms for the next six months. The sex was passionate and dirty, and it did the trick. As soon as we finished, I sat at the hotel desk and wrote while Savannah slept soundly. The screenplay was called *The Seven-Year Affair*, a fictitious story about my real affair. I wrote about Jane's own indiscretions, too. A web of lies and deceit that destroyed two souls, and the child that suffered the consequences.

After I was done, I felt horrible for writing it, for laying bare those truths.

I didn't give it to my agent.

I almost took a lighter to the script several times. I should have. But then I thought about the price I had to pay to write it.

I had no idea.

One night Jane found the script while rummaging through my desk.

"Do you have feelings for her?" she cried, holding the pages up to me in the kitchen.

"Not like you."

"Then what's this?" she asked.

"Fiction."

She let out a bitter laugh. "You used her like you used me."

"No," I protested, reaching out to her, but she recoiled. "Jane, I love you."

Her head shook in anger. "You never loved me. I was just your fucking muse. You wasted over a decade of my life, and now you found someone else."

"How could you say that?" I extended my hand again. "After everything we've been through."

She withdrew, and in one swift motion, hurled a wine glass toward my head. I ducked and the glass shattered against the wall.

"You fucked Jacob Perry," I seethed.

She closed her eyes, wiping away falling tears. "And there it is. Because your little ego will never recover. You can't see why I did it…You can't understand my pain because you refuse to look at your own."

"What the fuck was I doing in rehab?"

"Certainly not dealing with your shit. Because if you had, you wouldn't have had to write this," she shouted, thrusting the script to my face. "This is a cop out. This isn't real art. This is a sad attempt to hurt me."

She tossed the loose pages all over the kitchen.

"I can make it right."

She shook her head. "Don't you remember what I told you the first time we were together? I didn't need a fucking hero. I needed a partner."

I sat back dumbfounded.

"Pack your shit," she screamed. "Pack it and leave."

"Jane."

"Pack and leave," she screamed.

I went upstairs to find Pips hiding in the corner of her room. I held my daughter as long as I could. I read her one last chapter from a *Pipi Longstocking* book and then put her to bed. She didn't understand. She asked me if we could play with her tattered stuffed bear and dollhouse tomorrow, and I wrapped my arms around her and wept. I knew our relationship would never be the same. Then I left my house forever.

When was your divorce finalized?

Years later. Only because I ran from the divorce papers.

I moved into the penthouse suite at the Beverly Wilshire. Another feeble attempt at sobriety broken. *Impeachment* came out. It did well at the box office, but something was off with Jacob's performance. He hadn't been the same since he shot *The Canvas*. But it didn't matter. I was nominated for best screenplay. I invited Jane to the Oscars as a last-ditch effort to reconcile. But when she didn't respond, I ended up getting loaded and passing out in the hotel with my tux still on.

Thankfully, I didn't win.

Still, the nomination was good for my comeback. My agent certainly did his best to take advantage of the moment. He got me paid large sums to continue writing. And I delivered the worst shit of my life. *Vampires in Hollywood*. It was supposed to be a satire. It was a train wreck. I tried adapting *Slaughterhouse Five* for a remake. Garbage. I wrote a romantic comedy that read more like a funeral. Every time something flopped, I tried something else.

New drugs.

New locations.

I rented a shithole in Bangkok with a busted, flickering light bulb and water dripping from the ceiling. I abandoned my Hollywood assignments and penned a two-hundred-page novella called *Flickering Lights*. It had potential, but it was jumbled and choppy. It read more like a hellish nightmare. I sent it to my former editor, Stanley. He said he would take a look.

But I never heard back.

I was too scared to follow up. My fragile ego couldn't handle the rejection.

I showed up for Pips when I could, but custody was tough. The drugs and drinking didn't help. Jane refused to let me see her if I was high. Rightfully so. She turned me away dozens of times. I watched Pips grow up from afar.

But there were brief moments of happiness.

We'd take trips to the bookstore every Sunday, spinning around in awe and wonder at all the imagination and creativity in one place. She loved the smell of books like me. Just like my father. We'd sit at a nearby café and read stories and eat sugary pastries. I'd stare at her with a smile on my face, basking in her presence. She wanted to be a writer like me. I tried my best to tell her that she was loved. That she was good. That she was worthy. I always hugged her like it was our last time together. She used to wipe my tears and say, "Daddy, don't cry, we'll be together soon."

I prayed she wouldn't have a hole inside her like her father.

That I didn't pull her into my darkness.

Jane started dating someone else, an actor on her new TV series. A muscly thirtysomething who played the dumb cousin on her show. He wasn't right for her. He was a fill-in. He poisoned Jane to stop letting me see Pips. He pushed her to request full custody. And I made his job easy.

I was invited to professional day at my daughter's school.

Jane's boyfriend decided to show up just to piss me off. We exchanged words in the hallway; he called me a deadbeat, and I lost my shit. I shoved him against the locker and beat him to a pulp. I remember looking up at Pips, who stood there trembling with her pink backpack, tears cascading down her face. I tried to touch her, but she flinched, and my heart broke. I backed away.

I had proved myself right.

I was no good.

She was better off without me.

The judge granted Jane full custody.

I signed the divorce papers.

Pips became a teenager.

She started rebelling.

She wanted nothing to do with me.

I wrote her letters.

I wrote her cards.

I sent books.

I wrote her stories.

She never responded.

I retreated deeper and deeper.

Eventually, the money ran out. I blew it all on lavish hotel rooms, drugs, and material things. I didn't have stocks or savings, just a single checking account that I stuck a syringe into and drained. I was desperate to make a comeback. But I couldn't write any longer. I was a creative insomniac, tossing and turning on the blank page. I experimented with every drug there was. One night, I took a couple hits of LSD and mushrooms, and I had a script idea about a director with lucid dreams.

The police found me naked on a park bench, a mile away from the Warner Brothers lot.

When I woke up in the hospital, there was no Jane, no Pips. My agent didn't even send flowers. You know it's bad when your agent stops sending flowers.

I went home that day to my empty penthouse suite which I could only cover for one more month. My thoughts were dark. But this time, I didn't have a lifeline. I had burned all my bridges. In my desperation, I picked up and reread my favorite book for what I thought would be the last time. In the final chapter, Sal is forty-five years old, walking through the streets of New York in a daze. He had gotten his revenge. He had destroyed the people responsible for killing his parents. But it never satisfied his thirst. He lost everything in the process. His wife. His child . . . Nothing gave him meaning any longer.

I finished the final page, and then turned to the symbol, running my hands along the faded ink. I closed my eyes and put my index finger on it. The three cloaked shadows flashed before me. Then the three tiles. The old book merchant smiling, handing me the book. Then a creaky wooden sign, the oar logo.

Suddenly, I had this urge to find something, an old drawing that Pips had made for me in rehab. Me, Jane, and her sitting beneath the blue jacaranda trees. And when I looked closely, I saw something... the lines on the lawn were just a shade darker... *No. No. No*, I whispered, tracing the hidden symbol —XIIX.

I dropped the picture in horror.

I had passed evil onto my daughter.

* * *

Thirty-six hours, a plane, a tube, and a train later, I stood in front of the bookstore in the small village of Castle Combe. It was pouring rain, and I was drenched from head to toe. I pushed open the door, greeted by the familiar chime of the bell. The store was dark, cold, and unwelcoming. I moved through the rows, the creaky floorboards, heading straight toward the back. Charron's instruments were sitting out. Sewing kits. Book glue. Old bindings.

He was nowhere to be found.

"Hello," I shouted, lifting the employee partition and wading deeper into the shop. I saw a thin spiral staircase leading downward. I tiptoed along the metal stairs, entering a cavernous stone chamber. It was an ancient library of sorts, with pillars separating large shelving space. Modern electronic dials hung on the walls. The place was in disarray, with stacks of old books flung off the shelves, scattered across the stone floor. I bent down and picked up a red leather-bound book, flipped through the pages to the back.

The symbol stared back at me.

A shadow emerged from the darkness.

It was him, the man from my childhood, Charron. Time had not been kind. His wrinkles were etched deeper, his hair thinner, his eyes a shade darker.

"Strange you would pick up that book."

Charron edged closer in the light, his cane tapping on the stone ground. He coughed, holding a bloody handkerchief to his mouth. Peering at his skeletal face, a dark chill sped through my body.

"That book belonged to a cursed family," he continued. "Just like yours."

"How do you know my family?"

"Let me tell you a tale," Charron's voice hissed in the air.

"It's about the owner of that book," he said, pointing. "His name was Eli Kinsley, an English playwright, quite renowned in London for his turn of phrase and eloquent monologues. He lived in Soho with his wife and child. One day, Eli got a call from a colleague, inviting him to sunny California to assist him with a movie he was producing."

Charron kept pacing.

"From the moment they got off the plane, Eli's wife, Margarite, was smitten with Tinsel Town. She fell head over heels for the glamour and glitz. So when Eli's Hollywood job finished, she refused to return the family to London. She convinced Eli to move and start a new life in Hollywood, the city of angels.

"Within a few years, Eli's wife developed a thirst for the extravagant. Her demand for status and money became unquenchable. To keep her happy, Eli bought her everything her heart desired, houses, cars, clothes. But no matter what he bought, his wife wanted more. To make matters worse, Eli's scripts were no longer selling. The studios wanted watered down stories that could entertain the masses, not poetic works of art.

"In his desperation to keep his wife happy, Eli began to associate with unsavory folk, making bets that he was in no position to make. Eli's son, Bobby, was ten years old when he first saw his father shaken down by a large man in a black hat. After the altercation, Eli, bruised and bloodied, gazed over to his son and said the words that would define the child. *If you want someone to love you, you'll make it big in this town. You'll do whatever you have to do to succeed.*

"Two days later, Eli Kinsley was found dead in a Los Angeles dumpster. His wife married an actor known for playing a mobster in a film franchise, a bad man on and off screen. So young Bobby ran away at sixteen, left to fend for himself in the streets of Hollywood."

Without warning, Charron's knees gave out. He stumbled into a nearby chair, wheezing in exhaustion, the red book still in his hands. He held his bloody handkerchief to his mouth.

"What became of him?" I asked.

Charron looked up with tired eyes. "Like his father, Bobby became a writer. But he didn't write spectacular plays and eloquent dialogue. No. He wrote whatever the machine demanded. He did what his father couldn't. He made it big. He made loads of money. He found a woman who loved those things, too. If the studios asked him to write something, he wrote it. Anything for the right price.

"But one evening, everything changed." Charron grinned, looking down at the book. "Bobby found that red book that once belonged to his father. He found the symbol in the back, a symbol that he had seen in his father's study before. A symbol that Bobby had wondered about his entire life. As you might expect, he became obsessed with finding the truth, obsessed with seeking answers."

"And then?"

"Bobby Kinsley lost everything chasing that symbol. His family. His career. His sanity. He died in 1978. His body was never recovered, and his pregnant wife was shot to death in the suburbs of Hollywood. His death remains a mystery to this day."

"How do you know so much about this story?"

Charon ripped the book from my hands.

"I know about every man or woman who has gone in search of that symbol," he seethed. "No good has ever come to them, for the seeker must pass through the gates of hell." He put the book back onto the shelf, then pointed his cane at the symbol on my arm, still seething. "Forget that symbol, Kohl Reynolds. Forget that it ever came to you."

"I can't."

"You can, and you must," Charron protested. "You can live, write, be free. But if you chase it, there is no hope for you." His eyes fell on my father's ring. "You, like so many before you, will suffer a terrible fate."

Then he stepped up to face me, so I could see the dark rings around his eyes, the blotches of purple skin that had grown across his face like ivy. "Now go."

26

CONNER

Kohl rises, his gaze drawn to a sudden burst of light piercing through the blinds. He glances nervously at me before ripping open the curtains. Headlights cast a sharp glare into the room before flickering off. Kohl stares out into the darkness, his hand clutching his gun.

"Police?" I ask.

"Don't think so," he replies.

"Conner?" a faint voice calls out in the darkness. "Are you in there?"

Allie?

Kohl, eyes wide, turns to me. "Who did you tell?"

"Not a soul," I reply, peering out into the darkness.

"Shit," Kohl mutters, gun gesturing toward the door. "Well, go see who it is."

The cold air strikes me as I bound down the porch steps, toward the car's silhouette. The window rolls down, revealing a face I know all too well—Grace.

"Thank God." She lets out a sigh of relief. "Conner, get in. Now."

I jump into the passenger seat, still shocked at the turn of events. She doesn't turn the ignition. Instead, she grips the steering wheel with unease, her mouth shifting back and forth. And then the pieces fall into place. Her scattered freckles, the brown eyes, just like her father's. This was the reason she was so distraught about the story.

"You're Pips," I murmur softly.

"Penelope Grace," she whispers, then reaches for the key in the ignition.

I grab her hand. "We need to finish this," I insist.

She pauses, taking a deep breath. "You don't know everything."

She tries the ignition again, but I hold her hand more firmly. She falls back into the driver's seat.

"You know I idolized him growing up," she says. "Despite his flaws. Despite his addiction. I wanted to be like him. I used to watch his movies and read his screenplays over and over, dreaming of becoming a writer. But as I got older, I started to see who he truly was. Still, there was always a sliver of hope that we could mend things. That he could help me become the artist I wanted to be."

She finally turns to face me. "I went to find him. I wanted answers. He was living with Savannah by then, and let's just say, he wasn't my father any longer. He was someone, something else," she says.

"You know he loves you."

She laughs bitterly. "You know nothing, Conner."

"Come inside. Let's finish this together." I reach for her hand again, and she pulls it away.

"I'm not going in there," she says coldly. "I can't look at him knowing what he's done...and I *do* know what he's done. I know what he's capable of."

* * *

Ten minutes later, I walk back inside alone. Kohl is waiting in anticipation, the gun still in his hand. "So?"

"It's your daughter."

He staggers backward, collapsing to the couch. "Pips is here," he mumbles to himself.

"Yes."

"And she won't come in?" He glances up.

"You should go out and talk to her."

He nods absently.

Suddenly, the sound of helicopter blades and police sirens pierce the quiet. Kohl switches on the television. A reporter stands by a wooden sign indicating the San Bernardino Mountains. "Police have reportedly tracked Kohl Reynolds here. Sources claim he's with the young journalist, and they were spotted by a local gas station clerk."

The sirens grow louder.

Kohl picks up the gun, peering out into the darkness. He doesn't look surprised. He knew how this was going to end.

"She didn't publish the story," he murmurs, half smiling.

Kohl pauses, his smile fading as he glances back at me. "You can go now, Conner." He offers me a sad, half grin. "I'm sorry I couldn't finish the story for you."

"I'm staying," I declare firmly. "Right now, as far as anyone knows, I'm your hostage."

Kohl furrows his brow, deep in thought.

"You owe me the rest of the story," I insist. "Ever since I met you, there's been a stirring inside me. I need to know why the symbol came to me."

Kohl remains silent.

"Tell us all the truth," I add.

He chuckles, his eyes staring into the unknown. "Alright, but no more interruptions. No more questions."

I nod in agreement.

"Then the show must go on."

Part Two

THE UNTETHERING OF KOHL REYNOLDS

"The path to paradise begins in hell." —Dante Alighieri

27

I returned from London without a penny to my name. My Porsche was seized, and the hotel vacated my room due to nonpayment. Thankfully, my agent was still returning my calls. He promised to hunt down any paying gig. In the meantime, he encouraged me to use my network. In other words, call the biggest movie star in the world.

It was time to meet with Jacob.

But not about getting my career back.

I had other things in mind.

I was sitting at The Pig's bar top, swirling a glass of scotch, when he made his entrance. He stood in the entryway like a prodigal prince, shedding his high-end sunglasses and scanning the bar. His physical form had returned, ten pounds of added muscle beneath tan skin. He sat down, and the bartender shook his hand in admiration before pouring him a whisky.

"Well, I'm here." Jacob smirked. "I'm curious."

"I need answers."

He chuckled, taking a slow sip of whisky. "We had some good times in this bar, huh?"

"I didn't come here to reminisce."

"Humor me." He turned the glass in his hand. "Do you remember us as kids? Desperate to write something real, something meaningful."

I didn't answer.

"Do you remember what I told you back then…I wanted to be an artist who goes places others won't. I would dive deeper. Love harder. Suffer greater. Experience true darkness and divinity. I wanted greatness."

I scoffed. "Why are you telling me this?"

"Because we've always wanted different things. You chased fleeting pleasures while I pursued the truth."

"Fuck you." I slammed my hand on the bartop. "I was the one who showed you that goddamned symbol. I was the one who was meant to discover the meaning. You owe me." I stared coldly at him. He needed to know what he'd taken from me.

He evaded my gaze. "There's a cost for answers."

"Look at me," I said. "I have nothing left to lose."

Jacob downed his whisky and rose from his seat. He glanced at the wedding ring I still wore on my finger. "We'll see," he said, and he handed me a slip of paper.

* * *

The address Jacob gave me was an old diner on Vine Street, nestled in the heart of the iconic Hollywood Walk of Fame. As instructed, I donned an all-black attire. I spotted him alone in a red booth, a newspaper to his eyeline. He was dressed in black slacks and a turtleneck, his hair neatly slicked back. Catching sight of me, he folded the paper, a vile smirk twisting across his handsome face.

I was placing my trust in the devil.

Jacob walked past me without saying a word. I trailed him to the street where a limousine awaited. Before Jacob ducked inside, he glanced down at the grimy sidewalk beneath our feet. The Hollywood star stamped into the concrete belonged to Gary Vice, the actor Jacob had been obsessed with in our youth. The actor who had won an Oscar for his favorite movie, *The Scream*. The actor who had once vanished without a trace.

When I slid into the back seat, Jacob handed me a blindfold.

"Is this necessary?"

He didn't answer.

I put it on.

We drove for what felt like hours, through stoplights, onto the freeway. Then the steep incline of a winding road, turning my stomach over and over. In the darkness, I felt Jacob's watchful observation.

Finally, he broke the silence. "I searched for them for years, you know. Pursuing whisperings and rumblings. Many cautioned me to end my obsession with that symbol. But I couldn't...

"And one day they came for me."

A cold shiver raced down my spine.

"An anonymous script showed up in my trailer, the symbol engraved on the title page. I devoured the script in a single read, my heart racing in anticipation. I knew... This was it, the role I was searching for. To become the greatest villain this world has ever seen.

"The next morning, I received an unknown call. A man told me—if I were interested in the role, I'd go to Norway, to the National Museum, to the painting that inspired my favorite film.

"Standing before Munch's masterpiece, I was awestruck. The terror, the vulnerability bleeding onto the canvas. Engrossed by the work, I hardly noticed the vagrant-looking man beside me. His thick gray beard and wild hair made him unrecognizable at first. But his bright blue eyes gave him away. My idol, Gary Vice. He asked me what I saw. And I told him about that scream in my youth, the red elk deer in the meadow. The scream of God dying.

"Gary told me that if I wanted this role, I would have to find that scream again. I would have to journey into the darkest parts of my soul. I'd have to lose everything in order to be reborn."

The car came to a halt, and the groan of a metal gate echoed through the limo.

"You know, I envy you, in a way." Jacob's tone harshened. "How long it took me to uncover the truth. But you . . . They have a strange fascination with you. As if you've been chosen," he scoffed. "You don't deserve this."

"Who's they?"

The humming of the engine ceased.

"You can take off your blindfold."

When my eyes regained focus, Jacob was staring at me with cold, envious eyes. He handed me an elongated bronze theater mask with sunken cheeks, deep-set eyes, its mouth agape in a gnarled frown. When I looked up, Jacob adorned a similar mask.

"What the fuck is this?"

Jacob didn't answer. He stepped out of the car.

It was the grandest mansion I'd ever laid eyes on. A gothic manor at the end of a gravel driveway with castle-like turrets soaring high into the sky. Green ivy stretched across dark stone walls, framed by gas lamps on either side of massive doors. A realm far away from the glitz and glamor of Hollywood.

Jacob tapped on the door.

A peephole with spikes around its edges opened.

Jacob spoke. *"Per viam."*

The door opened.

My heart thrummed in my ears, excitement bubbling in my veins.

I was about to discover the truth.

A secret that had haunted me my entire life.

We walked through a dark hallway and into a stone hall. The room was dimly lit, but I could see the faint outline of at least a hundred cloaked figures kneeling in the center of the room, their backs turned, their hoods raised.

A dark voice spoke over us.

"I AM THE WAY INTO THE CITY OF WOE."

A large drum pounded.

"I AM THE WAY INTO ETERNAL SORROW."

And pounded.

"ABANDON ALL HOPE."

The drum stopped.

The cloaked guests stood up and dispersed into a circular formation. My eyes darted from one figure to the next, all adorning the same grotesque masks. But nothing compared to the beast in the center of the room. A spotlight fell on the looming figure chained to a throne-like chair. The man's body was disfigured with scars and burns, as if he had been tortured and mutilated. Only a loin cloth covered his genitals. He wore a red devil-like mask with two serpentine figures twisting out from the head. As the beast thrashed and gnawed at its restraints, a shadowy fear pulsed inside me.

The drum pounded again.

The demon stopped lashing.

The spotlight expanded, illuminating the ancient stone beneath us. Eleven circular rings separated us from the demon in the center. Two silhouettes entered the circle from opposite sides, standing before the demon-like figure together.

A masked figure came forth, delivering a silver tray with two chalices.

The two cloaked figures knelt before the beast, grabbing the metal cups, consuming the liquid within.

The enigmatic voice rumbled through the hall.

"IN THE MIDDLE OF THE JOURNEY OF OUR LIFE I FOUND MYSELF WITHIN A DARK WOOD WHERE THE STRAIGHT WAS LOST."

The inscription on the coin Charron had given me.

Upon this recital, the vast doors at the far end of the hall creaked open, and the pair walked together into the darkness.

One by one, each masked figure took the journey into the circle, kneeling before the demonic figure. Staring at the demon, a sense of dread seized my chest, stifling my breaths. I wildly scanned the exits, but the door had been sealed behind me.

And yet there was a part of me that desired whatever lay ahead. A strange pull, a darkness calling me forth.

I was coming home.

It was my turn.

I entered the ringed circle.

A slender silhouette stood across from me. We knelt before the demonic figure together. Up close, I could see the tendons and muscles beneath his burned skin. His mask was caked with spattered blood, and the snakes on his head looked scaly and lifelike. The demon tore at his chains, foaming at his mouth. I recoiled in fear. The figure next to me held steady.

The chalices were brought forth. I tilted the cup to the opening in my mask and downed the liquid. The drink was bitter and earthy, and instantly warmed my chest.

The double doors opened for us. I linked arms with the figure, and we walked into the next room. The effects of the drink were instant and all consuming. My insides vibrated, tingled, a sensation of ecstasy swimming through me. I was floating off the ground.

I was standing in another stone hall, this one lit up by a grand fireplace. Around us, dozens of cloaked figures with masks chanted in what sounded like Latin.

Undecim

Undecim

Undecim

The dark energy inside me roused, stirred, my own demon awakening from its long slumber. Called forth by the ancient chant. My eyes settled on the roaring fire at the end of the hall. Above it, a stone skeleton protruded, holding a medieval shield, the familiar symbol carved into stone. The drugs lowered my defenses, my muscles melting into the scene, my soul releasing its grip. I was entranced, grinning, gazing at the mystery in awe and wonder. I was freefalling in midair.

In my delight, I hardly remembered the figure beside me. It was only when they whispered, "Why did you come?" that I snapped back to reality. It was a woman's voice, full of fear and angst. I knew that voice. How did I know her? In a past life? This life?

A few feet from the blazing fire, we stopped. A man in a red theater mask peered down from the giant balcony above us. He was the source of the omnipotent, demonic voice.

Silence.

"Who are you?" I asked.

"I AM THE WAY."

The cloaked figures around us kept whispering incantations, edging closer.

Undecim

Undecim

"Why am I here?"

Undecim

"I HAVE COME TO LEAD YOU INTO ETERNAL DARKNESS, INTO FIRE AND ICE."

Undecim

Without warning, one of the masked figures rushed forward, grabbing the woman next to me. She screamed, and I lunged in protest. The figures behind me seized my arms, restraining me. They turned me to face the looming figure on the balcony.

His head tilted as he examined me. Behind the mask, his eyes were unmistakable. Where had I seen them? In a dream. In my subconscious. Without warning, another wave of dark energy barreled through my veins, bringing me to my knees. My heart quivered in terror, the darkness rising inside me like poisonous bile.

Undecim

Undecim

"ENTER THE FIRE," the man on the balcony roared.

I stared at the roaring flames in the hearth.

The masked men pulled me to a standing position. I turned around to resist, but at least a dozen masked men were chanting, pushing me toward the wild flames. The woman next to me was sobbing in terror. Suddenly, the men removed their masks, and my vision blurred. I couldn't see their faces, only their eyes. They were as black as the night sky. I seized in panic. I had no control. Only angst and fear and shadows surrounded me. The figures kept marching forward, chanting.

Undecim

Undecim

I held the weeping woman's hand as we backed into the fireplace, into the flames, toward our death.

The blaze enveloped us.

I was in a cold room.

Inside a vision.

It was the night of my parents' death. But this time, the memory felt so real, so close I could feel it. The breeze flowing through the window in my father's study. The old wooden floorboards creaking beneath my feet. The familiar sound of my father typing in madness. *Click. Click. Click.* I tiptoed into the room, pages swirling around me in a frenzy. My father didn't notice my presence. Something was wrong with him. The room was so cold.

I grabbed a loose sheet that had fallen to the ground. There was something written on the page. Something horrible, something unsettling. But when I tried to read the words, I couldn't. They went in and out of focus, until finally, they morphed into the symbol emanating from the page. Then my father looked up from the typewriter, his eyes lost in a sea of black. He chanted.

Undecim

He charged at me.

Undecim

He grabbed my shirt with his bloody hands, pulling me into his madness.

The memory disappeared.

The warmth of the fire was gone.

I was somewhere else.

A backyard.

A lavish garden.

A labyrinth of boxcar hedges.

Cool air whipped across my face.

The woman who entered the flames with me was weeping on a bench before the hedges, her dress ripped and burned. She was still wearing her mask. Spotting me, she quickly stood up, bringing her index finger to her lips. Then she rushed off into the entrance of the labyrinth, her black heels in hand.

I followed her into the maze.

Weaving in and out of the narrow hedges.

"Hello," I shouted, ripping the mask off my face.

I heard giggling.

Figures with masks groping.

Naked bodies.

Moaning. Thrusting. Writhing.

I kept moving.

A strange mist rolled upon my feet, rising and obscuring my path. My hands glided across the sharp green leaves. More laughing, giggling, crying. My name hissed through the air. "Kohhhl…"

Then another.

"Fatherrrr…."

Penelope?

My body seized with panic.

I ran as fast as I could.

Heart pounding.

Screaming my daughter's name.

Penelope! Penelope!

Running through row upon row of hedges.

For minutes, hours, there was no way of knowing.

Until finally, I was out of breath, and my body gave out.

I could only stumble forward, mumbling my daughter's name, weaving through the narrow path.

Just when I was about to give up, the maze opened to a small courtyard with a stone fountain, illuminated by three gas lamps on the perimeter. The woman was perched on the edge of the fountain, sobbing into her hands. For a brief moment, the fear inside me subsided, and swirls of warmth and euphoria rose back to the surface.

"Penelope?" I sat down next to her on the stone fountain. "Is that you?"

She shook her head, hands still covering her masked face.

"Let me see your face."

"No," she cried. "You won't love me."

I gently tilted her head to face me. Her hands fell away, and in between the slits of her eyes, I saw familiar seafoam irises.

"Savannah," I said, putting my hand to her mask.

She leaned in. "You shouldn't be here."

"Let me see your face."

She shook her head.

I ignored her warning. I lifted the mask off, and her shadowy face fell into the dim light. I recoiled at the sight. Her face was deformed, covered in oozing, reddish skin. Her right eye socket was sealed shut. The warmth inside me dissolved into cold terror.

"Who did this to you?" I screamed.

Her face went rigid in anger. "You did this to me," she hissed.

"Savannah—"

"You hurt the people you love," she seethed, covering her face again.

She began sobbing, and I ran my fingers through her hair. "I'm sorry," I said. "I didn't mean it." I glided my thumb across her jaw to her chin, tilting her face up. When she did, I withdrew in distress, falling off the stone bench. My daughter stared back at me.

"Pips."

"Get away from me," Pips screamed, as she shot up and sprinted back through the hedges. My sweet daughter. Why was she here? I tried to follow her, but the gas lamps extinguished.

Silence overwhelmed me.

Then darkness.

A rustling in the hedges.

Three lit candles entered the courtyard.

Three shadows.

They chanted.

Undecim

Undecim

It was the cloaked figures from my childhood, standing at the edge of the park. They walked toward me. Darkness and evil. Outwardly, my hands trembled in fear. Inside, the shadows screamed with anticipation. I had always known the truth. A demon lived inside me, deep inside my soul. My entire life. Begging to be released. And now, the basement door was open. It could sense its freedom. One of the figures removed his cloak.

Undecim

Undecim

The man in the red mask stepped forward. Everything inside me told me to run, but I was incapacitated by fear.

"Back away from me," I screamed. "Back away."

"WELCOME HOME, MY CHILD."

The others chanted in unison.

Undecim

Undecim

"YOUR RECKONING HAS BEGUN."

Undecim

Undecim

Closer.

"YOU WILL LOSE WHAT YOU LOVE MOST."

He paused a foot from me.

Silence.

"EVIL IS COMING FOR YOU."

I fell back against the stone fountain, trembling.

"What do you want?"

"DEATH."

The man removed his red mask, and I saw the face of my father.

My eyes widened as he pulled out a knife and slashed it forward, the piercing blade tearing into my flesh. My eyes widened in terror as the knife plunged deeper into my stomach. I glanced down at my bloody hands, as my knees collapsed beneath me. My head hit the gravel, blood spewing out of my mouth. The darkness and poison inside me seeping out. The three figures stood over me, watching me squirm to my death. They held candles to their demonic, wispy faces. As my body weakened, and the blood poured out, they put their fingers to their flames, and all light extinguished.

28

I woke up on pristine white sheets, sunlight dripping through an open window. I was in a tidy room with purple flowers in a vase. Beside me was a laundry basket filled with women's clothes. A cup of seltzer and two pills next to me on the nightstand.

Anything to subdue my pounding head.

I stumbled into the kitchen to find a slender woman in biker shorts and a tattered T-shirt, cooking while dancing with headphones on. I couldn't believe my eyes. Rushing over, I gently turned Savannah around to face me, putting my hand to her warm cheek and then wrapping her tightly into my arms. She was alive.

"Hey there," she said, giving me a perplexed look. "You okay?"

I dropped my weary body down onto the table, sinking my face into my shaky hands. "What the hell happened last night?"

She slid a plate of scrambled eggs my way, then leaned back against the countertop, arms folded. "You tell me."

I shook my head, trying to piece together the madness.

"You called at three in the morning," she began. "Asked if you could see me. Then you never showed." She handed me a steaming mug. "I was worried, so I called the police. Sure enough, they picked you up on Sunset Boulevard. You kept saying someone was chasing you. They were happy to release you into my custody." Savannah sighed deeply. "You were pretty fucked up."

Savannah passed me a backpack. "You had this on you as well."

I dumped out the belongings, hoping its contents would jog my memory. No mask. No knife. No bloody clothes. Just Drifter's book, my laptop, and a few shirts.

I remembered walking through the double doors into the stone hall. I remembered chasing after Savannah in the hedge maze. Or so I thought. Most of it didn't feel real. Something from a drug-induced dream. I remembered seeing my father's face.

"You weren't there last night? At the party?"

She gave me a puzzled glare. "I was out with my roommate."

"No." I stood up in a panic. "I saw you. You were at this mansion, and you were wearing a mask."

She stared at me with concern. Then she opened her phone, showing me a video of her and a young woman from her social media account. She pointed to the time stamp in the lower left-hand corner. *8h ago.*

I leaned back in the chair, dumbfounded.

"What party were *you* at?" Savannah looked worried.

"Jacob Perry took me to some mansion."

"Jacob Perry? I thought you hated him?" She gathered her dishes, taking them to the sink. "Also, the answer is yes." She sat back down.

I gave her an unwitting stare.

"Last night, you asked me if you could stay here for a little while until you got back on your feet. The answer is yes." She grabbed my hand and squeezed.

* * *

At ten, Savannah left for rehearsals. I wandered around her Venice Beach apartment. There were two bedrooms: a master, and a second bedroom for her roommate, another actress on the show. The place was clean and polished, full of rose gold frames and tasteful decorations.

I sat down at the desk in the living room, closing my eyes, trying to recall details from the previous night. I needed to untangle the fantasy from reality. But it was impossible. All I could see were demonic faces and cloaked figures. If Savannah hadn't been with me at the mansion, who was that woman? I opened my eyes in a panic.

I heard Pips last night.

I saw her face.

I quickly dialed Jane, no answer. I left a voicemail.

I didn't have my daughter's new number.

I opened up my computer, checking Penelope's social media accounts. She hadn't posted for three weeks. Nothing unusual for her. She was one of the few young people that hated sharing her life. I was pacing the apartment, waiting for her message when my agent texted.

Meeting with Lance Levy in twenty. Send me something to show him - Brad.

Finally, some good news. Lance Levy was a big-time film producer, and my best bet for quick money. I was wrong to chase the symbol. Jacob was right...We weren't cut from the same cloth. Unearthing the truth wasn't worth the risk to my loved ones. Nothing good could come from the evil inside that mansion. Nothing. I needed to focus on getting my life on track. I needed a steady paycheck.

Sitting down at the computer, I placed my lucky coin and my father's ring beside me. I opened the latest draft of a spec script I was writing. A story about an estranged married couple banding together during an extraterrestrial attack. It was perfect for Lance Levy.

Clicking on the file, I took a moment to close my eyes, visualizing the scene. A young couple sprinting through a dark forest. Chased by a shadowy, unfamiliar presence. The fear exhaling from their shallow breaths. Out of nowhere, the scene evaporated.

A sinister chill ran down my spine.

My imagination betrayed me.

The man with the red mask appeared in the mist of the dense forest. He advanced toward me, each step deliberate and foreboding. His voice, a chilling rasp, echoed in the air. "I have come to lead you into eternal darkness, into fire and into ice."

I was in my childhood home.

In my father's vacant study.

His vintage typewriter sat untouched at the desk, its pages whirling about the room. From beyond the window, the distant chatter of a police scanner broke the silence. When I looked outside, a jarring sight met my gaze. My father was rocking back and forth in a patrol car, mumbling under his breath, lost in a madness.

Undecim

Undecim

"You can't save him." I whipped my head around. The man in the red mask stood in the study. "He is lost to the darkness."

I slammed the computer shut, forcing the haunting images to vanish. My trembling fingers hovered over the keyboard. What was happening to me? Last night had unleashed something. Buried memories. Sinister forces. Things I couldn't control.

Putting my father's ring back on, my phone's display lit up with Brad's name.

"Tell me how good of an agent I am!" Brad shouted in excitement.

"I don't have anything for Levy yet."

"Screw Levy. I got something better. I just had a phone call with the highest-grossing director in this fucking town. He wants to meet you."

"Who?" I asked.

"Bruce Perryman."

I stood up.

"That's right," Brad shouted. "He's scouting locations in San Francisco for a new movie, and he asked if you could fly up and meet him. He believes you're the man to write this thing. And get this." Brad's voice amplified. "If you two mesh, he'll pay your full fucking quote for the script."

My full quote? That would be enough to get my life back on track. Enough to forget that any of this ever happened. As soon as I hung up the phone, the realization struck me.

I hadn't been back to San Francisco since I was a child.

Not since I'd left my grandmother's home.

29

I stole two Ambien from Savannah's cabinet so I could sleep on the plane. By the time I made it to the hotel, it was almost one, an hour before my meeting with Bruce. I grabbed three whiskys from the minibar, frantic to keep my mind in a perpetual haze. The recurring images flashed through my mind like broken movie reels. Savannah and Pips crying in the courtyard. The image of my father's face staring back at me, wrenching the knife into my stomach.

With my eyes closed, I touched the skin where the knife blade pierce my stomach. Not a single mark, though I could still feel the dark energy throbbing beneath the skin.

I just needed a good night's sleep.

I needed to make a good impression at the meeting. If I could smile, nod, write one more bullshit screenplay, than all my problems would vanish. I would cover up the symbol tattooed on my arm. I would never search for its meaning again.

I powered up my laptop to prepare for the meeting. Bruce Perryman was known for big franchises and summer blockbusters with over-the-top special effects. I'd had several chances to work with Bruce in my heyday. Back in the early 2000s, he tried to hire me to pen a screenplay for the Buck Rogers franchise. I told my agent to decline his offer. A luxury I could afford back then.

As I clicked through Bruce's IMDb page, I felt a strange pull to something else... Could it still be there after all the years?

I found myself typing my grandmother's address on the search screen, zooming in on her old Victorian home.

I wondered if the old hag was still alive. I pictured my grandmother reclined in that chair, a thick haze of smoke enveloping her. I leaned into the screen, staring at the overgrown yard, the weeds spilling out over the walkway. Chills bristled down my spine as I stared at my old prison.

As if my demons had been waiting for my return.

I met with Bruce and his team down at Fisherman's Wharf. The restaurant was overpriced and swanky, with white tablecloths and panoramic views of the Golden Gate Bridge. Bruce stood up when he saw me enter. He was a tall, heavyset man, with a brash and boisterous personality. His thin black hair contrasted an untamed grizzled beard.

"Kohl Reynolds," he bellowed, grabbing the attention of everyone in the dining room. "Best fucking screenwriter in Hollywood. Take a seat. Take a seat."

I smiled politely. Bruce slid a bowl of thick, creamy soup over to me.

"This place has the best chowder," he screamed. "And this bread . . . Waiter, can we get more fucking bread?" He waved his hand wildly in the air.

Bruce stared intently as I took a taste. I nodded and swallowed the lukewarm, fishy soup. There was something peculiar about the way he stared.

We made small talk. Bruce mentioned our history together. Slapping me on the back, he said, "Don't worry, Buck Rogers did just fine without a Kohl Reynolds script." Everyone at the table laughed. He made a few jabs about my recent track record of box office disasters. He talked about my divorce: "That's why you never marry an actress. I should know. I'm on my fourth." More laughter.

When the waiter cleared the last of the plates, a passionate grin swept across Bruce's face. He leaned in, as if revealing privileged information. "Well I have an idea that you can't pass on this time."

He pointed out across the bay.

"Alcatraz." He grinned, staring at the former island prison. "The place that once housed America's most notorious criminals: Capone. Machine Gun Kelly. Mickey Cohen. You ever see *Escape from Alcatraz*?" he asked, rubbing his hands together.

"Of course."

"I want to reimagine it." His eyebrows rose. "The story of Frank Morris and brothers John and Clarence Anglin, the most daring prison escape of all time. Three men sharpening harpoons to tear through prison walls. Sailing through the treacherous San Francisco Bay on a raft made of raincoats."

"A remake."

Bruce waved my comment off. "When they made the movie in 1979, the FBI didn't really know if they'd survived. But you heard about this letter from John Anglin, right?"

"Sure," I lied.

"I want Anglin to recount the story as an old man. I have this idea for an epic fucking ending. An eighty-nine-year-old Anglin falling to his knees as he stands in front of the FBI. A scene just as powerful as the old woman throwing that blue fucking necklace into the ocean in *Titanic*. Heartfelt, raw. We'll win an Oscar for this."

We wouldn't win an Oscar for this.

But I was thankful for the payday. I was thankful for the opportunity to get my life back on track.

We ate lunch, and I said the right things. I started filling in the gaps of John's life after Alcatraz. I began painting the picture of the former prisoner telling his story to a young journalist anxious to catch a break. Perryman ate it up.

"I told you this was our guy."

His "yes" men nodded in agreement, and all I could think about was earning enough money to get my own place.

When we finished the meeting, I could hardly stand. My entire body and mind were utterly drained. There was no denying it —something terrible happened to me at that mansion. It wasn't just the drugs; it was a crack in my psyche, allowing angst and fear to infiltrate every part of me.

I promised to meet Bruce and his team for late night drinks at their hotel bar. A hot shower and a few scotches would do me good.

Soon, my Uber arrived, and the driver navigated the steep streets of the familiar city.

As the sun began to set, memories started to flood back to me. The cold, narrow hallways of my grandmother's house. The creaky door to the old basement. The water-logged rope twisting like a boa constrictor across the cement floor. The damp black rug wilting in the center of the room. Something inside me yearned to see the place it all started. To see if it really stood after all these years.

"Can you take me to 174 North Washington Street?"

* * *

My grandmother's house sat upon the crest of Nob Hill, nestled at the end of a windy street. I stood timidly in front of the house, gazing at my childhood prison. Someone had tried to mask its decay. Fresh white paint coated its exterior, and the windows had been polished and cleaned. A 'For Sale' sign dangled from the black iron gate.

The old sack of bones had finally passed. I wasn't surprised no one reached out to me.

"Can I help you?" A woman dressed in a tailored pantsuit stood before me, a brochure in hand. "Are you interested in buying the property?"

"I used to live here."

"Oh." She sounded surprised. "This place has been in the family for decades." She turned back at the house. "When Mrs. Reynolds died, it passed to her sister, who sadly departed as well." She examined my reaction, wondering if she should offer condolences.

I gave her nothing.

"The house is quite the catch in today's market," she continued. "I told her children not to waste their time on a single renovation."

I didn't respond. I couldn't pull my gaze away from the house. The sound of my grandmother's oxygen tank banging on the stairs echoed through my bones. Those cloudy, wicked eyes. The hissing of her voice. When I came to, the real estate agent was staring nervously.

"You can go in. Just lock up when you're done," she said, before quickly leaving.

A part of me wanted to burn this place to the ground.

It never should have been passed on.

I tiptoed through the creaky front door. The smell of burnt sage hung in the air; a feeble attempt to mask the bitterness. The polished brown floorboards creaked with familiarity. The fireplace was filled with soot and ash, the furniture removed, only a small stain where my grandmother's recliner once stood. The room felt strange without the crackling fire and cloud of smoke lofting around my grandmother's chair. I ambled through the hallway to the basement door.

Staring at the door to my former dungeon, the demon within me stretched out his hands, the way a plant strains for light. But it wasn't light they were after. It hungered for the evil lingering in that basement. The heaviness. The darkness. To remember what that cold room felt like. To feed off the fear inside me. I tried my whole life to bury that pain, to keep those demons at bay. But now that they'd crawled out, they wanted more.

I should have run as far away as I could.

No good could come in that basement.

The moment my fingers touched the doorknob, an image ruptured through my mind. The three cloaked men in the mansion courtyard. My father's face staring back at me, a knife in his grasp. Withdrawing my hand, the haunting image vanished.

Despite the warning, I proceeded through the battered door. I gripped the black metal rails, descending slowly into the darkness. A gust of frigid, damp air swept across my face, bringing me back to my childhood—my grandma's withered hand, yanking me down the cement stairs. *You're no good like your father.*

Finally, my feet hit the floor. A small beam of light pierced through a narrow window to the street, illuminating the barren walls. The rug that once adorned the floor was missing, replaced by a dark, ominous stain. The only remaining object was the water-damaged rope, now nearly unraveled. So many days I'd spent picking at it, untwining each thread, imagining what would happen if I ever got to its end.

Suddenly, the shadows whispered in my ear.

Get on your knees.

Obediently, I knelt on the cold concrete, shutting my eyes. I remembered kneeling as a child, running my hands along the floor and pretending it was sand, or soil on a midwestern farm. Lava rocks on a volcanic island. Red dirt on an alien planet. Anywhere other than here.

I felt something.

A crack in the concrete.

Opening my eyes, I noticed a small "XI" carved into the floor. The rug must have covered it up. Beside it, a section of the floor seemed loose. I jiggled it back and forth, until the slab dislodged from the floor. Inside, a cloth-encased parcel.

I gently unraveled it.

An old hardbound book and a rusty fishing knife lay within. I read the title on the spine: *The Fisherman* by Jeffrey Altman. The pages were rigid and brittle, but still clung to the tattered binding. I had never heard of this book. Instinctively, I turned to the back.

The shadows inside me screamed in excitement.

The symbol matched the one from my copy of *The Jeweler*.

Three initials next to it.

"MAR."

Mitch Allen Reynolds.

This book belonged to my father.

30

Back at the hotel, I placed the book and knife on the desk beside me. I opened my computer, anxious to research the author, Jeffrey Altman. Just like Robert Drifter, he had only penned one novel. *The Fisherman* was out of print, less than a hundred reviews online.

The book was about a young man from an affluent family. He falls in love with a girl beneath his station. Against the family's wishes, the couple elopes to a quaint fishing village in Italy, where they decide to make a humble life. There, they meet a prosperous fisherman named Zed, who takes Abe under his wing. But Zed isn't what he seems.

A tale of love, murder, and betrayal.

I opened the book, thumbing through the same pages my father once did. They were worn and dog-eared just like my copy of *The Jeweler*. Maybe he used the book to escape his horrible childhood like me. To dream of a better life. Holding this book for the first time, I felt connected to a man I've never truly known. I read about Abe on his fishing boat, casting lines, casting his dreams, casting his fears.

And Zed. The good-looking, charming mentor who Abe idolized. But there was a darkness to Zed, a past life of sins.

The sudden buzz of my phone startled me in the darkness. It was nine p.m. I had been researching and reading for hours. It was my agent, Brad, telling me that Bruce and the other guys were waiting for me. I asked him to find out everything he could about the writer, Jeffrey Altman. I needed to find out who he was. Who represented the book *The Fisherman*.

I needed answers.

* * *

I walked the five blocks to the restaurant, the bitter wind swirling off the San Francisco Bay matching the turmoil inside me. My thoughts were on my father. What was his place in all this? Had I really seen him that night at the mansion? Could he possibly be alive? It couldn't be true.

I had watched his coffin lower into the ground. Or did I...

It was a cold and rainy afternoon, and a row of nearby pine trees cast shadows across a somber gathering. A solitary coffin rested upon damp earth. Clutching my father's ring, I couldn't shake the feeling that someone was watching me. Something evil. My father's family had come out of respect. But I could see the indifference in their faces. My grandma's dark eyes bored into me with hatred. She had disowned my father long before his death.

As the emotions welled up inside me, I turned away from the gravestones, gazing off into the distance, toward the bottom of the hill. A new memory bubbled to the surface like sludge in a sink. I had seen them that day, on the edge of the cemetery. The three cloaked figures. Had they always been watching me? Had they been waiting for me?

I was thankful when I spotted the neon sign for Aaron's Steakhouse. The drum of chatter and clinking plates drowned my intrusive thoughts. The familiar roar of obnoxious laughter directed me to a large red booth, where Bruce and his team were finishing up dinner, the bones of overpriced Tomahawk steaks scattered like fossils across the table.

"There he is—our screenwriter!" Bruce shouted.

I sat down, grinned, ordered a drink.

Make it a double.

Bruce and his team were reminiscing about his favorite directorial scenes. How he blew up an abandoned hotel in Laos. How he shoved a supermodel off a boat because she was too frightened to jump. How a stuntman sued him for using real samurai swords in a fight scene.

"Still, best story is when I was filming *99 Bullets,* and Jacob Perry demanded to do all his own stunts." Bruce glanced over to me.

I downed my third scotch of the evening.

"So we're shooting a scene where Jacob's character drives his motorcycle through a fucking wall," said Bruce, animatedly recalling the memory. "Suddenly, Perry says, 'Wait a second . . . did you strap an explosive to my helmet?' And I said, 'Yeah. That's why I gave you a goddamned helmet.'"

They roared with laugher.

I feigned amusement.

Bruce eyed me suspiciously.

"Didn't you used to work with Perry?" Bruce asked as the laughter died.

I didn't respond.

"Sure," he said, leisurely sipping his wine. "You worked with him on several films."

All eyes at the table were on me.

I nodded.

"You two were pals, right?" Bruce continued, casually swirling his glass.

I beckoned to the bartender for a refill. As I lifted my hand, a dizziness overcame me. My vision flickered like a flame in a candle, unsteady and wavering. I glanced down at my scotch, then reached for the water. The glass slipped out of my hands, sending a wave of liquid across the table. In the commotion, I stood up, mumbling. "I need to get some air."

I stumbled outside the restaurant, inhaling the crisp night.

With trembling hands, I reached for my cigarettes in my jacket, trying to strike a flame from a cheap lighter. I needed to get back to my hotel. Something terrible was happening to me... As if madness lingered beneath the surface of my skin. Like my mind could snap and freefall at any moment. I was hanging on by a thread.

Without warning, Bruce's large shadow sidled next to me on the sidewalk. "You okay?" He lit the end of my cigarette with a match.

Before I could inhale, I slipped off the curb, stumbling to get my footing.

"Whoa there, Kohl." He took a drag of his own cigarette. "You seem a bit jumpy."

"I'm sorry." I waved my hand in the air, trying to hail a cab. "I need to get out of here."

"You've had a tough go these last few years. Rehab. A divorce. Flop after flop. And yet they're still interested in you."

"What are you talking about?" I swayed left and right.

"Don't play fucking dumb with me." Bruce grinned, taking an aggressive step toward me. "They've been tracking you for years."

My eyes widened as Bruce's distorted shadow swelled over me.

"You know, in film school, I was considered the artsy director. They all thought I'd be the one to win a fucking Oscar." He snickered. "And now…I'm a goddamned hack. But all that can change. All that *will* change."

"What's that got to do with me?" I yelled, steadying myself on a nearby pole.

Bruce grinned. "I've heard things, whispers throughout the years. They are known as the Gods of Hollywood. They grant wishes or destroy careers. And it is always in your best interest to do what they ask. For then, the Gods will shine upon you."

Bruce stepped into the light, his face distorting, his laugh demonic.

I stumbled backward, fear gushing inside me like water bursting through pipes. I looked back into the restaurant window. He must have slipped something in my drink.

"I don't know who they are, or what you did," said Bruce, still inching toward me. "But you should be very afraid, Kohl Reynolds."

I fell backward into this street.

Headlights glared.

I thrust my hands onto the hood of a car, desperate to stand on my feet.

I stumbled to the other side of the road, far away from the roar of Bruce's evil laughter. Everything went in and out of focus, a sharp pain tearing through my gut—the very spot the knife blade had pierced me. Abruptly, I turned around.

And then I saw them.

Three cloaked figures appeared on the sidewalk, their faces concealed in darkness. *What the fuck?* They had returned. The same ones from my childhood. They were here to drag me into madness, into hell itself.

Another wave of fear and angst overcame me.

I broke into a run.

The shadows followed suit, gliding through the air like hooded demons.

I shoved myself through the bustling street, running as fast as I could, block after block. They were coming to kill me. It was no use. They were faster.

Every corner I turned, I saw the hooded figures.

I felt their shadowy vibrations reaching out to me.

They would never stop chasing me.

I ducked into an alleyway, running my hand along the brick wall. A memory flashed: I was running my hands along my father's desk, papers swirling about. I heard my father's teeth chattering in the background. He was muttering the phrase over, and over, *Undecim, Undecim.* I grabbed a sheet of paper from the ground, trying desperately to read the words. Once again, they were blurry, out of focus. But I knew there was something on that paper.

Something I needed to discover.

Something that would shed light on my entire life.

A dark secret, a horrible truth.

I tried to concentrate, but the words were just out of reach.

What had I read that night as a child?

The memory vanished. A chain link fence barred my path. There was nowhere to go. I turned to the entrance of the alleyway, and the three silhouettes stood still. I pressed my body against the fence, quivering with terror as they slowly glided toward me. I reached into my pocket and pulled out my father's knife. The cloaked men inched closer, chanting the phrase, over and over.

Undecim. Undecim. Undecim.

One of them stood in front of me.

Waves of darkness rolled off his face like smoke, an echo of the shadowy vibrations swirling inside me. His obsidian eyes gleamed with evil.

"I have come to lead you to the other shore," he said in a guttural voice. "Into eternal darkness, into fire and into ice." He stepped closer.

I closed my eyes, gripping the knife. I felt the cloaked man's cold breath on my neck. He reached his shadowy hand out, wrapping his skeletal fingers around my neck. The touch of his icy skin sent a shockwave of pain through my body. I screamed in agony. With his hand wrapped around my neck, I whipped the knife out and stabbed the cloaked figure in the stomach. I opened my eyes and stared back at his chilling, black eyes. He let out a piercing scream, falling backward as I ripped the blade from his stomach.

But when he looked up, a wicked grin stretched across his dark, swirling face. His raspy, demonic voice said, "You won't kill me that easily, Kohl Reynolds."

Then darkness consumed me.

31

THE FAMILIAR CHIME of a metal bell echoed in the darkness. I was standing beside my father, entering the dingy bookstore in San Francisco. He wore a cabbie hat and sported fresh stubble; his familiar bronze ring glinting in the light. He rifled through the shelves, searching for a specific book.

What will it be today, Kohl?

I awaited my father's selection with eager eyes. It was a fond memory. Until the memory shifted. I heard shouting, an altercation between my father and the shop owner. My father inquired about something or someone. In his hand, he held a piece of paper with the symbol drawn on it. The owner screamed at my father to leave the store. *I'll call the police if you don't leave right now.*

As soon as we were outside, my father lit a cigarette.

"What were you looking for, Dad?"

"Answers, son."

He held out the paper with the symbol.

"What does it mean?"

My dad looked down at me, his eyes cold and dark. "Greatness."

The clinking of metal on metal startled me awake. I came to, lying on a concrete slab, my teeth chattering in the frigid air. My head felt like it was tearing at the seams. I lifted my throbbing head, adjusting my eyes to my surroundings. A man with ripped jeans and a tattered shirt lay across from me, unconscious. There was a small metal toilet. I was surrounded by metal bars. How the hell did I wind up in jail?

Bruce Perryman was part of that fucking cult. He had drugged me. There was no doubt about it. It was the same twisted concoction they gave me at the mansion. Everything in my mind was blurry and out of focus, just like before. Unable to recall the details of the night, like grasping for a grain of sand in a swirling storm. What did these fucking people want from me? Hadn't they terrorized me enough?

Kohl Reynolds. I craned my neck to the voice. An officer stood at the other end of the cell. "There you are, nut job. The captain wants to see you."

The officer escorted me to a bland office, where a placard on the desk read: Captain Willard. The officer pointed to a chair, instructing me to wait.

Alone, I took inventory of myself. My collared shirt was missing, replaced by a white T-shirt and dirty jeans speckled with blood. Had I injured someone or myself last night? A memory surfaced. I was backed into a corner of an alleyway, three shadows skulking toward me. I remember thrusting my father's knife into their stomach. Was that real or a hallucination?

"Kohl Reynolds." A lean man with kind eyes and a crisp suit entered the office. He extended a mug of coffee toward me. "You all right, son?"

The coffee was bitter and strong, warming me from the inside. Captain Willard handed me a ziplock bag full of belongings, his gaze lingering uneasily on my father's ring in the bag. He then settled into his swivel chair, grabbing the file on the desk.

"Do you remember anything from last night?"

I shook my head.

"You don't remember the altercation between you and a homeless man?" Captain Willard dropped the file, adjusting his tie. "You stabbed him in the arm."

No. No. No. That couldn't be true.

"Don't worry; besides a few stitches, he's going to be okay," Captain Willard assured. "Didn't sound like he wanted to press charges."

A wave of nausea washed over me.

The captain's brow furrowed. Then he stood up and stared out the window. "There was a reason I wanted to talk to you." He took a long pause. "When I was a rookie detective, I was put on a strange case. A case that's bothered me for years. Never could quite let it go." He turned to face me.

"The perp was a local man. Came from a prestigious family. Got his master's in fine arts right here at San Francisco University. Real charismatic guy. Liked by everyone who met him. Then one day, he just snapped."

"And…"

The captain locked eyes with me.

"Your father was the perpetrator."

I held my breath.

"I met you, Kohl. On the night your father was arrested."

The grip on my porcelain mug slipped, shattering on impact.

Before me, I saw the night of my parent's accident. The details were morphing, reshaping. The babysitter wasn't there... No, I was left home alone that night. My father had returned, not my mother. But when he came home, something had changed in him. He was in a fit of madness. He entered his study, ignoring my presence. He went straight to the keyboard, typing, over and over. Pounding, screaming, uttering strange phrases.

Undecim.

Undecim.

I walked into his study, watching the pages dance across the room. I picked one up off the ground, and my father swiftly turned his head, malice emanating from his eyes. He rushed at me, tearing the page from my grasp, slamming the door, screaming in a state of madness.

Flashing police lights surrounded our apartment.

My father hadn't been in an accident.

He was being arrested.

"My father is still alive," I say out loud. "He didn't die that night."

The captain regarded me with concern.

"What happened?" I asked, frantic. "What happened to him?"

Captain Willard studied my expression. "What do you know?"

"They said it was a car accident."

He avoided my gaze. "That's not what happened."

"What do you mean?"

"Your father," the captain began, sighing heavily before pausing, as if he was too frightened to even say it. "He murdered your mother."

* * *

I threw up in the police department bathroom.

My grandmother was right all along. My father *was* an evil man. He chased the symbol into madness. He had sold his soul to the devil, committing an unforgivable sin. And now, this evil was passed down to me. I was like him. Evil like him. Whatever fear and darkness ran through my father's veins ran through mine.

"You okay in there?" the captain asked from behind the door.

I stepped out, wiping my mouth. Everyone in the station gawked in my direction. The captain motioned me toward the exit, escorting me into the lobby and handing me the bag with my possessions. Then he held out a folder. "The homeless man you stabbed said you were muttering something, over and over. You should really read your father's arrest report."

"What happened to my father?" I asked, grabbing the folder.

The captain shook his head. "The judge declared him insane, then transferred him to an institution. There's no record of him at all."

"Any leads?" I asked.

The captain glanced around nervously before speaking. "There was something that always bothered me. As part of my investigation, I tried interviewing your father's former professor. But I couldn't find him. He was a ghost. I was told by a few sources that he and your father had a... strange relationship. I kept trying to pursue the lead, but eventually, I was warned by higher-ups to drop the case—another thing that always rubbed me the wrong way. Someone didn't like me digging."

"Who was my father's professor?"

"He went by the name of Jeffrey Altman." The captain looked back to the station. "I've probably shared too much. Good luck. Take care of yourself." He pointed to the folder in my hand. "And read that report."

* * *

Back at the hotel, I threw up again after reading my father's police report. There had been an eyewitness who had seen an altercation on the Golden Gate Bridge. They witnessed my mother falling into the darkness, my father standing there with a knife, shaking, covered in my mother's blood. The truth was impossible to process. My father pushed my mother off the Golden Gate Bridge. When the police picked my father up from my house, he had been muttering the phrase, *Undecim. Undecim.* Eleven in Latin.

The same thing I was muttering when I stabbed the homeless man.

Staring at the symbol on my arm, the memory of the night I lost my parents took shape. Clearer than I'd ever seen it: the police dragging my father out of the room as he screamed the phrase, over and over. His eyes overrun with madness. The woman at the house wasn't my babysitter. She was from child services. She and the policeman were talking outside, staring at me on the front steps of our house. That was the moment I glanced across the street and saw them. Those cloaked men standing there, watching me. Waiting for me. That one memory that's always been present. My father was part of this cult. Passed from one generation to the next. The same way I passed it down to Pips.

I took a shower and put on clean clothes. Then I opened the computer and rattled off an email, ignoring calls from Savannah and my agent.

I took an Uber to the University of San Francisco. For some reason, I needed to walk the same grounds as my father. To retrace his steps. I needed to know who he was. What had really happened to him? Why had he followed this path to evil? From the small bits I remembered, he was a good man. A loving father. How could he have killed my mother? I would never hurt Jane. Never. But then again, I've always known there was something inside me fighting to escape. Demons with their own impulses. They screamed, breathed, fought to shape my reality. I used drugs to push them away. But what if I was capable of the same evil?

What if I was just like my father?

I never attended college, but the campus was exactly what I expected. Open grass knolls with students lying sprawled out on blankets. Beautiful red brick buildings and stoic trees. I walked past young students with ear pods, tattoos, and piercings. I was looking for Kender Hall, the home of the Creative Writing Department. I had researched the head of the department, Kathy Stein. She responded to my email within an hour, inviting me for a tour and visit. I took the elevator to her third-floor office.

"Kohl Reynolds." Kathy greeted me with a warm smile. She was in her mid-forties, with short, shiny auburn hair and bright red lipstick. She wore black slacks and a white blouse. Her office was small and tidy, with bookshelves lining both sides of the wall. She looked me up and down, staring at my tattoos with curiosity.

"What a treat to get an email from Kohl Reynolds. I have your novel right here," she said, pulling a paperback copy off the bookcase.

I politely smiled, taking a seat.

"What can I help you with?" she asked.

"As I mentioned in the email, my father got his degree here."

"Who was your father again?"

"Mitch Reynolds."

"Doesn't ring a bell."

"How about his professor, Jeffrey Altman?"

She put her hand to her chin. "Vaguely. I believe he had a short tenure back in maybe the late '60s, early '70s maybe."

"Do you have any information on him?"

"Sorry." She shrugged. "It was before my time."

A realization struck her. "Actually, we did find some old boxes in storage last year. The custodian said it was from that era. You're more than welcome to dig through them if you want."

Kathy walked me through the halls of the department. I couldn't help but picture my father as a young man, following his mentor to this program. The author of his favorite novel. The novel that made him want to be a writer. I imagined I would have done the same if Robert Drifter had ever taught a writing course. What was the strange relationship that Altman and my father had shared?

"Here it is." Kathy opened the storage closet, revealing long metal shelves holding cardboard boxes and supplies. She scanned a row of boxes, until she found one with Altman's name written in sharpie.

"Do you mind if I have a moment?" I asked.

"Sure." Kathy smiled. "Take your time."

As soon as she left, I shimmied the hefty box from the shelf, blowing the thin layer of dust off the top, ripping the masking tape with my hands. The box contained old books, thick stacks of papers, and manila envelopes holding paperwork. My eyes gravitated to a stack of essays. I raced through the names, desperately searching for my father's name.

But it wasn't my father's name I found.

It was my mother's, Jessi Ross, her maiden name. Was this how my parents met? They were both students, both writers. I skimmed the essay. It was about a young woman who fell in love with an older man. There were notes in the margin, presumably from Altman: *This has potential.*

I scrolled through the rest of the essays until I found my father's name.

There was a title page.

THE UNTETHERING by Mitch Reynolds

Chapter 1.

I read the chapter in a hurry, my father's voice singing off the page. It was about a young creative writing student who moves to a small university town to study under his favorite novelist. He had moved there with his fiancée, who he cherished more than anything. They were excited for the fresh start. He was eager to learn from his mentor. I scanned the notes scribbled in red, my eyes gravitating to one note in particular.

You're not ready.

Eager to continue, I dumped out the rest of the contents of the box. Most of it was rubbish, old newspapers, paperwork. Finally, I came across a class photo at Vesuvio Café, a famous bar in San Francisco frequented by Jack Kerouac and other Beat Generation writers. I spotted my parents in the front. They were wearing blue jeans and white T-shirts, beaming from head to toe. My father's arm wrapped around my mother's. Both young and carefree. In the middle of the photo was their professor, Jeffrey Altman. He was tall and striking, with a tweed jacket and brimmed hat. My eyes narrowed. There was something familiar about him. I'd seen the man before. But I couldn't quite place him. My eyes gravitated back to my father. As I ran my finger over his handsome face, an image of the hooded man in the courtyard flashed before my eyes. The knife piercing my stomach.

My father was still alive.

As the realization settled, bitterness and anger rose in its wake. Why had he never made contact, never reached out? His only contribution to my life had been passing this evil legacy onto me. A man who murdered my own mother.

I exited the storage closet and staggered down the halls, deep in thought.

"Mr. Reynolds."

An older woman with untamed curly gray hair was peering at me from a small office. She sat behind a disorganized desk, her beady eyes staring at me with fascination.

"How do you know my name?" I lingered in her doorway.

"Not every day a famous writer visits our department," she croaked. "You're here about Altman, aren't you?"

I stepped into her office. "How did you know that?"

I closed the door behind me.

The woman leaned in, adjusting her thick-framed glasses.

"What do you know about him?"

She looked around, as if she'd been holding these secrets for years. "The kids used to say Altman was a tough professor. Very hard on his students. I'll admit, I was curious myself. So I sat in on a lecture. I saw him belittle a kid, berating his lack of imagination. Calling him spineless. I never forgot it... Well, a year later, that kid snapped. Shoved his wife off the bridge. I presume it's your father."

"Do you know how I can get a hold of Altman?"

She shrugged. "Some detective came here asking the same question years ago. But I only had one conversation with Professor Altman. I was writing a novel, and I asked if he knew anyone in New York that could represent me. He gave me his own editor's info. Never replied to any of my submissions or letters, but I still kept the card all these years." She opened the desk, then handed me the creased card.

I stared at the logo.

Bravado Press.

I flipped the card over.

My editor's name was on the back—Stanley Davis.

32

I RETURNED to Los Angeles the next morning, exhausted. I staggered into Savannah's apartment, my body collapsing into her bed. The poison depleted me. I slept for two days straight, stirring only occasionally to research my mother's murder. I scoured the internet for a single detail, any information about my father's arrest, or a woman being pushed off the Golden Gate Bridge. There was nothing.

I turned my focus to Stanley Davis. His name had been removed from the Bravado website. There was only one article about him in an obscure trade magazine: LONGTIME EDITOR FIRED OVER SEXUAL MISCONDUCT. The report was vague. A male assistant had come forward with allegations. That was it. There was no contact information anywhere online. I was surprised that no one from the publishing company had contacted me. I asked Brad to continue digging for me.

My dreams became more vivid, my father showing up clearer than I'd ever seen him. The creases around his brown eyes, his prominent jawline. He stared at his reflection in the mirror, mumbling the phrase, over and over, his irises drowning in a sea of black. Suddenly, my own reflection stared back.

I woke up sweating to find Savannah nuzzling her head into the crook of my neck, her lips gently kissing my collarbone.

She nursed me back to life.

By the third day, I felt well rested. Noticing Savannah's side of the bed was vacant, I reached for my phone and found a voicemail from my agent. According to him, Bruce loved our meeting and was eager to read the first pages of my script. *That's strange,* I thought, climbing out of bed. Was poisoning me all part of his method?

The conversation we'd had outside the restaurant was blurry. But I knew one thing: He knew about these people...these shadows. Whoever they were, they were dangerous. If I kept chasing these clues, I would suffer the same fate as my father.

I was determined to write Bruce's five crappy pages and get my life back on track. Sitting down on the kitchen table, I opened my computer to a blank page. I took off my ring and set my lucky coin beside me. Then I began to type...

The frigid air howling off the San Francisco Bay.

The blare of ship horns passing beneath the bridge.

The dark, ominous island materialized in the fog, Alcatraz.

I typed the opening scene, then moved to the next. But as I envisioned the dark and cold prison cell, the scene altered in my mind. I saw my grandmother's basement. My father sitting in the corner as a young boy, reading his copy of *The Fisherman*. Suddenly, my father looked up, a fishing knife clenched in his hand. My pulse raced to a halt. My father's face was gone. Pips's reflection stared back.

My phone rang, interrupting my session.

It was my agent.

I tore my eyes from the screen, picking up on the third ring.

"Kohl, how's the script coming along?"

I glanced down at the words blanketing the pages.

"I have the first five pages."

"Perfect. Send them over, and I'll make them cut the check."

Changing the subject, I asked. "Did you find anything on Altman?"

"Nothing."

"What about my editor, Stanley Davis?"

Brad paused. "He moved to Los Angeles about five years ago."

"Great," I said, standing up in anticipation. "Do you have an address?"

"Yeah, but it's not going to do you much good."

"Why?"

"The guy's dead."

Stanley's final resting place was a cemetery in the Hollywood Hills, right across the street from the Warner Brothers Studio. I wasn't sure why I'd made the forty-minute drive. Our relationship was strictly professional. He was important to me for a single reason: He was my one and only connection to Robert Drifter. His editorial hand had touched both of our books. Somehow, that made me feel closer to a man who had been more of a father to me than my own.

As I drove, Brad disclosed the full story. Stanley had suffered a heart attack while driving through the Malibu canyon. His car and body had been discovered off the side of the road.

The towering black iron gates of the cemetery stirred memories of my own parents' gravesite. Or perhaps it was just my mother… Since visiting the police station, I had begun to recall the day of their funeral more vividly. I'd driven in a limo that morning with my grandmother, clutching my father's ring for dear life, desperate to keep the shadows at bay.

"Your father deserved what he got," my grandmother said. "He was a horrible man."

My grandma had known the truth.

That was why she called me evil.

I was his spawn.

But did she know he was still alive?

The memory vanished.

I parked my car and began my ascent up the cemetery's steep rolling green hills. I held the location of Stanley's bronze headstone on a scrap of paper. It took me a half an hour to find Stanley's name next to a shady oak tree.

I paid my respects, trying to recall my brief time with Stanley. The last time I'd emailed him was after finishing *Flickering*

Lights from that rundown hotel in Thailand. I had sent him the manuscript to his office and eagerly awaited his feedback. But it never came. It was all done on a typewriter, so I never had a backup copy. At the time, I'd been so high and insecure that I didn't follow up. I never requested the manuscript to be returned. I never contacted him again.

Out of the corner of my eye, a dark figure caught my attention, standing near the tree line. An elderly man, draped in a pea coat and wearing a cabbie hat, stood watching me. Was he one of them? Had he been following me? As soon as our gazes met, the man hobbled away.

I started walking toward him, but he quickened his pace. I trailed him down the hill to the road.

"Who are you?" I screamed, narrowing my distance between us.

I watched the old man ease into a luxury sedan.

Reaching the car, I saw him nervously fumbling with his keys. I smacked my hand on the window, demanding, "Open up."

Again and again.

The car window rolled down, followed by a shaky revolver.

"Back away or I'll shoot," the man wheezed, the gun trembling in his hand.

I held my hands up.

"Why were you at Stanley's gravesite?" he pressed.

"My name is Kohl Reynolds," I said. "Stanley was my editor."

His eyes registered my name, and the tension on his face washed away. He gave a slight head nod and lowered the gun. Both of us took a deep breath.

"I thought you were one of them," he said.

"Them?"

I met his tired gaze. "The people who killed Stanley."

* * *

In a dimly lit diner, we sat opposite each other, cradling cups of lukewarm coffee. He introduced himself as Gregory, Stanley's partner of thirty-eight years. Grief and age had taken their toll, with thick under-eye circles and sparse patches of gray stubble over weathered skin.

We made small talk between cups of coffee. After Stanley's firing, the two had moved to Los Angeles to make a fresh start. It didn't last long. The funeral had been a small gathering. Most of Stanley's friends in New York had abandoned him once the allegations came out. According to Gregory, the sexual harassment charge was completely fabricated.

"Well, he was an incredible editor," I said, trying to lighten the mood.

Gregory scoffed. "Stanley was a fraud."

I blinked in surprise. "Excuse me?"

"You don't know, do you?"

"Know what?"

Gregory took a shaky sip of coffee. "Stanley ever tell you how he got his start in publishing?"

I shook my head.

"A mailroom." Gregory smiled. "Worked his way up to assistant for the top editor at Bravado. Back then it was Eli Trotter. One day Trotter gets a call from a Hollywood executive who says he has a manuscript to sell. But somebody had to fly out to Los Angeles to fetch the thing. So Trotter sent Stanley in his stead.

"When Stanley got there, he met with an assistant who made Stanley read the book in one sitting. It was a fantastic novel called *The Fisherman*."

I leaned in, eyes wide.

"The assistant told Stanley that the people he represented would have more for him to sell, but that Bravado couldn't ask questions. He just had to publish the books they gave them. In rare cases, as it was with *The Fisherman*, the author could not be contacted. All communication went through him.

"Because the manuscript was so fantastic, Stanley didn't argue with the terms. But when he returned to New York, Trotter was furious. No one told Trotter which books he could and could not publish. He told Stanley to send word to Los Angeles that they would not be publishing this, or any of his books."

"But Stanley couldn't let the novel go. He became obsessed with the damn thing. So he decided to take the book to the executives at Bravado. When they read it, they also became enamored. They congratulated Stanley for finding it and awarded him with a promotion. Stanley became the youngest editor at Bravado. And it was the first of many times that Stanley took credit for finding a book he didn't actually find."

"What are you saying?" I asked.

"Stanley was a pawn," Gregory growled. "He didn't find any of those books. In the beginning of his career, the assistant would mail Stanley a book, and Stanley would publish it. No questions asked. He didn't lay his editorial hand on a single one of them. He didn't have to. They were all perfect. Most of Stanley's authors went on to write multiple books, except a select few, which always bothered Stanley." Gregory's eyes narrowed on me.

"So what happened?"

"By the early 2000s, the books stopped coming. And Stanley's other authors had a habit of burning out quickly and dying too soon. So for the first time in Stanley's career, he had to find his own books. But he was rubbish at hunting down winners. That's when Stanley did something he wasn't supposed to do. He disobeyed them."

"How?"

"He tried to publish your book, *Flickering Lights*."

"But it was never published."

"You're right," Gregory croaked. "They made sure your book never saw the light of day. And Stanley... He was punished for his betrayal."

Gregory continued: "I hoped that moving to Los Angeles would be a fresh start. But Stanley was determined to find these people. He thought he could reengage them. Convince them to restore his career and reputation. He became obsessed with tracking them down, following strange rumors, following that damn symbol." Gregory pointed to the tattoo on my arm.

"And what happened?"

Gregory downed his final swig of coffee. "One evening, he left the house and never returned. They found his body at the bottom of Malibu Canyon."

"You think they killed him?"

"I know they did," he snarled. "They are dangerous people—and you'd be smart not to go looking for them." Gregory reached into his coat and pulled out a letter.

"What's that?"

Gregory stared at the letter in his hands. "I'm not sure how, but Stanley knew that one day you would come looking for answers. He told me to give this to you when the time came. I've been carrying it with me ever since he died."

I was taken aback.

"Stanley used to pick up the manuscripts from a PO Box in Brooklyn. One day, a letter was attached to one of the manuscripts. The letter was addressed to you."

He handed me the letter.

Robert Drifter's name was on the envelope.

I sat up in disbelief, staring at my mentor's name. So many nights I had spent drafting letters to that man. Needing to know whether Sal's adventures were real. Telling him about the accident that had killed my parents. Confessing to him my dream of becoming a writer. Begging him for his advice. And there it was…He had written back. When I looked up, Gregory had deserted the booth. He hobbled out of the deli, cane in hand.

33

Dear Kohl,

If you ever make it to Los Angeles, go see the irises in bloom. Make sure you mention that you know the gardener.

-Robert Drifter

I pored over the letter again and again, dissecting every word. The thick blue ink and smooth-scripted handwriting of my idol, my mentor, Robert Drifter. Touching the signature was like touching a piece of him. He was real. Not just a figment of my imagination. *Go see the irises in bloom.* All those years writing personal letters, and he sends one mysterious riddle back.

I put the letter into the binding of *The Jeweler*, flipping to the symbol in the back of the book. What if Drifter was giving me a clue? He knew my fate, that one day I would migrate to Los

Angeles to seek out the symbol and truth. But what if the truth led me down the same evil path as my father? Whoever these people were, they held no restraint. They hurt people. My parents. Stanley. What had become of Robert Drifter? I needed to know my own destiny. Most of all, whether my daughter was in danger.

"Take a break." Savannah walked into the room. "I have some good news." She smiled, draping her arm across my shoulder.

I leaned into her warm skin.

"I just read the script for season two, and I have a bigger role," she squealed, then kissed my neck and danced away towards the bedroom.

"Come to my cast party tonight," she yelled from the bedroom.

I was about to close my computer when my phone buzzed.

"Kohl," Savannah yelled from the other room. "Did you hear me?"

I reread the name several times just to make sure it was real. Pips wanted to visit me.

* * *

Savannah agreed to leave the apartment early. After sending Pips the address, she promptly texted back that she was en route. It had been three years since our last visit…

She was in her final year of high school, and we met at a food court near the Grove. She was sitting at a table when I arrived, backpack in hand. She was a mirror of her mother's beauty and quirks, but she had my dark olive skin and hair. I sat across from her, and I couldn't stop staring. I was so proud of her. She asked me tough questions about the divorce, my career, about my addiction. I was candid about everything. I told her about *The Seven-Year Affair* screenplay, and how her mother found it. I told her that I had broken our marital vows. I used someone else as a muse. I didn't tell her about Jacob. I didn't have the heart to do it.

When Pips left, I felt hopeful. Hopeful that we could mend our relationship. A week later, I got a call from the head of the school paper, asking if they had permission to run Pips's exposé. The teacher emailed it to me—a personal tale about the toxicity of Hollywood on our family, including my affair with Savannah. Seventeen and she was already writing hard-hitting pieces. I pleaded with the teacher not to run it, that everything was off the record. They killed her first big story. I tried to reach out and explain to Pips why I did it. But she never returned my calls.

The sound of the buzzer interrupted my thoughts. *My daughter was here.* I pressed the button to let her in, then paced the apartment, trying to steady my nerves. I was terrified of what she would think of me. My appearance was unsettling. I had lost weight these past few weeks. My eyes were swollen and red, and the color had drained from my fatigued face. Worse, I was living in Savannah's house, a woman she likely blamed for our family's demise. I opened the door.

She was wearing one of Jane's old collegiate sweatshirts, her hair tied in a messy bun. In her presence, the darkness from the past few days withdrew. I could almost feel her tiny hands wrapped around my neck, the thrill of young fatherhood. Her eager voice when she begged for another story. But those days felt like another lifetime. She was a grown woman. She mustered a faint smile before stepping inside, her eyes darting around the room.

"So you're living with her?"

"It's not like that."

Her eyebrows arched.

"Can I get you anything to drink?"

She took a deep breath, her mouth shifting back and forth. She was nervous around me, and that was what stung the most.

"Coffee?" I asked.

She nodded, then settled on the sofa.

I joined her. "I'm so glad you texted. I've miss—" I stopped mid-sentence, watching her eyes avert. I learned the hard way —emotions made Pips withdraw. When she finally looked back up, her face had hardened.

"I'm doing a story about Jacob Perry," she said coldly.

I flinched at his name.

"What about him?" I asked, and it came out harshly. "Is that the reason you came? Another story?"

She shrugged, turning away.

"I've really missed you."

She stood up, her eyes gravitating to my copy of *The Jeweler* on the table. She walked over and picked it up, flipping to the book's end, her gaze fixated on the symbol.

Suddenly, a memory returned. The childhood picture with the symbol hidden in the grass. Her voice on the night of the mansion. Was that a figment of my imagination or was she already marked? My daughter would not make the same mistakes as me. A fatherly instinct gripped me.

I ripped my father's ring off my finger, holding it out to her. All those nights I held it to keep the demons at bay. Maybe it could protect my daughter in the same way. At least a little bit longer, until I figured this out.

Her expression softened as she took the ring. Then she looked up, pleading. "Please, just tell me what it all means?"

"I don't know…But please, Pips." I reached for her hand. "Don't go looking for that symbol."

"It's too late." Her tone sharpened. "I need answers."

Then she ran her fingers over the inky emblem on the back of my book, as if the symbol was whispering to her, the devil begging her to follow.

In a swift motion, I snatched the book from her grasp, startling her.

She backed up, her eyes blazing with fury.

"What does it mean?" she screamed. "That fucking symbol. You've always been obsessed with it. Tattooed on your arm. Written on your book. I've seen that symbol my entire life. What is it?"

"Please, trust me. Nothing good can come of it."

"Always with the secrets," she scoffed. "Mom used to tell me that Jacob and you were fanatical about it."

"Pips," I said, trying to steady my voice.

"Don't fucking call me that," she screamed, her hand trembling. "My name is Grace."

Reaching out, I whispered, "I'm sorry."

"I deserve to know." She recoiled.

I remained silent.

"Well if you won't tell me, I know Jacob will."

"No," I seethed. "Stay away from him!"

"Why should I listen to you?" she screamed back. "You left us, remember? You know why I stopped writing my novel? Why I gave up my dream? Because I was scared of ending up like you. Scared of disappointing Mom. Scared of being an unreliable addict and a liar. That's why I gave up the name "Pips" and "Reynolds" and whatever bullshit identity that connected me to you. So I can finally be free of your lies. So yes, I *will* go to Jacob. Maybe he has the guts to tell me the truth."

Before I could stop her, the door slammed in my face. I keeled over in disbelief, regret flooding my body. I just sent my child into the hands of a monster.

* * *

I spent the rest of the afternoon trying to hunt down Jacob, but his phone went straight to voicemail. Brad gave me his new address, guiding me to the Palisades. Desperate, I kicked and pounded on his iron-clad gates. He didn't answer. Neither did Jane or my daughter. It was nightfall by the time I gave up my pursuit.

With nowhere else to go, I drove north to find Savannah. I didn't want to be alone. I didn't trust myself. Not with all the guilt and fear and sadness swirling inside me. Savannah and her show's cast were celebrating in a grand Brentwood mansion.

The place was alive with partygoers, the sound of laughter and celebration filling the air. Savannah spotted me in the crowd, beaming with fondness. She was the only person who still believed in me. The only person that still cared. I didn't deserve her.

Proudly, she introduced me to her colleagues. I smiled, desperate to make a good impression. To make small talk and play my part as her doting boyfriend. But my mind, my body, every part of me was spiraling out of control. I was desperate to work out all the pieces in my head.

The picture of Altman with my parents.

Stanley's death.

The letter from Drifter.

For my daughter's sake, I needed to understand what it all meant.

Time was running out.

While refilling our drinks, I noticed a striking woman from the show's poster—Savannah's roommate. Her cascading blonde hair contrasted with her dark, cherry lips. She weaved in and out of the crowd, whispering to me from across the party, mouthing something. But I couldn't focus. I couldn't see straight. I was about to approach when Savannah suddenly grabbed my arm.

"There you are." She smiled. "Come meet my director."

When I looked back, the woman had disappeared. Savannah ushered me to the balcony, bathing in the glow of the setting sun. A middle-aged man with a beanie and scraggily beard was smoking a cigarette on the porch, conversing with a producer of the show. He glanced my way, a flicker of curiosity in his eyes.

"Howard, this is Kohl Reynolds," Savannah announced. "Kohl, this is our director."

"Pleasure." Howard shook my hand, taking a sip of scotch. "I've admired your work for a long time. In fact, the final scene in *The Offering* inspired me to cast Savannah as Geneva... A woman that could decimate powerful men with a single glance."

"You made an excellent choice," I said. "The show is fantastic."

Howard grinned. "Got to love the Old Testament. So much good source material."

I nodded, my thoughts drifting back inside. What was that woman trying to tell me? Or was I seeing things? My mind couldn't be trusted.

Howard continued. "I was actually inspired by a painting in the Getty," he began, pointing to the hill above us, where Los Angeles's biggest art museum stood. "I was staring at this old painting of King David—David and the Penitence—and suddenly I was struck with this divine inspiration. I just saw the man so vividly on screen. This looming, powerful, dark, complicated figure.... Have you seen the painting?" the director asked.

"Huh? No," I replied, refocusing. "Actually, I've never actually been to the Getty. My wife—my ex-wife tried to get me to go, but—" I stopped midsentence.

"Oh, well you have to go," he cut in. "Some fantastic works of art. Rembrandt. Van Gogh."

"I love Van Gogh," Savannah squealed.

"Absolutely. You must see the *Irises*."

I flinched at the word. "What did you say?"

"That you guys should—"

"No," I said with urgency. "You said there's a painting in the Getty called *Irises*."

"Yes," the director said. "One of Van Gogh's masterpieces."

I glanced toward the sloping mountains above us. Even from here, I could see the peak of the Getty's sprawling buildings rising over the crest. Drifter's code became abundantly clear; whatever he wanted me to find was inside that building. *Come when the Irises are in bloom.*

34

The Getty Center sat atop the Santa Monica Mountains, overlooking the entire city. By the time I parked and boarded the museum tram, it was half past six. The tram climbed up the mountain's steep incline toward the main entrance.

Savannah had offered to come along with me, but I refused.

No one else would be dragged into this. This was my burden to bear.

There were five other people on board, all of them glancing in my direction as the trolly twisted and turned up the mountainside. I closed my eyes, focusing my attention on the dark energy humming inside me. The closer I got to the museum, the more my body came alive. I couldn't pretend any longer. Ever since my shadows awakened at the mansion, I wanted more. I savored the madness swirling in my veins. I craved its power. I wanted to feed the demon that lived and breathed inside me.

I needed more.

Bursting out of the tram, I stepped into the main plaza, past the fountain and into the museum pavilion. I didn't have a map; I didn't need one. Something else was guiding me like a quivering needle on a compass. I sped through the viewing halls, past the hordes of onlookers.

I was there for one painting.

It was hanging among three others on the wall. A small group had just departed, leaving me alone with Van Gogh's masterpiece. The waves of madness radiated from the brushstrokes, echoing the dark vibrations buzzing in my fingertips. The same dark energy I once felt standing in front of Diego's painting in London. But this time, I wasn't afraid. I was enthralled, mesmerized, overwhelmed. Lost in its power. A twisted smile moved across my face as streams of colors floated from the painting, encircling me like smoke in the air. I could almost feel the pain behind every stroke, every flower. The artist's suffering, bleeding out onto the canvas. I no longer pushed it away.

I wanted to absorb it.

Closing my eyes, I visualized black paint washing over the canvas, three cloaked men emerging from the background. The symbol painted beneath the colorful strokes. In my mind, I watched Van Gogh painting the symbol over and over again, XIIX, lost in madness.

The sound of boots on the wooden floor interrupted my absorption.

"Can I help you, sir?" A uniformed curator stood next to me. "The museum will be closing soon."

"Just here to see the *Irises*." I stared at the painting, then back to the man. He wanted me to say it. He needed me to say it. "I know the gardener."

His eyes widened, as if he had waited a long time for someone to utter those words. "Very well." He reached into his coat and handed me a plain white key card. Then tilted his head and exited, leaving me alone in the room.

Except I wasn't alone.

A shadow lingered at the door.

Jacob Perry walked into the viewing hall, dressed in black jeans and a green bomber jacket, mala beads draped across his chest.

"Don't make a scene," he whispered, standing beside me.

"Where's my daughter?" I seethed.

Jacob ignored me, beckoning to the painting. "Are you enjoying Van Gogh's work?"

I didn't respond.

"Do you know why this painting is so special?" he continued. "Van Gogh painted this right after a fit of madness, a horrific journey into hell that caused him to mutilate his ear. Then, when it was over, in the calming of the storm, he began to see for the first time. He began to understand his role, his purpose. God's true vision for him. And that's when he painted this… In the garden of an asylum."

I didn't respond.

"Your daughter contacted me," Jacob said.

I swallowed the impulse to strike him.

"She wanted to know about the symbol. Perhaps she is ready to begin her own journey. To follow in the footsteps of her old man."

I spun around, foaming. "Don't you dare—"

Jacob grabbed my neck, pulling me into his body. I recoiled, but it was too late. A sharp needle plunged into my skin.

"You have about five minutes until the effect kicks in," he whispered in my ear, then released me. Stunned, I staggered backward.

"Use them wisely," he taunted.

Moments after he vanished, an unsettling ringing pulsed in my ears. The familiar effects of the drugs kicked in. My vision was the first to go, blurring in and out. Only one thing ran through my mind: *I must stop Jacob from harming my daughter.* Fury burned inside me as I trailed Jacob's path through the gallery, barreling through a small crowd and descending a staircase. Jacob disappeared through a discreet metal door. Instinctively, I reached for the metal card in my jacket, scanning it across a mounted keypad.

Click.

Inside, a sterile corridor with white linoleum floors, fluorescent lights buzzing overhead. Jacob's silhouette moved through a doorway at the end of the hallway.

I trailed him into an elevator room, encountering yet another key scanner. The lights on the elevator panel lit up, revealing Jacob's destination: the basement level.

As I waited, I felt the poison flood my veins, amplifying the voice of my inner demon. Domineering my mind, body, and soul. The elevator doors slid open, and my reflection stared back from a glass panel. Three cloaked figures stood next to me in the steel lift. Shutting my eyes, I felt the icy breath of the cloaked figures run down my neck, leaving behind a trail of dark, prickly goosebumps. The elevator dropped, my mind along with it. I descended into madness. Into nothingness. I reached the basement level, and the door opened to complete darkness. Absolute silence.

I stepped out shakily onto the concrete floor.

"Jacob," I yelled. "Show yourself."

Whispers surrounded me.

"Undecim."

"Undecim."

"Undecim."

I followed the voices.

A single flickering light emerged down the dark hallway, buzzing on and off. Illuminating a metal door. When I stood in front of it, the shadows released their grip. The ringing in my ears ceased. My vision cleared and my heartbeat calmed. I gazed inside the small glass panel.

The flickering lights illuminated an older man in all white, hunched in the corner with his back to me. He was carving into the walls with a sharp rock. As I observed, the shadows inside me screamed in excitement. The man turned toward me, shielding his eyes from the blinking light.

He lifted his arms away from his bearded face.

A recognizable face stared back.

My father.

His eyes drowning in darkness.

Mumbling the phrase, over and over.

"Undecim."

"Undecim."

I smacked the door, violently. "Father! Father."

He was still alive.

The lights in the room brightened.

And that's when I saw it.

Thousands and thousands of symbols were etched into the cement walls, covering every inch of his cell. My father was beaming, admiring his masterpiece, spinning around the room in ecstasy. I fell backward, my hands clasped over my mouth in horror. My father rushed to the door, a wicked grin stretching across his face. My future staring back at me with dark obsidian eyes. Lost into madness. I had to get away. I had to run.

I had to escape this fate.

I came out onto the street.

Headlights glared.

I ran.

Just as I had done my entire life. Away from the horrible evil inside me. Away from my past. Away from my father. Away from my reckoning.

I was on a bridge.

Waves crashed below me.

The silhouette of a beautiful woman appeared.

The streetlight illuminated Savannah's face. She crept toward me on the bridge, the glint of a metal blade in her hand.

"Have you always known?" She stopped, standing still.

"Known what?"

"I am the demon who will drag you into hell," she hissed, lunging at me with the knife. I shoved her away, pushing her against the bridge railing, grasping her neck. I screamed in anger. *You are a snake. A devil. You did this.* When I realized what I was doing, I released her... But it was too late. She stumbled backward against the railing, flaring over the edge and into darkness. Then silence.

The vision changed.

I was in my old house.

I walked into the kitchen.

Jane sat in the kitchen table, tears streaming down her face. Loose pages from my script, *The Seven-Year Affair*, blew wildly across the room. It was the night I left my family.

I ignored Jane and slowly ascended the staircase, trailing my hands along the metal banister. The chime of a toy music box echoed through the house. Pips was sitting on the floor in her room, playing quietly with her toys. My sweet daughter. She glanced up, smiling, then reached for her favorite book, handing it to me. She wanted me to read it. But when I opened the binding, every page was blank. Flipping to the back, the symbol stared back at me. I looked back up to Pips in alarm, only to find she was no longer a child. She was older, with long jet-black hair. Black veins ran the length of her neck, spreading wildly on her face. Her eyes were obsidian, just like my father's. She stood up, rushing toward me, hissing. *Look what you've done to me. Look what I've become.*

She plunged a knife into my stomach, smiling, whispering in my ear, "You should have kept running, Father."

35

"Help!" I tried to call out, but no sound escaped my lips. The steady ping of a machine in rhythm with my heartbeat rang in my ear. I found myself in an elevated bed in a stark white room. The pungent smell of antiseptic filled the air. I jerked my arms and legs against restraints. *Why was I restrained?*

I lurched again with frustration, tugging at the straps. To my left, a monitor spiked, giving sound to my alarm. Quickly, a nurse entered, gazing with unease behind a cotton mask.

"Please relax." She fidgeted with the IV behind me, and my muscles melted into the bed, slowing my heartbeat, dulling my senses.

"Where am I?" I murmured through cracked lips. "What happened?"

"You're at Cedars Hospital in Los Angeles," the nurse informed, maintaining a cautious distance from my bed.

"What happened?"

She quickly checked my vitals, tearing the blood pressure cuff off my arm. "The doctor will be with you shortly."

She left me to my bewilderment.

I breathed deeply, closing my eyes, desperate to make sense of everything that happened. The last place I remembered . . . The Getty. Everything after that was a blur. Except for one face, a familiar face—my father. He was still alive. In some dungeon-style facility beneath the Getty Museum? That couldn't be possible. I'd also seen Pips. Or had that been a dream also? Another burst of adrenaline barreled through me, overrunning the medication. I tore at the restraints. I was about to scream again when a man in a white lab coat walked through the doorway.

"Mr. Reynolds." The doctor glanced down at the chart. "Welcome back. That was quite the night. How are you feeling?"

I didn't respond.

"Your bloodwork came back." He chuckled. "You had enough drugs to put down an elephant."

I remember the needle plunging into my neck.

Jacob Perry.

He was meeting with Pips.

He was helping her chase the symbol.

The doctor's gaze shifted to the spiking monitor, then back to me with concern.

"When did I come in?" I asked.

"Let's see." The doctor traced his finger along the chart. "You came in at five thirty a.m. They found you in a neighborhood in the Hollywood Hills."

My old neighborhood... So it wasn't a dream. I'd really been at my old house last night.

He put the chart away and swiveled closer to me, stethoscope in hand. "You're going to need to take it easy on the hallucinogens," he said, smiling.

He believed I did this to myself.

He unbuckled my restraints. "Sorry about that. The nurses said you were in quite a state. Not a lot of minds can withstand the quantity of drugs you ingested. The fact that we are talking is quite an accomplishment."

Rubbing my aching wrists, I fell back onto the bed.

"One more thing..." the doctor said, his eyes darting nervously to the door. "The police are outside. They wanted a word with you."

Before I had a chance to respond, the doctor hastily grabbed my chart and made a swift exit. Moments later, two suited men shuffled in behind him. One sported a thick mustache with slicked-back hair. His companion, a burly man with a ginger flattop.

"How are we doing, Mr. Reynolds?" The redheaded officer flashed his badge. "My name is Detective Rollinson, and this is my partner, Detective Rodriguez. Can we ask you a few questions about last night?"

They positioned themselves at my beside.

"What do you remember?" Rollinson asked.

He was waiting for me to lie.

"I was at the Getty Museum. That's the last place I remember."

"And then?"

"Nothing. I remember nothing."

He glanced sideways at his partner.

"Did you see Savannah Beck last night?"

"We attended a party earlier. But after that, no."

Detective Rollinson's gaze narrowed in suspicion.

"A report came in about disturbances at Ms. Beck's apartment. A man was heard shouting inside her apartment. The same phrase over and over."

Undecim.

"Do you remember any of that?" Detective Rodriguez asked.

I shook my head.

"Then, at one thirty-five a.m., they found you up on Wilson Drive in the Hollywood Hills," Detective Rollinson continued.

"My ex-wife and daughter... Are they ok?" I managed to ask.

The detective glanced down at his report. "Did you visit your old residence last night, Mr. Reynolds?"

"I don't remember," I said. "I think I was drugged."

"Drugged?" Detective Rollinson's eyebrows rose.

"Yes, with a needle," I said, reaching for the spot Jacob grabbed me. There was no mark.

"Who drugged you?" asked Detective Rodriguez.

"Jacob Perry."

"The actor?" Both detectives restrained grins.

"Well, if you have nothing more for us." Detective Rollinson closed his notepad.

"Is everyone okay? Did I hurt anyone?"

The detectives looked at each other, withholding. "We'll be in touch, Mr. Reynolds."

* * *

An hour later, I was discharged from the hospital. Brad was waiting in the lobby with his suit and sunglasses on. Spotting me, he shook his head in disbelief. "Jesus you look like shit!"

On the way to his Malibu home, I confessed everything: Jacob, the mysterious mansion, the symbol, the night in San Francisco with Bruce, my father. I knew how it all sounded. He didn't believe me. How could he? When we were done, he handed me his phone and told me to call Pips and Jane and make sure they were safe. When neither of them answered, he grabbed the phone back.

"I need to tell you something," he said, taking a deep breath. "Savannah Beck's manager called me. They filed a restraining order against you. You need to stay away from her. We'll get you back in rehab before the press get wind of this."

A restraining order.

"They said you got violent with her last night."

"You know me, Brad. I didn't do this."

He exhaled deeply. "Let's just hope those pages you sent over to Bruce were good. That should be enough money to get you into a facility. In the meantime, don't go back to Savannah's."

I nodded in agreement, but deep down, I couldn't see a way out of this. There was no end in sight. These people. This entity. They wouldn't stop pursuing me until I was dead. I had seen too much.

At Brad's house, I took a long, hot shower, trying to wash the grime and fatigue from my swollen face. To no avail...I stared at my haunted eyes in the steamy mirror. The evil eyes of my father. I could almost sense the three cloaked shadows looming behind me, their silent smiles chilling. The untethering had begun. My fate had been sealed.

I staggered out into the living room. "I need to borrow a car, Brad. I need to see if my daughter is okay."

Brad sighed, throwing me the keys to his spare car. "Fine. But find her and that's it. I'm not bailing you out again."

* * *

My old residence was a forty-five-minute drive from Brad's house. I had spent decades imagining my return home. In my fantasy, Jane and Pips awaited me in the driveway. Pips would rush forward, her arms encircling me in a warm embrace, while Jane's smile lit up the background. We would eat dinner as a family. Talk and laugh deep into the night.

We would be whole again.

The way it had been in our cabin.

Us against the world.

The gate opened, and I drove up the steep driveway to our home—the Hollywood castle I had once purchased for Jane, hoping it would save us. Enough room to have several kids. A place we could have grown old together. Turning the ignition off, a tidal wave of emotions struck me, the weight of the last few days crashing down. For a life that could have been. I should have fought harder. I should have let go of my feud with Jacob. I let my pride consume me. I should have never followed that symbol into that mansion. But now, it was too late. I had gone too far. My family was never coming back.

Jane stood outside the door, her arms crossed.

She was just as beautiful as the day I'd met her. Her skin never aged, her freckles never dulled. Dressed in sweats and a sports bra, her hair was pulled in a disheveled bun—the same way our daughter wore it. Just the sight of her brought tears to my eyes. I missed her more than life itself.

"Jesus, Kohl. Are you okay?"

I couldn't get the words out.

I had never been this broken.

"Come in," she urged gently.

I trailed her into our house, into the sunken living room. Memories flooded back. Pips playing with blocks on the floor, while Jane read scripts on the couch across from me. Those little but profound moments. Now, the paintings were gone. The play mat and toys removed. The brown leather couches were replaced with blue sofas.

I sat on the couch, burying my face into my hands. Jane crossed her legs, hands folded, leaning back.

"Did I see you last night?" I finally asked.

Jane's eyes met mine, and she slowly shook her head.

I nodded in relief.

"But—" Her voice strengthened. "A couple detectives came by this morning. They asked me if I saw you."

"He's alive, Jane."

"Who?"

"My father."

Her eyes widened in disbelief.

"And he murdered my mother."

She leaned forward, brow furrowed. "You said you went to your parents' funeral."

"It was just my mother's. It wasn't a car accident... My father snapped. He lost his mind. And I'm following in his path. I'm slipping, Jane. Just like him. I need help."

Her mouth twisted back and forth with concern. But then she glanced at the clock, her emotions retreating. I wasn't her problem anymore. "Listen, Kohl. I'm sorry. Aaron's going to be home, and—"

Before she could finish, I got up and sat beside her, reaching for her hand. She stiffened, but she didn't leave. "I'm sorry," I pleaded. "I'm sorry I ruined us. I'm sorry I hurt you both."

I squeezed Jane's hand, and she closed her eyes, a single tear rolling down her cheek, proof that her vows on our wedding day rang true. She would always love me, the way I had always loved her. But she wiped her emotions away, regaining her composure.

"When's the last time you saw Pips?" I asked.

"She came home the other night for dinner. She went into her room to get some of her old things."

"I need to see what she was looking at," I said with urgency.

Jane looked at me strangely but nodded. "Don't tell her I let you in."

Climbing the stairs, I tiptoed into my daughter's room. I trailed my hands across her enormous bookshelf, catching a thin layer of dust. Childhood memories flashed as I stared at the books. She used to love the greats. Bradbury. Angelou. Poems by Leonard Cohen. I scanned the walls. My movie posters had been replaced with reprints of artists she admired. Just like her mother, she loved art, favoring impressionists and expressionism above all. There were Rembrandts and Monets. Edvard Munch's *The Scream*. Van Gogh's *Irises*.

I didn't believe in coincidences any longer.

My eyes gravitated to a stack of black-and-white marbled notebooks on the coffee table. I noticed one notebook open on her neatly made bed. I sat down, peeling open the dog-eared page to find a journal entry from her childhood. I needed to read it. I needed to know.

There's a childhood memory that follows me around like a shadow. It was late, and I heard my parents screaming downstairs while I played in my room. I was worried, so I tiptoed to the kitchen to check on them. The concrete floors were especially cold that night. The house was pitch black, except for the spotlights over the kitchen island. My mother was angry. She had thrown a script at my father, who was pleading with her. I stood at the edge of the stairs, and a page from my father's script floated down to my feet. I picked it up, staring down at the typewriter font. As soon as I read the words, my entire body seized in shock. I had this urge to run upstairs and hide, to curl up in a ball. I felt physically ill. As if something evil had been planted inside me, some energy or darkness. To this day, I can't remember what I read. But I need to know. What secret did those pages reveal?

Flipping to the next page of the journal, I covered my mouth in fright. The symbol covered the page, inked wildly in ballpoint pen, large and small. My daughter didn't just recognize the symbol. She was obsessed with it, just like me. She was seeking answers, just like me. I walked down the steps, bewildered. What had I done? Jane was at the bottom of the staircase, waiting to escort me out. Before I walked out the door, I turned to her.

"She went to Jacob for answers," I said.

A shade of horror struck her face. "You need to fix this," Jane murmured tensely. "Don't let him hurt her."

Her eyes went cold. She was about to slam the door but stopped, sighing heavily. "The police asked me about Savannah. Whether or not you've ever been violent with her or with me. What did you do to that girl?"

Swallowing hard, I confessed, "I don't know."

She lingered at the door, biting her lip.

"What is it?"

"There was a phone call, years ago. After your tour with Blitz Cab. Jacob called me." Jane avoided my gaze. "He was drunk. But he told me about your affair with Savannah."

"You already knew."

She paused, then nodded. "He said something else. That Savannah was an alias. Jacob called her Beatrice. He kept saying that she was sent to punish you."

I fell backward off the doorstep as the door slammed in my face.

36

It took me thirty minutes to get to Savannah's apartment. Driving over, I replayed every interaction we've ever had. Our initial encounter was in that audition room... Or was it? There was something peculiar about the way she looked at me. That night she arrived at my hotel room during production, leaning against the door, her vibrant eyes peering into mine. Had our paths crossed previously?

Her real name is Beatrice.

I carefully unlocked her apartment door and entered with caution. Stepping inside, I was struck by the scene before me. Everything in the apartment was upended. Potted plants had been tipped over, spilling clumps of dark soil across the hardwood floors. Broken frames lay shattered on the floor. Clearly there had been some sort of altercation. A vivid flashback of our confrontation on the bridge appeared in my mind. My hands gripping tightly around her neck, her body falling over the bridge railing, into the darkness. But it wasn't real. It couldn't be . . . And yet. The police had known something. Savannah filed a restraining order.

In the bedroom, everything appeared in its place, yet something caught my eye, a framed poster of her TV show above a small desk. My gaze narrowed on a familiar face: the striking blonde at Savannah's cast party. She had tried to catch my attention. Her words had been a whisper then, but suddenly, staring at her photo, they echoed loudly in my mind: *Nothing is real.*

My phone rang, interrupting my concentration.

I answered.

"What the fuck, Kohl!" Brad shouted on the line.

I didn't respond.

I sauntered into the hallway.

"I just got through speaking with the fucking police."

I didn't respond.

I stood in front of her roommate's door.

"Savannah didn't show up at her fucking table read."

I didn't respond.

"They think you have something to do with it."

A grin twisted across my face.

"Where are you?"

"I'm at her house," I said calmly.

"Are you fucking serious?" Brad screamed. "Get the fuck out of there!"

Nothing is real.

"Something isn't right," I whispered into the phone.

Brad screamed, "Of course it's not. You're in fucking deep. Oh, and thanks for those pages you sent over for Bruce. Was that some sort of joke?"

"What are you talking about?" I muttered.

"I'll send you the screenshot he sent me."

I looked down at my screen.

Line after line, XIIX, blanketing the page. I hadn't written a fucking thing. I laughed. The woman at the party was right. *Nothing is real.* This wasn't real. This was madness. I lost my sanity. Dropping the phone, I braced my shoulder and rammed into the door. One. Two. The lock snapped, and the door burst open. I ambled in, taking in my surroundings. It wasn't a bedroom at all.

Centered in the room was a large oak desk surrounded by an enormous bookshelf. There were holes punched in the wall, a bat discarded on the floor. The aftermath of rage. I stepped across the debris, gazing at the shattered photos on the ground. Candid shots of Savannah and me from set, including a grainy photo of the back of my head between her legs.

Amongst the chaos, I walked to an untouched photo on the desk, an older polaroid of Savannah and me at a bookstore. I didn't remember taking this. She looked much younger in the picture, less polished, with highlighter blonde streaking through her hair. I looked fatigued, drunk, and bloated.

Frantically opening the drawer, I scattered its contents on the desk. There were multiple passports, hotel keys, handwritten letters. I quickly rifled through the stack.

You have done well.

We are pleased with you.

You will be rewarded.

All signed with the symbol.

What the fuck is this?

Then I saw it at the bottom of the drawer, a bronze theater mask. The mysterious woman from the mansion. Of course it was her. Next to the mask was a copy of my book. Tattered and torn, as if it had been someone's most treasured possession. The way *The Jeweler* had been for me. The way *The Fisherman* had been my father's. I flipped to the back, the symbol staring back at me. Tucked behind the pages was a cryptic note.

He must uncover the truth on his own. The answer has always been with him.

I didn't need to decipher.

I knew what it was.

Reaching inside my pocket, I grabbed my lucky coin, rubbing the bronze metal over in my hand. A keepsake given to me by the bookseller. The bookseller who set me on this journey—Charron. He had said something on the day he gave me that coin: *Everything good comes out of fire.*

I held the tip of my lighter to my lucky coin.

Under the heat, a tiny fragment of metal melted off, revealing a tiny compartment. From it, I shimmied out a strip of paper. An address was stamped across the back. It was all coming to an end. I would save my daughter. I would destroy them all.

37

The address led me to the corner of Pico and Hyland, a grimy intersection several blocks from the renowned Chinese Theater. The sidewalk was filled with the names of Hollywood stars. I stood in front of an abandoned liquor store, its yellow lettering peeling off the windows. Two homeless men huddled underneath the awning. Long ago, a celebration had taken place in this spot. Visitors had honored the stars memorialized into its sidewalk. But like so many, they had been forgotten. Like tombstones in an overgrown cemetery, walked over and sullied.

At my feet was a star dedicated to Bob Kinsley. I recognized the name. Charron had told me the man's tragic story. Once, he had gone in search of the symbol, and death had come for his entire family. I stared out into the street, unsure of what came next.

A voice rang out behind me, startling me.

"The shades are coming."

I spun around, spotting a pair of eyes from a tattered sleeping bag.

He warned again, "The shades are coming."

The man's beard and eyes blended into the darkness. He held a bottle to his mouth, pointing to the wall next to him. I craned my neck to see what he was showing me. There, carved into the wall, the symbol, written over and over. In a rush of desperation, I seized his grimy sweatshirt. "Who are they?" I seethed. "What do they want?"

He laughed in my face, laughed in madness, displaying his last few corroded teeth. Stumbling backward, I lost my footing on the curb. Headlights glared. I shielded my eyes.

The car came to a halt.

It was them.

When I opened the limousine door, a familiar face stared back. Charron.

He had cleaned up since our last encounter, dressed in a tailored suit with a colorful pocket square. His gray hair was cropped short again, combed neatly to the side. He swirled a glass of scotch in his hand.

I sat in the seat across from him, bracing myself for the truth.

The car began moving.

He extended a glass to me, and I quickly chugged the smooth brown whisky. He poured me another.

"Just moments ago, you stood on Bob Kinsley's Hollywood star." Charron smiled in the dim light. "On the night he was honored with that star, Bob sat in a bar, drowning in regret. On paper, he made a fortune in Hollywood. He had a beautiful home and wife, who was pregnant with their first child. But there was something missing in Bob's life…Power and purpose.

"As I told you, Bob's father had planted a lie in his child's heart. That love was conditional upon his fame and wealth. So, Bob did what his father couldn't do. He penned scripts for loads of money, showered his wife with lavish gifts. But despite all of Bob's earthly possessions, his soul wasted away. His art was mediocre and forgettable.

"Sulking at the bar, a Hollywood friend came and presented him with the symbol—the very one from his father's book. The man posed a question: Would he risk everything to discover the truth? Miserable and drunk, Bob said yes." Charron refilled my glass. "And so his ritual began.

"Soon, clues about his father's death appeared out of thin air. Bob tried to forget his quest; he tried to get back to work, but the reckoning was underway. Bob was overcome with haunting images: the assailant in the black hat who had shaken down his father after the horse race. Images of his mother's indiscretions. Bob's mind unraveled, and despite his attempts to stop the madness, he became obsessed with finding his father's killers, hell-bent on seeking revenge.

"But the closer Bob got to the truth, the more dangerous his quest became. In the end, Bob paid the ultimate cost. His entire family was murdered by the same people who killed his father."

I hung on every word.

"With nothing left to lose, Bob sought his vengeance. And when it was all over, when the enemy's blood sullied his hands, the man once known as Bob Kinsley ceased to exist. From his ruins, Robert Drifter was born. He became a true artist. He wrote a piece of work that poor Bob could have never written. His magnum opus."

Charron took another slow sip.

"Did you know him?" I asked. "Drifter?"

He smirked. "Altman. Drifter. You are chasing ghosts, my friend."

"Then what am I doing here?"

"You tell me. You are the one seeeekiiii . . ."

The words drawled out of Charron's mouth. I glared down at the scotch, my vision weaving in and out of focus. How could I have been so foolish?

"I am merely a guide ferrying you to the other side of hell." Charron's face blurred, glitched, moved.

"Do not fight it." Charron stared coldly. "Lean into its power. Or like your father, your soul will be lost."

The metallic groan of an iron gate opening echoed through the car.

Falling deeper into the plush leather seats, I could feel the drugs seeping into my body. The shadows bubbling beneath my skin, tingling, screaming in anticipation. Waiting for their time in power. Waiting to be released.

The car climbed the steep driveway, coming to a halt.

The door to the mansion stood open.

Leaving Charron behind, I ventured into the dimly lit foyer and walked down the familiar stone hall with candlelight flickering along the walls. This time, there was no ceremony. No masked figures. No chained demon. The giant double doors to the next hall stood unguarded. I walked through them, my eyes gravitating to the banister above the stone fireplace. There he was, alone—the towering, omnipotent figure. Watching me. Haunting me my entire life. Tonight, he wore no mask, but his face was hidden in shadows.

I made haste.

I took a set of stairs upward through a long corridor, drawn to a warm glow radiating from a room at the end. I stepped into a grand study lit by a roaring fire. Gothic medieval oil paintings draped every inch of the walls. I tiptoed through the room, taking in the surroundings, pushing down the shadows swirling inside me.

My eyes gravitated to a giant bookcase, laden with ancient tomes. I ran my fingers across the antique bindings, stopping at one. A weathered brown leather book.

"Good choice," a deep voice bellowed behind me.

The looming figure from the staircase stood before me. He was a striking older man, with deep lines carved into his face. He was tall, with dark eyes and a foreboding smile. A distinct pink scar traced from his cheek down to his chin.

"We've met before," I said.

"We have," he affirmed.

"On the set of *The Offering*. You made us cast Savannah Beck. You go by Virgil."

He nodded, gesturing to the book in my hands.

"They consider that one of Dante's original manuscripts of *The Divine Comedy*. From the Medici library itself. A true first edition."

He inched closer.

"Did you know Dante was a forgettable politician? Had he not penned that masterpiece, he'd have vanished into obscurity. Only in seclusion, after losing everything he held dear, his status, his country, only then did he unearth his true greatness. Only through hell could he summon his greatest work."

Virgil stepped closer, inspecting me with curiosity.

"Who are you?" I asked.

He circled me like a predator stalking its prey.

"I have many names. Many personas. Your father knew me as Jeffrey Altman."

The admission sent me staggering backward. Suddenly, the lights in the room flickered and darkness rushed through my limbs, into the back of my throat. I couldn't move, couldn't talk. My vision kept moving in and out of focus. I took a deep breath, desperately trying to push back the madness, to thwart my demons from seizing control.

Not until I heard the truth.

Virgil poured himself a glass of scotch.

"Your father attended my first book signing at The Gate Bookshop, accompanied by your grandmother. In his eyes, I recognized a pain, a familiar torment, an evil cast down upon him by harsh, cruel parents. That day, I signed a book for your father and etched the symbol on its final page. The rest, I left to destiny."

He continued. "Your father found ambition in the pages of my book, a newfound purpose. He corresponded with me weekly, admitting his obsession with the symbol. Asking why I had given it to him. My story gave him the courage to escape his father's business and pursue his gifts. For he was a true artist."

Overwhelmed, my knees buckled, and I reached for a nearby desk to steady myself. Just a little longer…

"My father. What happed to him?" I whispered.

Virgil paced the hearth, observing me with fascination. "For years, I watched him, curious what he would make of his life. But your father was terrified of his tormenters. When fate made me his professor, your father was eager to please me. He idolized me, and I sought to bring greatness out of him. To make him confront the evil inside him."

Virgil drew closer, his tall stature casting a shadow across the room. The deep, jagged scar on his face more prominent in the firelight.

"You see, your father's greatest fear was proving his parents right. That he would amount to nothing. That he had chosen the wrong path. And if you tugged at the right strings, he would do anything to avoid that cold truth. He would abandon everything in pursuit of that greatness."

"What did you do?" I seethed.

"You father began writing the beginning of what should've been his defining masterpiece—*The Untethering*. But for years, he toiled away at the typewriter fruitlessly. He sought inspiration in your mother, but it was no use. The real artistry lurked behind his shadows, not the light. The monsters and demons needed liberation for genius to emerge."

He paused, his gaze unwavering. "So I returned to ferry your father into the gates of hell. Sadly, he was not up for the task. His soul was not strong enough to endure the monster within. I was there the night he was arrested."

Visions of the three cloaked figures standing across from me at the park flashed in my mind. One of them removed their cloak.

I staggered back, crashing into the bookshelf behind me.

"Yes, Kohl." He stepped closer, until his wicked face was inches from mine. "It was me, standing across the street that night. I've been watching you, the same way I watched your father, waiting for this moment. For like him, you have squandered your life away. A tormented artist who refuses to journey into the darkest parts of your soul."

"Who are you?"

"Like I said, I have many names. Virgil. The Primus Creator. The Devil. To your father, I was Jeffrey Altman."

The details of his face flickered in and out.

His powerful, sinister voice echoed through the room.

"To you, I am something else."

His irises darkened.

"And I am your final path to Inferno. Now come, my child. Your destiny awaits."

38

A CONCEALED DOORWAY in the bookshelf creaked open, and I followed Virgil into the darkness, staggering down an unlit, extended corridor. Each step felt like a descent deeper into hell's sanctum, the bitter air tightening around my throat, evil crawling down my skin.

Downward and downward.

Until the passage opened to a large chasm, a sunken arena surrounded by dark stone bleachers. Flickering torches burned along the wall, casting light on rows of cloaked men with theater masks, each one staring down at me.

They chanted:

"Undecim."

Louder, in rhythm.

"Undecim."

My body was giving out.

I fell to my knees.

Then silence.

Virgil advanced onto the platform beside me, donning the grotesque red theater mask, a dark cloak.

Silence overcame the chasm.

He circled around me, orating: "Long ago, a valiant group of patrons, excommunicated from the church, received a divine vision. The artists, not the clergy, were the true shepherds of this world, possessing sacred gifts that could pave the path to divinity for God's children.

"And thus, under the patronage of the illustrious Medici, a sacred conclave was born. With the wealth of this noble house, the Order would guide the visionaries, the artistic souls of the world, to lead them into their divine callings, so they might fulfill their destinies and become shepherds of God."

I collapsed onto the ground.

Undecim.

I could hardly see.

But I could hear every word.

"As time passed, the order witnessed the self-destruction pervasive amongst these gifted but tortured souls. They watched them squander their gifts, rotting in their own skin, distracted by carnal pleasures. These divine beings, these virtuosos were reduced to sheep, living and dying in filth and sin."

Undecim.

"To combat this regression, the order initiated a series of rituals and sacrifices aimed at purging the artist of their inner shadow. To propel them through the gates of hell and into God's paradise. There, they would experience the divine. For it was written in Deuteronomy IV, 'It was a journey of eleven days that took forty years... And so, the Holy Order of the Eleven began.'"

They chanted:

"Undecim."

"No longer would these gifted souls be allowed to squander their talents, wasting away for years in the wilderness. No longer would they be allowed to die without fully realizing God's vision. Instead, they would be given guides and muses to lead them into hell. They would be stripped bare and taken through an eleven-day journey with their tormenters. For in the fire, they will witness God's divine being, and thus, have access to His power."

Virgil paused, turning to face me.

"And now, as your Virgil, your Primus Creator, I offer this artist to you as sacrifice."

"Undecim."

I was swimming in a pool of black blood.

Surrounded by snakes.

And wispy shadows.

And pure darkness.

"It is time, Kohl Reynolds."

Silence.

A figure rose from the crowd, discarding his cloak and mask. Jacob Perry descended down the stairs, exiting a stone archway beyond the arena. Anger aroused my poisoned body, and a renewed sense of resolve brought me to my shaky knees. I trailed Jacob into the archway, finding myself in a stone chamber encircled by mirrors. Jacob's reflection stared back, and I pounded my fist against the mirrors.

"I warned you," he called out, pacing behind the glass. "You will lose everything in your pursuit."

"And what did you lose?" I cried.

His face hardened. "I lost her."

And I knew he meant Jane.

"She was going to leave you before she got pregnant, you know."

"You're lying."

He continued. "My ritual brought me back to my childhood home, my father's decrepit cabin in the Black Forest. By the time I found him, he was a shell of a man. Bitterness, rage and alcohol had warped his physical body, though his ugly spirit remained intact.

"I stayed with him for days, watching him, observing him. I despised how much I craved this crippled man's affection.

"But if I were to play the most despicable villain of all time, I knew what must be done...One morning, I invited him on a hunt, guiding him back through the chilled mist of the forest, back to the meadow from my childhood, now a barren and desolate patch.

"In the stillness of the clearing, I faced him, gun raised. This time, I wouldn't cower. I wouldn't back down. I stared down the barrel of the gun, into my father's pathetic eyes."

"'Do it,' he seethed. 'Put me out of my misery.'

"He scoffed at my hesitation. 'Or are you still the scared little boy I once knew.'

"With that, my gun lowered, and I ran away from my destiny.

"I sought solace in the only thing that's ever tethered me to the light. The only woman I've ever loved." He paused. "It was Jane."

I slammed my hands against the mirror, tears streaming down my eyes.

"Bonded by our pain, Jane found herself at a crossroads," he continued. "She spilled her deepest confessions. She regretted the day she left with you in Park City. That her life would have been so much happier had she chosen me. She had never stopped loving me."

"You're lying," I cried.

"In the morning, after our night together, Gary Vice appeared once more, offering me my final test. The decision between greatness or happiness. A life of bliss with Jane or the role of a lifetime. As you know, I chose what was necessary. I chose to follow the symbol through my personal hell. I took my father back to that meadow, and this time, I didn't hesitate.

"By the time they found me, I was wandering the streets of Germany in a state of madness. But the rage and violence within me had dissipated. I had made allies with my tormenters. I was free to make peace with them. I would become the greatest villain this world has ever seen. A role that would make me a Hollywood God.

"Don't you see? I killed my past to create something truly extraordinary."

"I'm going to kill you!" I pounded the mirror.

"Good," he screamed. "Lean into your anger. Lean into the madness."

Jane never wanted you.

Your father never wanted you.

Your own daughter doesn't want you.

Jacob gazed deeply into my eyes. "Sit with the truth, Kohl. You will never be as good as me. You will always be unworthy, unwanted, unloved." He stepped into the room. The glass no longer separated us.

"When you began this, I warned you. You will lose everything you hold dear."

Two cloaked figures stepped into the room, restraining someone with a black bag over their head. The prisoner screamed: "Dad! Dad!"

"Pips!" I screamed, lunging forward, but my legs gave out. I face-planted into the stone floor, my head rattling, my body dissolving into nothingness. I could only watch as they dragged my daughter out of the room, screaming. I crawled on my hands and knees, desperate.

"Pips," I mumbled before collapsing again.

Jacob crouched down and leaned in, whispering as I faded into darkness. "Before this is over, you will have to make your choice. Don't make the same mistake your father made."

39

In the evil depths of my grandmother's basement, loose typewriter sheets danced across the cold concrete floor, driven by an unseen force. Amongst them, one sheet stood still, begging me to come forth. I lifted the partially typed page up, its ink still fresh.

The key to unlocking all of this.

But just as the words were about to reveal themselves, a subtle movement caught my eye. A shadowy figure lurked in the corner of the room, facing the wall. They were whispering incantations, frantically untethering the thick rope of my youth. I edged closer, cautiously. Finally, they turned, and my daughter stood before me, mumbling *Undecim*, over and over, her eyes rolling in the back of her head. All I could see were the whites of her eyes.

An evil grin slithered across her face. "Time is running out."

I awoke in a panic, drenched in sweat. The shrill ringing of a landline pierced the silence. I was lying on crisp hotel sheets, with bright sunlight dripping through the blinds. My usual suite at the Beverly Wilshire. With a surge of adrenaline, I jolted upright, grabbing the hotel phone.

"Hello?" I bellowed into the phone.

"Mr. Reynolds?" I recognized the desk attendant's voice. "I thought you'd appreciate the heads-up. Two officers are on their way up to your suite."

"Thank you," I murmured, before hanging up the phone, my eyes scanning the room for my clothes. I had to get out of here; the haunting image of my daughter in their grasp replayed in my mind. They had taken her. They had kidnapped her.

Swiftly, I jetted out the door and descended the grand staircase. As I entered the lobby, the front desk attendant spotted me. He motioned to multiple squad cars parked outside the entrance.

This hotel had more than one way out.

I hurried down a corridor through the hotel lounge, stepping out into the daylight, shielding my eyes from the sun. My gaze darted left and right, desperate for an escape. Around me, Beverly Hills was coming alive as shop owners unlocked their doors.

From a distance, a voice shouted, "There he is."

I made haste, sprinting across the intersection, amidst the honking cars, seeking refuge in a nearby alley. To my luck, a man was pulling a chalkboard out onto the patio of a bar. Passing the curious stares of the waitstaff, I made a beeline to the restroom in the back, locking the door behind me.

I stuck my head in the sink, running water over my matted hair, then gazing at my reflection. The untethering was almost complete. My face had withered to the bone, my eyes overrun with evil. Still, I knew there was one demon, one monster still concealed inside me. Waiting to be unleashed. To drag me into Inferno and take the last thread of sanity with him.

I couldn't hold it back forever.

I walked back into the restaurant, straight to the bar. The bartender was filling his garnish tray, gazing up at a news station on the big screen. I pulled out a twenty and set it on the bar top, signaling for a drink. Reading my mind, he reached for a bottle of scotch, pouring as I scrolled through my phone.

I called Jane. No answer.

My agent. No answer.

Savannah's number went straight to voicemail.

Finally, I called Jacob.

"I'm sorry, the phone number you are trying to reach is disconnected . . ."

I downed the last of my scotch just as a youthful image of Savannah flashed across the television. Beside her, a newscaster began to narrate.

"Will you turn that up?"

The bartender grabbed the remote.

Actress Savannah Beck has been reported missing by authorities.

A wave of nausea overcame me. Had I done this? Just like my father, I was capable of dreadful things. This was the cost of chasing the symbol. Everyone I loved would suffer. Starting with Savannah. I was the evil that threatened my daughter and my family.

I made up my mind…

Exiting the bar, I walked toward the commotion, toward the police vehicles and gawking pedestrians scattered across the block. This was my only choice. I had to do something my father couldn't. It was the only way to save Pips. As I raised my hands in surrender, a red Porsche screeched to the curb.

And there, behind the wheel, was Savannah Beck.

* * *

Savannah steered us westward toward the Pacific Coast Highway, a compact revolver resting in her lap. Silence enveloped the car. She stared at the road with determined eyes, biting her bottom lip, pulling at her earlobe. She wore an oversized sweatshirt, her hair pulled back into a disheveled ponytail. Ever since I met her, she had always been so put together, so even-keeled—but now…

Unable to hold back, I pressed. "Where is my daughter?"

"I need to keep you safe," she said, turning onto the highway. The skies were overcast now, casting shadows on the crashing waves beside us.

"Who are you?" I asked.

"Give me a minute," she exclaimed.

Before I could respond, she turned up the volume on the radio. "I need to think," she shouted over the noise.

The song playing was unmistakably familiar: a haunting score from our movie, *The Offering*. As the dramatic notes amplified, a single tear trickled down Savannah's cheek. She put on her blinker and turned right into the mountain pass.

I reached for her hand. "Tell me the truth."

The car sped into a tunnel along the steep road. When we emerged into the light, tears streamed down her cheeks without restraint.

"I did this to you," she sobbed.

"Savannah," I whispered.

"This is my fault."

She sped faster around the sharp turns, the car careening from side to side, the orchestrated soundtrack intensifying the fear.

"Slow down, Savannah."

A haunting smile turned in the corners of her lip, even as the tears fell. "You know your words have power, Kohl."

"Savannah?"

She inhaled deeply, turning down the radio. "I spent my childhood fantasizing about this world...The glam and glitz of Hollywood. Whenever awful things happened, I locked myself in my room and lost myself in films, all those happy endings. That was my dream, Kohl. To live like the stars on the screen, to never have to be me."

Her face hardened. "I was recruited by them when I was nineteen. I came to Los Angeles to be an actress and ended up penniless, nearly selling my soul in the process. But then he came... Virgil was charming and cunning, and he promised me something that no one else could—a purpose. My first assignment was you."

I was taken aback.

"You don't remember, but I attended your book signing in Los Angeles. I was anxious to meet you. I had read your book, absorbed your beautiful words, and I thought you were so talented. But standing in front of you that day, stoned and wasted, I knew you needed our help. You were my purpose. To be your guide, your muse, like Beatrice was for Dante. I would lead you through hell, into the divine.

"But then I betrayed him, Kohl," she cried.

"I'm not following, Savannah."

"I was ordered to begin our affair on the set of *The Offering*. But I couldn't do it. I didn't want to hurt you. I sacrificed everything for you." She whipped around the turn.

I reached for the dashboard, my eyes widening in terror. "Slow down, Savannah."

She pressed harder on the accelerator, the car screeching around the bend. Savannah jerked the car back into our lane just as a car flew by, horns blaring.

"What the fuck, Savannah?"

"And for what?" She laughed bitterly. "I will never be Jane."

"Where's my daughter?" I demanded.

The engine throttled again.

"I will never be good enough for you."

We entered a tunnel.

She turned up the radio, the finale of *The Offering*.

"Stop!" I shouted.

"This is the only way."

In the darkness, she screamed, "We will never be free of them. We will never get our happily ever after."

Exiting the tunnel, our path was headed straight toward the guardrail.

She glanced at me, her tears making her green eyes shimmer. "I loved you, Kohl Reynolds."

A sad smile extended across Savannah's face as the world blurred and we flew off the mountain pass.

40

The compact sports car crashed down the side of the mountain, bouncing violently over the rocky terrain. The sound of metal screeching and branches snapping filled the air. I braced for impact, anticipating the bone-jarring collision.

Then, darkness.

When I came to, my ears were ringing, my legs wedged between the twisted metal. The car was wrapped around the tree, smoke rising steadily from the engine. Besides the blood trickling down my face, I avoided serious injury.

Craning my stiff neck, I noticed Savannah's seat was empty. I shimmied my way out of the front seat, shoving my shoulder into the door and rolling out onto the dirt. I staggered to my feet, screaming her name. *Savannah*. The ringing in my ears became voices.

"You okay?"

A bystander stood on the road, gazing down at the wreckage.

He called out again. "You okay?"

I turned my attention back to the wreckage.

The glovebox was open.

Inside, a key from the Hollywood Roosevelt Hotel. "Room 11" was stamped onto the plastic.

Instinctively, I knew—this is where it ended.

"I've called the police," the man above me yelled.

No. A dark voice resonated from deep inside me. The authorities couldn't do what needed to be done. They couldn't stop this evil. Savannah's revolver was on the ground. Snatching it up, I sprinted away from the highway, descending the slope as sirens echoed in the distance.

* * *

The rain had begun to fall, thunder ripping across the skyline, backlighting the city of angels. I stared at the grand façade of the Hollywood Roosevelt ready to uncage my final demon.

Before entering, I secured Savannah's gun in the back of my waistband. A scene I've described in countless screenplays. The line between fiction and reality blurring. I entered the familiar lobby of the Hollywood Roosevelt, my resolve hardening with every step.

I would destroy them all.

I ascended to the eleventh floor.

Closing my eyes, I felt the rough, tethered rope of my childhood in my hands, pulling apart the final few threads. This was the end of the line. I was prepared for death.

The elevator door opened.

Room eleven was a suite, the largest one in the hotel. I placed the key to the door pad, it pinged green. Tiptoeing in, I cocked my gun, sweeping through the suite. The room was shrouded in darkness, only the dim flicker of candlelight lay on the floor. A warm breeze fluttered through the room, rustling the curtains. My gun remained raised.

In the low lighting, a silhouette caught my attention, a figure bound to a chair, writhing and screaming behind a hooded mask. *Pips.*

Looming behind her were three cloaked men.

I aimed the gun toward them.

The tallest of the cloaked men stepped forward. He removed his mask. A sinister grin stretched across Virgil's marred face. "Drop the weapon," he demanded, turning back to Pips. One of the masked men held a knife to her throat.

I did what they asked.

Virgil paced around me.

"Welcome to the final layer of hell," he said, presenting me with a gold chalice.

I didn't hesitate. I swallowed the bitter potion, then tossed it aside.

Quickly, the liquid took effect, rousing my demon from its slumber.

A surge of darkness roared from deep within.

But this time, I didn't fight it. I welcomed the shadows.

I would use it to destroy my enemy.

"Not long ago, your father was in this very position," Virgil continued, circling me. "Do you know what his novel, *The Untethering* was about. An aspiring writer attends university to learn from his idol. There, the professor puts him through a harrowing trial to embrace his greatness. Yet in that pursuit, he becomes consumed by ambitions, forsaking his true love. And who was there to keep her warm? The mentor, the professor—the ultimate betrayal."

The cloaked figures closed in, surrounding me.

"Close your eyes now, Kohl," Virgil whispered. "Revisit the night of the accident. Do you recall what your father wrote on that page you found?"

As he spoke, the demon inside me rumbled again. The monster, tearing at its chains, begging to be freed.

Virgil's voiced dripped with malice. "You see them. The words on that page, echoing through your life, leaking into your soul. Words your father never wanted you to read."

Squeezing my knuckles, the demon thrashed from side to side, its chains loosening from the floor.

"Your father's ritual culminated on the Golden Gate Bridge," Virgil continued. "There, he was given a photo—his beloved wife in the arms of his mentor, me."

And when I emerged from the darkness that night, onto the bridge, your father had to confront that betrayal, that dark truth. A truth you've known your entire life, Kohl." Virgil paced around me. "I saw you from the window that night. You picked up a page that your father typed.

"Those words have been blurry your whole life. Until now."

With one last tug, the demon ripped the chains from the floor.

A tidal wave of terror emptied into my veins.

Rage. Anger. Shame. Guilt.

Overwhelming my body.

My lips turned cold.

My limbs numbed.

I stood in the room, a young boy, holding the thick typewriter page. The unfocused words sharpened. I read them aloud: "I was betrayed. The child is not mine. He is a spawn of evil. The embodiment of my deepest fears, my worst impulses, my unchecked ambitions. I brought this upon us, this pain, this evil. Now I will never escape this hell. The child is cursed. Destined to follow in my footsteps."

Suddenly, the vision faded, and Virgil's dark presence stood before me.

"It can't be true," I whispered.

"It is," Virgil said. "That night, I revealed the depth of your mother's betrayal. That the result was you, Kohl. The child he raised was not his own. In his already fragile state, your father snapped. He attempted to kill me, taking a knife to the side of my face." Virgil ran his hands along his scar. "Your mother intervened, and in the chaos, she fell to her death."

"It's a lie," I screamed, as the buzz of darkness ripped through my limbs.

"And in his darkest hour, with the stain of his wife's death upon him, he attempted to write the ending to his masterpiece.

That *you* were the product of that betrayal. His darkest fear coming to fruition. So when he stared at you that night, he was staring at his own reflection, his darkness. On that day, a demon was planted inside your soul, allowed to fester for decades. You were cursed, just like your father predicted. A spawn of his evil deed. That you were unworthy and defective.

"Your life has been a replication of your father's sin.

"But this time, I wasn't the traitor. It was another."

A cloaked figure stepped forward, removing his mask.

It was Jacob. "Three months after our affair," he began. "Jane called me and told me she was pregnant."

"Don't say it," I shouted, fists clenched.

"She told me . . ."

"Don't say it," I seethed.

"I was the father," he finished.

"It's not true," I screamed.

"She asked me to raise the child. To give her the life she deserved. A life that you couldn't provide. Because you were incapable of anything good. But alas, I had made my choice. I abandoned Jane." He turned to Pips. "And my child."

My greatest fear.

I was nothing without her.

I had no attachment to this world.

I was everything they said I was.

Everything my father had been, everything he foretold.

"And now." Virgil stepped forward. "The symbol demands a sacrifice." He handed me a knife. "Kill the man who stole your life. Just like Drifter, lean into the madness. Seek your revenge. Do what your father couldn't. Kill him. He has fulfilled his purpose. Now it's time to fulfill yours."

I shut my eyes, summoning the darkness to my fingertips. The power coursing through my veins. The demons stretching across my heart, casting out the last bit of light inside me. It was taking control. I was transforming. I would become the monster within.

Gripping the knife, I stepped forward. This was for my father. For my mother. For Savannah and Pips and Jane. For the brokenness of the world that had rooted its shadow inside me. It was time. I surrendered to its authority. I lunged toward him, sending Jacob sprawling to the ground. He tried to resist, but the power inside me was too great. The shadows empowered me. They were me. Standing over him, the knife edged closer and closer to Jacob, until the tip of the blade rested on his flesh. His eyes went wide in fright. With one final surge, I rammed it through his stomach. His flesh was soft; my hands were steady.

Plunging the knife deeper, a terrible ache swelled within me. The demon inside me screamed in agony, a piercing screech that sent swells of pain through my body. When I looked down, I realized what I had done.

I had stabbed myself.

Collapsing to the ground, blood seeped from my stomach, bubbling at my lips. Swiftly, I removed the dagger from my flesh. The shadows shrieked again, and a wave of black blood swept across the floor. The grief and shame and pain that had lived inside me. Too weak to move, I surrendered to death.

Virgil towered above me, grinning, as if admiring a work of art, his ultimate masterpiece.

My vision blurred, and I felt myself slipping away. But just as the darkness overtook me, I saw a figure in the corner of the room. Pips. She'd freed herself from her restraints. Unnoticed by Virgil, she removed her hood.

But it wasn't Pips.

It was Savannah.

Her face etched with rage.

With a gun in her hand, she lunged at Virgil, screaming, "I wield the power!" as the sound of gunshots rang out.

Virgil screamed in agony.

The cloaked men swiftly subdued Savannah. Struggling to rise, I tried crawling on my hands and knees to help, but it was too late.

More gunshots rang.

A loud thud sounded beside me.

Turning weakly, I found Savannah lying beside me.

Blood trickled from her lips, her once vibrant eyes dimming. I scooted closer, cradling her, rocking her back and forth. "It's going to be ok," I choked out.

"I love you, Kohl," she whispered.

"I'm sorry," I said, as her eyes began to close. "I'm sorry for everything."

I held her as long as I could.

Until the final breath escaped her lungs.

41

I woke up in a bare concrete room, no bigger than the basement from my childhood. I was leaning against the wall, the wound in my stomach leaking through the bandages. The room was sparsely furnished with only a steel desk and a typewriter. I was weak and drained, but for the first time in a long while, my mind was lucid.

With strained effort, I climbed into the chair. I inserted blank pages into the typewriter, cranked the ribbon, and began to type…

I appear in a desert wasteland, scorched earth, the sun beating down. I am dragging my father through the wilderness, his body littered with gashes and bloody bandages. Both of us adorning beige military jumpsuits. We are returning home from a never-ending war, a battle he has been fighting my entire life. I enlisted into the war to find him. I left my wife and daughter to bring home a man I've never known.

I put another page into the typewriter, cranked the ribbon.

I kept writing.

The battle was nothing I'd expected. The enemy was strong, shadowy cloaked men with vicious fangs filled with poison. I ventured across enemy lines, where darkness devoured the land. Armed with an iron sword, I fought demon after demon, their black blood spattering across my face. The enemy camp was full of grotesque beasts and creatures, discarded bones laying bare across the land. I found my father in a cell constructed of human bones. He was barely alive.

Somehow, we escaped.

Our odyssey home began.

I make a fire for him. I care for him.

He has sharp green eyes, black hair just like mine.

His wound, and his imminent death, make him vulnerable.

"I should have never left my family," he murmurs, clutching his sides. "I should have been there for you. I should have given you guidance, and love. Instead, I dragged you into this hell."

I share stories about his granddaughter. About our trips to the bookstore, just like he used to take with me.

Closing his eyes, a grin stretches across his face. "End this cycle," he pleads. "Return home. Mend the things that need mending. I was wrong for believing that greatness was out here. It was in front of me this entire time." He put his hand to my cheek. "I fought out of fear. Fear that I wasn't enough. But you, child, you are enough."

Tears stream down our faces, falling to the parched dirt.

We travel.

Past the bodies of allies and enemies. Soldiers and cloaked demons.

Finally, my father is too weak to stand, falling to the bare ground. He reaches out for my face. "I'm sorry," he cries.

I hold him and weep.

For the father I never had.

For the guidance and love I never received.

For the brokenness that he passed down.

May it die in this desert.

"I forgive you."

Then I bury my father in the wasteland.

Shedding tears for a man I never knew.

But I had known him. I was him. His mistakes. His creativity. His false ambition. I was his fears and dreams. I stare out into the horizon. It isn't too late. There is still hope for me.

The trip is long.

I am dehydrated.

The hallucinations come. Visions of my family dance before me. Jane, spinning joyfully in our kitchen, reaching her hand out to me. Our daughter, grabbing a book from the shelves to read, her bright smile, so full of life, curling up in my lap. "I want to be a writer just like you, Daddy."

The emotions well up inside me.

You will be better, daughter.

You will be a ray of light for this world.

Just as you were for me.

You were the reason I kept going.

The reason I made it this far.

Reaching out to her, I collapse to the scorched earth, unable to move. My mouth as dry as the sand whirling about. My family stands off in the distance, their faces coming in and out of focus. I know it isn't real, but it is real. When I close my eyes, I feel their love and their light. The first time I kissed Jane in front of that doorstep. The way my daughter wrapped her tiny arms around me. I hear their laughs. Their voices. They loved me without the fame and the money. Without the success. Without any of it.

I can't lose them again.

I can't die here. Not in this wasteland.

I fight to stand, fight with everything I have left. I stagger to my feet, stumbling through the battlefield, over the rotting bodies. With each step, the corpses disappear. All the fears I spent my entire life running away from evaporate in the dry air. They aren't real. I take one step forward. I am going home.

I am coming back for both of you.

42

A BLINDING light dispersed across the room, illuminating the cement floor covered in blood-soaked typewriter pages. I lifted my head from the cold cement, pain jolting throughout my body. Two men hoisted me up and swiftly placed me on a gurney. A familiar face loomed over me. It was Charron. Before I could ask what happened to me, doctors surrounded me with instruments, my consciousness wavering.

And then, all was black.

When I finally came to, Charron was sitting at my bedside. Warm sunlight burst through the window, casting a glow on dust mites floating softly around me.

"How long have I been out?" I muttered.

"Six days," he replied, a hint of a smile on his face. "Let's go outside. Some fresh air will do you good."

I dressed and gingerly stepped foot into the corridor, exiting into the warmth of the sun. The unmistakable architecture of the Getty Museum lay before me. Charron guided me through the manicured gardens, weaving passed cheerful tourists and onto a bench overlooking the city.

I took a deep, painful breath, my eyes fixated on the horizon. I glanced over at Charron. In the harsh daylight, the lines on his face were more pronounced, his eyes heavy with fatigue.

"I'm sorry for all this," Charron broke the silence, holding his gaze on the skyline.

"Is Savannah dead?" I asked.

He nodded.

"And my father?"

Charron's gaze softened. "He passed three hours ago."

The weight of the news pressed down on me, and I could only nod in response.

"You know he had been committed for decades," Charron continued. "Completely lost to madness. Yet in those final moments, they say he found peace. They discovered him leaning against the wall, a satisfied grin on his face."

Charron took a long pause, then offered a faint smile. "But you . . . You endured." He patted my leg, presenting me with a thick set of pages. "And you came out the other side with this."

"What is that?"

"A script. I've read it several times already. You wrote it these past few days, before your body gave out. It will be your defining masterpiece."

I vaguely remembered typing the story, but it all felt so distant.

"You entitled it *The Wasteland*," Charron added.

"So that's what this was all about?" I asked, staring at the script. "A piece of art? Is this why Savannah had to die? Why my parents are dead?"

"It's complicated," Charron sighed. "After my own ritual, the man Hollywood knew as Bob Kinsley perished, and in that death, Robert Drifter was born."

I didn't react. Deep down, I had always known. Charron was the one guiding me from the very beginning. He had set me on this path.

"Why did you only write one book?"

"That was the best I could offer this world."

"So that's all this is? Rituals that kill and destroy for the sake of art?"

Charron chuckled. "That's no small feat. The order has left its mark on some of the world's greatest artists. Dante Alighieri. Leonardo DaVinci. Van Gogh. And that's just the tip of the iceberg."

I sat back.

"But you're right… Perhaps all this is too great a price to pay. For years, I believed wholeheartedly in the Order's work. That passing through these rituals was the only way to reach true greatness. That it was worth losing everything for a glimpse of divinity. To produce a work of art that would endure long after the artist passed."

"You don't believe any longer?"

"I have often wondered if the Order has it all wrong."

"How so?"

"These rituals are manufactured, forced encounters. Therefore, the artist never learns the true path of self-discovery. They never build the strength and courage required for the next journey. For sadly, this is not the end of your tormentors."

"I don't understand."

"The rituals began to mimic the journey of the Israelites. As you know, it took forty years to pass through the wilderness, on a path that should have taken eleven days. But I have begun to believe that artists need those forty years. A lifetime to learn how to survive in the darkness, to fail, to pick themselves up, to obtain true strength and grit. Then and only then do they earn their place in the promised land. Only then could they teach the next generation how to make the journey themselves.

"Or not." Charron glanced at me, then back down to my script. "Perhaps the Order was right. Like so many tortured artists before you, you may have never unveiled your true genius without our help. You would have continued throwing your life away. Fleeing from your shadows and squandering your talents. And this—this piece of work—it holds the potential to move the needle of humanity forward, ever so slightly. Or at the very least, inspire someone the way my novel inspired you.

"But at what cost?" Charron shook his head. "At what cost?"

Charron inhaled deeply, his gaze drifting. "I do believe that the Order has lost its way, entangled in a web of its own archaic and unyielding traditions, unwilling to evolve. Blinded by power, our Primus Creator, Virgil, now acts with unchecked tyranny. He is dangerous, and he must be stopped."

"So he survived?"

Charron nodded, glancing down at my script.

"So what happens next?"

"You shall be invited to the mansion tonight to be initiated into the Order." He held out a gold ring to me, half of the symbol carved into the metal. Then he held out his own ring with the same markings. When he touched them together the full symbol formed—XIIX. "The mission of the creator and his subject fulfilled. They will reward us for our faithfulness."

"And if we defy them?"

"Their war chest is large." He glanced around the museum campus. "Their power is substantial. They have the ability to destroy you."

"What if I go to the police?"

He looked saddened. "Will anyone believe you? Right now, Savannah Beck is dead, and your fingerprints are in the hotel room and on the gun. As soon as you skip your ceremony, you will be their number one target. But if you remain in the Order, all will be forgiven. The police will never touch you."

"And Savannah will what? Remain an unsolved murder?"

"Savannah was inducted at a very young age, indoctrinated with unbending loyalty. But she defied her Primus Creator twice. She defied him because of the words you gave her in

The Offering. 'I wield the power.' Her final words as she shot a bullet into Virgil."

With that, Charron rose off the bench.

"Where will you go?"

"I would like to try to become someone or something else—not a person who ferries souls across hell." Charron's gaze was distant, hopeful. "Good luck, Kohl. I'm truly sorry… For everything."

He plopped the manuscript down on the bench.

"You're giving this to me?"

He grinned. "Indeed. I believe this is your work, not the Order's nor humanities. You shall decide what comes next… Make it count."

43

CONNER

"You can turn it off now." Kohl exhales a lifetime's worth of air. Setting his gun on the table, he strides to a nearby cabinet, grabbing two scotch glasses and a sealed bottle of whisky.

"This was given to me by my agent," Kohl says, studying the label. "After my nomination for *Impeachment*. Seems like a fitting time to drink it."

He pours the drinks neatly, then hands me a glass.

I refuse. "So that's it? You're giving up? You're going to let some radical cult get away with this? Let them murder and kill under false pretenses of somehow bettering the world for the sake of what…Art? This is insane."

Kohl smirks, setting the glass down and re-corking the scotch. "You don't believe what I've told you? That some of the greatest artists in this world have been guided by the Order?"

"No. Of course not. You do?"

Kohl casually swirls around his glass. "Of course. And you should too."

"And why is that?"

"Because you are part of it."

I sneer.

"The symbol brought you to me," Kohl adds.

"No." I shake my head. "Your book brought me here. Not this symbol."

"And how do you think you came across my book?"

"Chance," I assert, my pulse quickening. "Because I needed guidance, and I found an author who taught me perseverance, not surrender." I get up from the seat.

"You really believe you found my book by chance?" Kohl says, reaching for my copy of *When the Lights Go Out*.

He takes the novel, then opens to the inside cover. In one swift motion, he rips the library pocket from the book and turns it back to me, revealing the symbol etched in black ink. It had been there all along.

I am speechless.

"I'll admit, when I first reached out to your magazine, I had hoped my daughter would be the one to find me. But it made sense that you would be my subject."

"What are you talking about?"

"Do you recall a movie called *Encounters*?" He chuckles at my blank face. "No surprise. It was a shit Midwest alien film. But it was filmed two hours away from where you grew up, in Breckenridge. Your father… He came to the set looking for work as an extra. I knew right away he was an addict like me.

"For the next few weeks, I found myself partying with your father. He got us the drugs, and we spent all night consuming them. He told me how special you and your mother were. How he never thought he deserved either of you. He believed he wasn't worthy and that he was going to hurt you. I guess we were kindred souls that way.

"But then his biggest fear came true.

"We got arrested one night, and your mother got his one phone call. She drove at two a.m. to come pick him up, and... Well, you know that part of the story." Kohl sits down on the couch, studying me.

I avoid his gaze, reeling from his words. It can't be true. It can't

"I was in the hospital lobby that night, Conner. I went with your father. He... He was a frightened man. Scared of responsibility. Scared of living without your mom. He thought you were better off without him. He and your aunt had a heated exchange, and he made the choice to leave you behind."

"You were there that night," I mutter.

Kohl studies my expression. "You remember, don't you? Just like I remembered those three cloaked men. I was the one staring at you from across the room. I was the shadow you remember."

I shake my head in confusion. Kohl continues.

"As for me," he continues. "I never forgot about you, that reflection of my childhood self. I returned to your hometown years later. I just needed to make sure you were okay. So I drove to your school, and I don't know why, but I went into the library, and I grabbed my book. I peeled off the library card, and I added the symbol. This was before I knew what it was. Maybe I wanted to do for you what Drifter did for me. Give you a way out. Offer you hope. I found you in the gymnasium, and I knew right then and there, I was marking you. I was setting you on this path."

"That can't be," I mutter. "That's impossible."

Kohl smirks. "I sported a beard and wore a hat, so I knew you wouldn't recognize me as the young man on the back cover. But yes. That was me. I gave you my book the same way Drifter gave me his book in that shop in San Francisco."

Chills race down my spine, my mind struggling to process.

"And I knew one day you would find me. The same way I searched for Drifter. The symbol is powerful."

"This is ridiculous—just a bunch of coincidences." I pause, staring at Kohl, a man I idolized my whole life. And yet—he was partly responsible for my mother's accident. For ruining my entire life. "So my father is alive?"

"I don't know."

He downs the rest of his scotch.

Suddenly, loud voices and stomping boots echo through the house. With a deafening crash, a metal ram throws the door off its hinges and armed men with Kevlar vests flood the small cabin. Amidst shouting and commotion, we drop to the ground, raising our hands in surrender.

44

CONNER

IT TAKES hours for the police to take my statement. I sit in a trance, recounting the entire week. I explain to the detective that I wasn't a hostage, just a reporter chasing a wild story. I attempt to tell them about Jacob Perry, the Order, the rituals, but they can only shake their heads in dismay.

"Sounds like you're pitching us a Hollywood screenplay."

They refuse to listen to my recording.

And for a second, when the commotion dies down, with Kohl no longer in front of me, the magic of his storytelling begins to dissipate, and I wonder if they're right. What if everything he said was fiction? What if he was manipulating me this entire time? He wasn't someone worth idolizing. He had ruined my life. He had ruined Grace's life.

An hour later, the police pack up, and the media vans pull out. Grace kindly offers to take me home. As we drive, I play her the entire recording. She stares out into the darkness, her face etched in sadness, listening to the tragic tale of her father's life.

It's two in the morning by the time the recording finishes in front of my apartment. Grace wipes away a tear, maintaining her silence. I collect the recorder and gather my things. Just as I'm about to get out of the car, a nagging question escapes my lips.

"Do you actually believe him? All that stuff about cults and initiations. You said so yourself, 'He does this for a living.' What if he killed Savannah Beck and this is just another one of his far-fetched stories?"

She reclines in her seat, a faint smile playing on her lips. "Ever since you met my father, something's changed in you. You seem…different." She hesitates, her expression softening. "I'm sorry about your parents."

"I'm sorry too," I respond. "I can't imagine what you're going through."

She nods gently. "You know I found out when I was a kid. I remember walking into the living room to find my parents fighting. And all these pages of my father's script scattered across the floor. I remember picking up one of the pages and reading it, this unsettling truth, just like my father read that page in *his* father's study. And just like him, it took me years to reckon with it. But now I can see those words clear as ever. He wrote about my mom's affair, and he wasn't sure if I was his child."

She continues. "His words made me doubt who I was. Whether or not I was a real writer like my father. Whether or not he really loved me. Whether or not I was a Reynolds. That's why I changed my name.

"But hearing his story, something feels different. Maybe I understand him for the first time ever." She pauses, then smiles. "Maybe the healing can finally begin."

Without thinking, I reach for her hand, and she takes it.

Suddenly, I'm aware of the loud thumping of my heart. All the fear and uncertainty that I was feeling dissolves. I inch closer, and for a second, Grace's face lingers. But just when I'm about to reach her lips, she turns away.

I retract, embarrassed. "Grace, I'm—"

She starts, "I just don't think—"

"It's okay," I interrupt, swinging the car door open. "It's been a long day. I'll talk to you tomorrow."

* * *

I wake up the next morning at the crack of dawn. The television is replaying details from last night's arrest. I see my name and photo. *The journalist Conner Daniels held hostage.* I'm flattered that they called me a journalist, considering my employment status with the magazine. I watch footage of the police dragging Kohl away in handcuffs. Everything about the last few days feels surreal. As if the events were still buffering in my consciousness.

I still don't know what to believe.

When I get to the office, reporters are lined up outside. I rush past their extended mics and the barrage of questions, opting for the winding stairs that lead to the third-floor office. When I walk in, someone whistles, prompting everyone to stand up and applaud.

The blood rushes to my face. It is everything I've wanted since I began working here. Recognition. Validation. And yet . . . My gaze travels to Grace's empty desk. Something is missing.

Settling into my chair, Allie flashes a mischievous smile.

"If it isn't the man, the myth, the legend." She laughs. "I wouldn't get too comfortable."

Right on cue, Tom Arnold bellows, "Conner! My office now!"

Entering his office, I spot four men in suits lounging on the couches. They all appear eager and excited to see me.

"Conner, meet our investors. They're here for the occasion." The suited men nod, and Tom beckons for me to take a seat.

"So where is it?" he asks.

"Where's what?" I glance around the room.

"Oh, I don't know," he mocks. "The story of a fucking lifetime. I have a staffer who was in the center of a hostage situation, and I have nothing to put on the front page. Nothing," he snarls. "When can I expect this story? This afternoon, tonight?"

Locking eyes with him, a rush of confidence swells in my chest.

"It will be ready when it's ready." I stand up. "Is that all?"

Tom raises his eyebrows. "Listen, you get me that story, and not only will you be a staff writer, but I'll make you a star. You got that?"

* * *

Back at my desk, Allie is holding up my phone. "Who's Aunt Laura?" she asks. "She just called three times."

I wonder if my family has seen my face on the news. I ignore the missed calls. I ignore the sinking feeling in my gut when I stare at Grace's empty desk. I ignore everything. I put my headphones on, and I push play on the tape recorder.

The office comes and goes, but I don't leave my seat. I sit and type. I retell Kohl's story the best way I can. I sense my own skepticism when I mention the Order. There's a part of me that still believes this whole thing is fabricated. It takes me six hours to get everything down on paper. I don't bother reading it over. I walk into Tom's office and slam the story on his desk. His forehead crinkles as he stares at the pages.

"The Eleven?" He picks up the pages. "What the fuck is this?"

"It's the story."

His gaze shifts from the paper to me.

"Oh . . . and I quit."

***

That afternoon, I clean my entire apartment, scrubbing every dish, counter and tile. I've decided to make Los Angeles my home. The call to Aunt Laura wasn't easy, but I know my mother would affirm my decision. She wouldn't want me wasting my whole life in Breckenridge. She'd want me to pursue my dream.

Starting now.

Seated at my desk, I open my laptop and stare at the blank page. Five minutes. Ten minutes. Nothing comes. Fear inches its way in through the back door, whispering in my ear: *You made a mistake by quitting. You aren't a writer. You'll never be good enough to make it. You're just like every sucker in this town. Are you really going to leave your own mother? Who are you to write anything meaningful? You aren't worthy of anything.*

There's a knock at the door.

When I open it, Grace stands across from me. My entire body lights up in her presence. But it's different than before. It used to thrash with nerves; now it beats in anticipation. She wears a heavy black coat with no makeup, her father's bronze ring hanging on a chain around her neck.

I step back to let her in. "Come in."

She lingers at the door. "Listen, I have to be quick. Tom let me see the story. Quite the read."

"Are you going somewhere?" I ask, glancing at her large coat.

"I'm taking a trip to London. Finally work on that novel."

A brief silence ensues, both of us unsure what comes next.

"I meant to—" I begin.

"I wanted to thank you," she gently interrupts. "For not listening to me, and for fighting for him. For writing his story." She smiles, then pulls out a bronze coin from her pocket, scorch marks seared around the edges. It was Kohl's lucky coin.

"I went to visit my father," she said, turning the coin over in her hands. "He wanted you to have this."

"Why?" I ask.

"For centuries, that symbol stood for a cult that tormented the minds of artists, making them expendable and powerless. And this...This is the shell of what the Order was. My father said that we will reign in a new era, one in which a parent or mentor doesn't pass on their brokenness and suffering. One that uses love instead of fear to influence. One that gives *all* artists a chance to prosper."

Grabbing the coin, I meet Grace's eyes.

Her smile widens as she casually tucks a strand of hair behind her ear.

As she does, my body leans toward her like a tree straining for sunlight. She doesn't back away. The moment our lips meet, a million shockwaves ripple through me, tingling my arms and legs, flooding into my veins, pumping to every corner of my body. When we separate, I feel like I'm hovering in midair. I'm smiling so wide that it hurts my face.

"See you around, Conner."

When the door closes, I feel something. A rush. A pull to the desk. I sit at the computer, my mouth still tingling in the aftermath. Putting the coin beside me, my mind races with inspiration. My hands vibrate. Images burst into my consciousness, scenes, characters. I look down, and to my astonishment, my fingertips are gliding across the computer, the words streaking faster than I can type.

A NOTE FROM THE AUTHOR

THIS BOOK BEGAN during the pandemic, a few months after the birth of my first daughter. It was a complex time. On one hand, our daughter brought so much light and love to our little family. On the other hand, becoming new parents amidst so much chaos and uncertainty in the world was difficult.

During this transition, a few destructive patterns from my past resurfaced, including panic attacks and intrusive thoughts. Things that made me feel even more out of control.

Alas, the one thing I could control was showing up to the blank page. It became my therapy. I created Kohl to represent everything that was surfacing, including the scariest question of all — *What if I passed down my traumas and wounds to my innocent daughter?*

The book was actually finished at the end of 2020, but it took another three years to feel like it was ready to see the light of day. I needed my own journey of self-discovery in order to complete Kohl's.

That's why this book is so meaningful to me.

While finishing this book, I started going to therapy to confront the childhood wounds that went unmarked and unreflected for so much of my life. The past shadows that subconsciously tormented me for so long. In many ways, finishing this book was my way of healing.

It was my way of stating that the generational trauma in my family ends with me.

It will not be passed down to my children.

Of course, unlike *The Eleven*, there was no shortcut, no ritual, no secret society that forced me to endure that pain. Each day, I had to make a choice to face the shame, grief, and pain inside me.

One of my favorite quotes is from the American priest and writer, Richard Rohr. He says, "Shadowy material resides inside of all of us, but the man who is willing to face his own capacity for darkness will discover his deepest inner goodness and the presence of the divine within him."

I'm truly grateful for this journey from dark to light, and thankful that I'm able to share it with you. Thanks for reading.

-Kyle

DIED FAMOUS

ABOUT THIS SERIES:

I began writing the DIED FAMOUS series ten years ago. *She Died Famous* was my first novel in the series. At the time, I questioned why the story coming out of me was so dark, why the main characters were so flawed and broken.

Steven Pressfield says, 'The more scared we are of a work or calling, the more sure we can be that we have to do it."

So I kept writing.

Year after year, the stories began to unfold in mysterious ways. The more I trusted the void, the more the patterns and themes emerged.

It wasn't until this book that I realized how this broken but hopeful universe connected. It only took me a decade… :)

The Died Famous Manifesto.

We are Artists & Anti-Heroes—flawed artists and creators. To us, creativity is a spiritual act, our highest expression of self. Therefore, we reject the allure of serving algorithms and fame. Our obligation is to create meaningful work. Often, this requires us to journey into the deepest parts of our souls, to overcome inner resistance, and to confront our deepest fears. We use our brokenness and pain as the raw materials for our creations. By sharing these works, we inspire others to embrace their unique paths. Above all else, make good art.

If this manifesto resonates with you, please join me at my newsletter— creativeritual.substack.com.

ACKNOWLEDGEMENTS

Thank you to my friends and family for all your love and encouragement. Thank you to my editor Julie Tibbott. Thank you to my newsletter friends for sticking around. Thank you to Anamaria Stefan for creating the Died Famous branding.

Most of all, thank you to my wife for always believing me, and my daughters for inspiring me to keep following my dream.

ALSO BY KYLE RUTKIN

She Died Famous

Tik Tik Gone

Influencer Island

Join my newsletter at creativeritual.substack.com

Made in the USA
Columbia, SC
31 March 2024